JOSS THE SEVEN

GUILD OF SEVENS, BOOK 1

J. PHILIP HORNE

For news of upcoming works,
please join Mr. Horne's email list at www.jphiliphorne.com
or visit him on facebook.com/jphiliphorne

ALSO BY J. PHILIP HORNE

The Lodestone (2011)

Guild of Sevens
Joss the Seven (2016)
Guardian Angel (2017)

Cover illustration by Justin Stewart
www.justifii.com

ISBN: 1533150362
ISBN-13: 978-1533150363

For Tricia
I have so many dreams
but live the best one

TABLE OF CONTENTS

Chapter 1

ONE LAST DAY

"WE'RE GONNA GO out with a bang," I said. "Come on."

I yanked Thomas toward the bathroom door. At least, I tried to. He'd grown a ton during eighth grade. It felt like pulling on a tree.

"Geez, Joss," Thomas said, "do we have to go in there?"

I pushed open the door and held it for him. "Come on."

The smell of chemical cleaners, mildew, and urinals used by boys who had trouble aiming washed over me. Everyone knew you avoided the bathroom closest to the cafeteria. In my book, that made it the perfect place to plot.

Thomas rolled his eyes, but stepped past me. I slapped him on the back and took a last glance down the hall. A flash of motion caught my eye, and I jerked my head back around. The hall was empty. I frowned and let the door close behind me.

"Did you see a cat or something out there?"

"What are you talking about?" Thomas folded his arms across his chest. "What'd you want?"

"Right." I shook my head. I was sure I'd seen something small and furry dart around the corner at the end of the hall. "Look, we said eighth grade wasn't going to be a repeat of seventh, right?"

"Yeah. We've done pretty good."

"Here's the deal," I said. "We're about to be on the bottom again. Freshmen. Losers. But we've been making a name for ourselves. If we go out big, they're gonna remember us."

"And?" Thomas hiked up his shorts as he spoke. His

1

mom kept trying to get ahead of his growth by buying him clothes that were way too big.

"Mr. Sanders had us make homemade ice cream in first period, right? Who knew ice cream was science? What was the word?"

"Colloid," Thomas said.

"A colloid. So there's a bunch of ice cream in the freezer between the science classrooms. It's still going to be a colloid when we're done, it's just going to include hand soap."

Thomas's eyes got large, and his face split in a grin. "That's brilliant. Evil, but brilliant."

I stepped to the sink, swiped the small, clear bottle of liquid soap off the counter, and tucked it into my back pocket. "Let's do this."

Mr. Michaels' science room was empty except for the oppressive odor of formaldehyde. I grabbed one of the stirring spoons drying in the sink and followed Thomas into the utility room. The faint sounds of Mr. Sanders lecturing his class penetrated the door opposite us.

The big freezer stood against the wall just to our left. Thomas eased it open and we were greeted by a wave of cold air. Nine silver cylinders sat on the three shelves. I handed the wooden spoon to Thomas and pulled the soap out of my pocket.

"All of them?" Thomas mouthed at me.

I nodded. "Ours, too. Avoid suspicion."

One by one, we lifted the canisters out and stirred in several pumps of soap. The ice cream was getting thick, so we took turns stirring and were done in a few minutes. Once the containers were back in the freezer, Thomas started giggling. It felt contagious, but there was no time to laugh. We had to get back to the hall before the bell rang.

"Let's move," I whispered, and went to the door. I cracked it open. The room was still empty. I gave the spoon a quick rinse in the sink and put it with the others before we walked out like we owned the place. A moment later, the bell rang and students flooded the hall.

"We've got to get back there right after school," Thomas

said. "I want to see their reactions when they eat it."

I held out my fist, and he bumped it.

That feeling of victory lasted until twenty-nine minutes into seventh period. That was when Ms. Arnett's phone intercom buzzed. She picked up the handset.

"Yes? Well, I see... Yes, of course.... I'll send him right over."

She hung up, and as she did, her gaze swung up from her desk and fell on me. Ms. Arnett was pretty cute for a teacher, but right then I felt like Frodo trying to hide from Sauron's gaze, except my desk offered no shelter from the glare.

"Joss," Ms. Arnett said, "I believe you're wanted in the office. Please report to Mr. Nichols immediately."

"Yes, ma'am," I said.

"Take your bag with you. I doubt you'll have time to come back before seventh period ends."

I shambled out of the room and headed toward the office. How had they known? The ice cream wasn't going to be eaten until after school. No one should have even opened the freezer for another half a period. I paused at the door to the office and took a look around. A flicker of motion tickled the corner of my eye, but when I looked down the hall, there was nothing.

What the heck? Was I going crazy? Why did I keep seeing mystery animals? I took a deep breath and opened the door.

Mrs. Diebold perched at her spotless desk behind the chest-high counter. She gave me a hard look, her pudgy face looking like it was carved from stone. Very pudgy stone, with wispy, graying hair creating a halo around it. Her smelly perfume dominated the room. Without saying a word, she pointed toward Mr. Nichols' office on the far side of the room.

I went in.

"Ah, Joss," Mr. Nichols said. "Please, have a seat."

Mr. Nichols sat behind his big, wooden desk. As always, the desk held his laptop and about twelve stacks of papers and notebooks. He was a long man in every way. Long body. Long face. Long nose. His thin, dark hair seemed lost on the top of his long forehead.

I sat down in one of the two chairs facing his desk. It needed a cushion. Mr. Nichols leaned forward with his elbows on the desk and his hands steepled, his chin resting on his thumbs. He sat there for a moment, his eyes flickering over me. My stomach clenched.

He sat back in his chair.

"Heard an interesting story this afternoon from Mr. Talbot," he said. "You probably had Mr. Talbot for math last year. You remember him, I'm sure."

"Sure," I said. His eyebrows lifted. "Uh, yes, sir."

"It seems," Mr. Nichols said, his eyebrows coming back down, "that Mr. Talbot learned of a certain science experiment being performed today. A study of colloids, I believe. Why, I believe you were in the class that made the colloids, yes?"

"Colloids. Yes, sir. We made colloids in first period science." My stomach climbed up my throat. My parents were not going to be happy with me.

"And these, ah, colloids were placed in the freezer. They were pure examples of colloids. Untampered with. And it seems, when Mr. Talbot learned of these colloids, he took it upon himself to, uh, study them. And what better way to study such colloids than to sample them?"

Oh. Not good.

"Suffice to say," Mr. Nichols continued, "that I have confirmed with Mr. Sanders that the middle of his sixth period class was disrupted when Mr. Talbot burst into the room from the utility room. You know, the room that has the freezer containing the colloids? Mr. Talbot burst in and proceeded to rinse his mouth out at the classroom sink. He rinsed it vigorously. And strangely, the 'colloids' he had sampled bubbled up in the sink. Soapy bubbles."

My shoulders sagged. It was a double whammy. I was about to be busted, and I had not gotten to witness the legendary awesomeness of my prank. I wanted something for my efforts.

"So are you saying," I said, "that bubbles came out of his mouth?"

"Of course not. But there were some bubbles in the sink when he rinsed out the ice… the colloids he spit in the sink."

"Oh." Disappointment after disappointment. There had been no bubbles. I had been sure there would be bubbles.

"Mr. Talbot was quite confident that it would be beneficial to talk to you," Mr. Nichols said. "So here you are. Please, enlighten me."

A sudden realization smacked me on the side of the head. They didn't know. There had been no witnesses. Mr. Talbot was gunning for me, but he had no proof. My stomach stopped clenching, and started floating. I had to play this right.

"Well," I said, "I'm not sure what to say. Why do you think it was soap?"

I made sure I didn't glance at my backpack. The backpack that held a bottle of hand soap.

"I had a skilled scientist on hand to make that difficult call," Mr. Nichols said. "You'll recall Mr. Sanders previously taught chemistry at the high school level. No? Well, he did. Mr. Sanders confirmed that the bubbles looked distinctly soapy, corroborating Mr. Talbot's judgment that he tasted soap."

Holy cow. Mr. Nichols was being sarcastic. I was in uncharted territory.

"Mr. Nichols, it sounds like someone picked my name at random, and messed up my last day of school. Today is really important to me, and I hate to take time away from my teachers."

It was a beautiful statement. One of my best. It was wasted.

The door to Mr. Nichols' office banged open. I whipped my head around. Mrs. Diebold filled the doorway, her hand to her mouth. Her perfume surged into the room and tried to gag me.

"Mr. Nichols!" she said. "We have reports of a large dog

roaming the halls!"

Now that was interesting. Maybe I hadn't been seeing things. I turned back to Mr. Nichols. His frown pulled his eyebrows together into a single, fuzzy line. I glanced back and forth, trying to watch both of them.

"A large dog?" he asked, his voice pitched higher than normal.

Mrs. Diebold nodded, her chins bouncing. "Or a wolf. But that's ludicrous."

Mr. Nichols' chair banged into the wall behind him as he surged to his feet. "A wolf?"

"Two of the teachers who called me said wolf. One said dog," she said. "All three teachers are in classrooms off Hallway C, back half."

"Two of the teachers said it was a wolf?" he asked. "Remarkable. Do you know anything about this?"

I thought the last question was directed at me, but Mr. Nichols was staring forward over my head, his eyes intense. Well, I had nothing to do with a wolf. I kept my mouth shut. Maybe, just maybe, I could get out of here.

Mr. Nichols jerked his head in a quick nod. "Mrs. Diebold, please buzz Officer Trent's office. Tell him to meet me in Hallway C straight away."

"Dogs at school," she said, throwing up her hands as she stepped out of sight toward her desk.

Mr. Nichols lowered his gaze to me. "We are not through. I've got you for another ten minutes at least. I'll be back shortly after I see to this foolishness."

With that, he strode out of the room.

What a disaster. Not only was I busted, but I'd probably be stuck in his office way after school let out for the summer.

Wait a second. I played back what I'd just heard. Sure, he'd said he had me for a few more minutes, but he'd never said I had to stay in his office. Maybe he'd just meant I shouldn't leave the school until the final period ended. Good enough for me.

I rose, grabbed my backpack, and headed out. I gave Mrs. Diebold a big smile and ignored her glare as I left the office. She was too busy fumbling with her phone to stop me. Out in the hall, I saw Mr. Nichols disappear around the corner of the cross-hall that led to Hallway C. I let out a long whistle. A giant dog-wolf roamed the halls. I really hadn't thought the animals I'd seen had been that big.

The large digital clock at the near-end of the hall revealed there were only eight minutes left of junior high. I headed for my locker, going the way Mr. Nichols had just gone. Then it clicked. My locker was off Hallway C, near the back of the building.

I stopped to think. Should I follow Mr. Nichols? What would he do if he saw me at my locker? And what would I do if there was a wolf guarding it? It had to be nonsense, but the teachers had seen something. Heck, I'd seen something moving in the halls. I was sure of it. I glanced back at the clock. How had I been standing there for three minutes? I started down the hall in the direction of my locker.

At that moment, the school security alarm started shrieking.

Chapter 2

THE BUTTERFLY SEAL

I TOOK OFF at a dead run toward my locker. In moments the classes would line up and let out into the hall. If a teacher spotted me, I'd be pulled into a line of kids and marched outside. I wasn't going to sit around in the parking lot and then be made to go back into the school to clean out my locker. Or worse, end up back in Mr. Nichols' office.

I ran full speed through the halls, the seconds tripping by silently in my head as I counted. I figured I had about twenty seconds. I got to my locker in eighteen. A few seconds later, students poured out of the classrooms behind me. I was hidden from view by a bend in the hallway as long as I stayed mashed up against the wall by my locker. A quick glance showed everyone had turned toward the exits at the front of the school.

The hallway bent back about twenty lockers further on. If Mr. Nichols was here, he was somewhere past that second bend. There were no classrooms on that side, just a couple utility closets and an emergency exit. I took a few deep breaths to steady myself, and unlocked my locker. I reached in to grab my notebooks along with my stash of gum. My hand froze.

A white envelope with a thick, red wax seal sat on top of my notebooks. At least, I thought it was a wax seal. It wasn't like I received mail sealed with wax very often. I picked up the envelope and checked it against the small vents on the locker door. Yep, it would fit through. So someone had probably put it into my locker without picking the lock.

The security alarm continued its crazy-loud beeping, but

the noise of students dropped off as they marched away. Between the beeps, I realized I was hearing voices coming from the other end of the hall toward the emergency exit. That had to be Mr. Nichols with Officer Trent. I grabbed the notebooks and pushed them with the envelope into my backpack. As I turned to head back down the hallway, I heard what they were saying.

"We're agreed, then, what..."

That was Mr. Nichols for sure, though I lost a couple words to the alarm's beeping.

"Uh, yeah, I guess so."

That was Officer Trent. He had one of the deepest voices I'd ever heard.

"A dog stood and pulled down the security bar, then pushed through the door?" Mr. Nichols asked.

"Yeah, but I still say it was a wolf," Officer Trent said.

"A *dog* stood and pulled down the security bar," Mr. Nichols said. "Look, we're going to sound odd as it is. Can we drop the wolf bit?"

"Yeah, alright. But just so you know, it was a wolf."

Wait a second. The voices were getting louder. They were coming this way. I took off running, cutting over a couple hallways, and headed toward the entrance to the school. I burst through the front doors into controlled chaos.

The summer heat slammed into me as I took a quick glance around. Kids clustered together by class in the parking lot. Sirens wailed as fire trucks and police cars came to a stop in front of the school. Uniformed men spilled out and headed toward the school entrances. I kept my head low and hurried down the front steps to the parking lot. After a quick glance around, I headed for the closest group of kids.

Once in with the students, I found my way to Ms. Arnett's class and sat down on the pavement to think. Could Mr. Nichols still bust me once school was out? I thought I was in the clear, so long as he didn't see me. And what was going on with the wolf-dog and the security alarm?

More importantly, what was that letter I'd found in my

locker? The letter with a red wax seal. Who uses wax to seal a letter? Did it have anything to do with the dog-wolf setting off the alarm?

I thought about the questions until the cops determined there was no threat to the school and released us for the summer. I saw Thomas and Deion heading back into the school to empty their lockers among the masses of students, but Mr. Nichols was standing near them, so I didn't dare go talk to them. It was okay. My friends all lived near my neighborhood. We'd meet up soon enough. For now, that letter consumed me. I headed out.

Beedle Junior High was about three quarters of a mile from my house, but I didn't go directly home. I didn't want to risk the letter being seen by anyone until I'd had a chance to open it. I cut over on Milken Street to Beckler Park. It had all the usual stuff—jungle gym, swings, merry-go-round—made out of steel pipes painted bright blue and yellow. It also had a big oak tree that reached out over one end of the playground.

I went straight to the swing set and sat down in the green swing on the end that was shaded by the tree. My skin was prickling from the summer heat, and the shade felt glorious. I unzipped my backpack and pulled out the envelope. The red seal was about an inch around and stamped with a flower or something. I picked at the edge of the seal. It felt like hardened wax. I sniffed at the tiny piece lodged under my fingernail. It smelled like a candle. Definitely wax. I turned the envelope over in my hands. There were no other markings.

I held the envelope close to get a good look at the seal, and my breath caught in my throat. It wasn't a plant. It was the outline of a butterfly. A butterfly that mirrored the shape of an odd birthmark I had on the back of my right shoulder. My birthmark was so exact, so much like a small butterfly clinging to my shoulder, that my doctor had thought it was a tattoo the first time he'd seen it.

I never went without a shirt around other kids. What teenage boy wanted to be known for having a butterfly tattoo? Thomas and Arjeet had seen it at a sleepover when I'd been careless and taken off my shirt, but I'd sworn them to secrecy.

The wax seal was imprinted with the same shape. My heart raced. I looked around, and saw two seventh graders I didn't know walking home on Milken Street. I took some deep breaths with my eyes closed and tried to calm down. Thomas and Arjeet must have made the seal. No one else knew about it. I didn't know how they could have done it from memory, but there was no other explanation. I looked around again. Nobody was in sight other than the two kids.

"Thomas! Arjeet!" I called. "You can come out now!"

The two kids stared at me but kept walking. No one popped out of hiding. It had to be a prank, but what was the point of a prank if there was nobody to witness it?

I ran a finger under the edge of the envelope flap where it wasn't glued shut and tore it open along the top of the envelope to keep the seal intact. A single, tri-folded piece of white paper was nestled inside. I pulled the paper out and put the empty envelope back in my backpack. After one last look around, I unfolded the paper.

Perfect lines of handwriting covered the page. Some of the I's had little hearts instead of dots above them. The cursive script was a girl's, no doubt about it. I read.

> *Dear Joss,*
>
> *You don't know me, but I know of you. I hope you saw the seal and realized I know about your birthmark. The butterfly, symbol of an old, prestigious family. That's your seal on the front, not mine.*
>
> *I'm going to show you that you have a special ability, and then I'm going to help you learn how to use it to help the world. I know that will sound odd to you, but it is the honest truth. Let me prove it to you.*
>
> *I've listed seven tests below. Tonight, before bed, try them out. Do them carefully, and keep it secret. If you do the tests, I'm confident you'll want to talk to me. I'll be at Beckler Park tomorrow at noon if you want to learn more.*
>
> *Sincerely, Mara*

I glanced around, turning my head this way and that, trying to catch whoever was messing with me. The letter's author knew about Beckler Park. They knew about my locker, and about the birthmark. The birthmark was the key. How had Thomas and Arjeet made the wax seal? I looked back at the letter.

THE TESTS
1. Relax your mind and body. Concentrate on your index finger (either hand). Concentrate hard. Pretend it isn't solid. Pretend it is a ghost finger. Hold this image in your mind for a full minute. Then tap on something hard with that finger.

That test was eight kinds of crazy. I felt agitated and couldn't finish the letter. I glanced down the page. There were six more tests listed.

So, was Mara a real person or just a name used to set up an elaborate hoax? What were the facts? First, the letter had appeared in my locker right when a wolf-dog was seen near my locker. Second, the letter writer knew about my birthmark. Third, though the test was insane, it wasn't big and bold. If I did the test, it wouldn't embarrass me. No one would even know. The test didn't require I climb a flagpole with no pants on, like I'd tricked Davey Talbot into doing last year. What was the point? It made no sense.

Wait a second. Maybe that was why Mr. Talbot had tried to get me in trouble today. Was he still mad about me humiliating his son? I couldn't hold onto the thought. I couldn't hold onto any thought.

I opened my backpack and dropped the letter in beside the envelope. I quickly looked around, but still didn't see anyone watching. My mind buzzed. I couldn't make any sense of it. The facts didn't line up. They didn't tell me anything. I felt like there were butterflies in my stomach, not just one on my back.

Freaking out didn't help, so I tried to stop. Deep, calm

breaths. I'd do the test and be done with it. There would be no witnesses.

I checked my watch. It would just take one minute of my life. Relax your mind and body. Easy enough. I lifted my right index finger in front of my face and slumped against the swing chain. I tried to quiet my thoughts, and concentrated on the finger. I imagined the finger becoming something less than solid. Something still visible, but insubstantial.

I glanced at my watch. I must have gotten into it, because I was startled to see a minute and a half had gone by. I leaned way over and tapped the steel swing-set pole. My finger hit the metal.

Only, it didn't.

My finger slid *through* the pole.

My vision swam and my eyelids sagged closed. I was so tired.

My finger...

Something was wrong. My head felt like an over-filled water balloon the moment before it burst. I forced my eyes open. My vision was cloudy around the edges and too bright in the middle. I swayed on the swing and struggled to stay upright. What had just happened?

The summer before, Dad and I had gone fishing with a bucket full of minnows for bait. There had been so many minnows in the bucket, but I hadn't been able to grab any. My thoughts were like those minnows in a bucket, slipping between my fingers. Finally, I caught one.

Home. I had to get home. I grabbed my backpack and stumbled forward in a fog of tiredness and confusion. It was less than a quarter mile, but my legs didn't want to work, and I struggled with each step. My mind played tricks on me. Something about my finger. My finger and a metal pole. What had happened?

I got home, crawled up the stairs before Mom could track me down to ask about school, and collapsed in my bed.

I passed out.

Chapter 3

GHOST FINGER

I WOKE SATURDAY morning at 9:27. I didn't think I could have stayed up until 7:30 the previous night if not for the two-hour nap I'd taken after passing out. On the plus side, I felt rested.

I thought I'd showered before crashing, but my memories of the previous day were fuzzy. I could remember school, the alarm, going to the park, and collapsing into my bed, but that was about it. I lifted my arm and did a quick check. The fine, manly scent of fresh deodorant greeted my nose.

I don't know why deodorant triggered my memories, but the vision of my finger passing through steel came back in a rush, my arm still up, my nose poised in the act of checking things out. The letter. The test. My finger going through a steel pole.

I sat down hard on my bed. What was my game plan? The letter had said something about today. I got up and found my shorts from yesterday on the floor. The pockets were empty other than a few pieces of gum, which I dumped on my desk. I found my backpack under my bed and pulled it out.

There it was. The letter and the envelope with the butterfly seal. I unfolded the letter and read the intro again, and then folded it back up. I wasn't ready to read another six tests. First, I needed to know I hadn't gone crazy.

Beckler Park. Mara would be at Beckler Park today at noon. I grabbed my phone off my desk and texted Thomas.

Need backup. Beckler Park. 11am

That should get his attention. I threw on some clothes, and stuck the letter and envelope in my pocket.

"Well, good morning, sunshine!" Mom said when I walked into the kitchen looking for food. She sat at the breakfast table, her laptop open. My sister Janey sat across from her finishing a bowl of cereal, with a book held open on the table. I grabbed a bowl and went to the pantry to see what we had.

"Hey Mom," I said. "You cool if I hang out with Thomas today? We're thinking of meeting at the park. Maybe riding our bikes over to Taco Bell for lunch."

Mom stood up and crossed over to me. She was wearing her favorite morning outfit, a pair of black-and-white polka dot sleep pants with a gray fleece. She put her hand on my forehead and then looked into my eyes.

"Just so long as you're okay." She patted my cheek and headed back to her seat. "I don't think I've ever seen you go to bed at 7:30 before."

"Yeah, I don't know what the deal was," I said. "I was probably just playing catch up on all the sleep I'd missed this past school year. Where's Dad?"

"The gym."

"Right," I said. "So about the park, and Taco Bell. What do you think?"

"That's fine, honey." She turned her attention back to her laptop.

I grabbed the Fruity Circles and poured a bowl. As I headed to the breakfast table, Janey closed her book and went to the sink. She stuck her tongue out at me as we passed. I threw an elbow, but she twisted to the side and I missed her by an inch. Man, she was quick. Had to give credit where credit was due.

My family was a prime specimen of suburban perfection. We had a minivan. We had an SUV. We had a trampoline in the backyard. One dad, who was an accountant. His hair was curly like mine, but he kept it trimmed super short. He was just over six feet tall, which gave me hope that I might catch up with Thomas one day.

One mom, who worked part time as a physician's assistant with a nearby doctor. In her spare time, she wrestled alligators. Not really, but it would be easier than all the work she did at home.

There was me, of course. Janey was twelve but thought she was seventeen and acted like she was five, at least when she was with me and there were no witnesses. She had inherited Mom's reddish-brown, straight hair, which Mom wore just past her shoulders, while Janey's went halfway down her back.

I felt my phone buzz. I pulled it out of my pocket but kept it hidden under the table.

Backup? Whatever. But okay

I texted Thomas back, ignoring the attitude.

Good. Lunch at Taco Bell? Need to show
u something crazy

That got his attention. His response was immediate.

Sure

Good. Thomas's size made him a solid wingman. I figured the two of us could handle anything that went down. I ate my cereal and helped clean up from breakfast. I was crafty and dropped a few complaints about being roped into chores on my first weekend of summer break just to make sure Mom didn't think anything was out of the ordinary.

I rode my bike to the park and arrived about ten minutes early. No one was there. With a few minutes to burn, I practiced my parkour moves on the jungle gym. It's not something I wanted to do with other people around because, well, my parkour moves deserved to be in scare quotes. As in, my parkour "moves."

Around 11:10 I started worrying that Thomas had blown me off, but he rode up a couple minutes later. Though Thomas had grown a lot in the past couple years, he was still riding his mountain bike from about three years ago. It was smaller than mine. That poor bike looked like it belonged in a circus with him riding it.

He set his bike on the ground and followed me over to

the merry-go-round.

"Got pretty crazy at the end yesterday," Thomas said. "Messed up our 'colloid' prank."

Thomas pushed his straight, brown hair out of his eyes as he spoke. The dude was always messing with his bangs. The rest of his hair was pretty short, but those bangs. It made my hands itch.

"Not quite," I said. "It was already messed up when Mr. Talbot snuck some during sixth period and made a scene in Mr. Sanders' room."

Thomas's eyes widened. "For real?"

"Oh yeah. Heard about it from Mr. Nichols."

His eyes got wider. "Mr. Nichols?"

"Yep. Got to go visit him during seventh period."

"Were you busted?"

"Nope. Some teachers spotted a dog or wolf or something. He left, and I walked out. Then the alarm went off."

Thomas let out a low whistle. "I heard about the dog. Didn't know it had helped you. Man, I wish I'd seen Mr. Talbot with soap bubbles coming out his mouth."

"Yeah, me too." I didn't mention there hadn't been any bubbles. "There's more."

I pulled the envelope out of my back pocket. Good. The creases had left the seal intact. I held up the envelope so Thomas could see the seal.

"What does that look like?" I asked him. "Look closely."

Thomas stuck his face right up next to the envelope for a few seconds and then sat back. "A butterfly."

I handed him the envelope.

"Not just any butterfly. Remember my birthmark? The one you saw at the sleepover? That one I keep secret 'cause, you know, it looks like a butterfly tattoo?" I stood and lifted up my shirt. I turned around so Thomas could see my back. "Compare them."

I strained my neck around to watch Thomas out of the corner of my eye. He looked at the envelope. Then he stood up and looked at my birthmark. Envelope. Birthmark.

Envelope. Birthmark.

"They're the same. I mean, identical. Not the same size, but the shape is the exact same. Where'd you get this?" Thomas asked, holding up the envelope.

I pulled down my shirt, took the envelope, and sat down beside him. "In my locker. I grabbed some gum before seventh period, so I know someone put it there between the start of seventh and the alarm going off. And that's not the strange part."

I pulled the letter out of the envelope and started reading it aloud. Thomas leaned in to look over my shoulder. I got about four sentences in before Thomas interrupted.

"Stop. What the heck are you up to? Isn't this a lot of work just to set me up for one of your ridiculous pranks?"

"Just listen," I said. "Do you really think I could write that neatly?"

I read down to Mara's name and stopped.

"Noon? Beckler Park?" Thomas glanced at his watch. "That's in half an hour. Dude, this is way too much effort to go to just to mess with me. I'm not hanging around to be the punch line to a prank."

"Thomas, there's no punch line, and I think I can prove it to you, though I'm not sure. Yesterday after school is kinda fuzzy."

"What are you talking about?"

"The tests," I said. "I haven't even read all of them. Just the first one. It was enough. I... I wanted a witness when I tried to do it again. I want to make sure I'm not going crazy. Like I said, we're not to the strange part yet."

"Joss," Thomas said, "I'm not getting suckered in no matter how innocent you sound."

My mouth tightened. He didn't believe me! I read the first test out loud.

THE TESTS

1. Relax your mind and body. Concentrate on your index finger (either hand). Concentrate hard. Pretend it isn't solid. Pretend it is a ghost finger. Hold this image in

*your mind for a full minute. Then tap on something hard
with that finger.*

"What. The. Heck." Thomas stood. "I'm outta here."

"Watch!"

As I relaxed and concentrated on my finger, I saw him
hesitate and then stop at the edge of my vision. I stared at
my finger and imagined it made of fog. Then I concentrated
some more, and worked even harder to relax. Relaxing was
hard work, but I did it.

I reached out and stuck my finger through the bar next
to me on the merry-go-round. I had desperately wanted to
feel my finger hit steel. No such luck.

"WHOA!" Thomas said. "What just happened? What
was THAT?"

I ignored him and held my focus on my ghost finger. I
inserted the finger straight into the pole. Around the second
knuckle I felt a resistance and couldn't push it in further, but
half my finger was inside the pole. I moved my finger
around. No real resistance short of the second knuckle, just
a slight pressure, like floating in calm water.

I pulled it out and let go of my thoughts. Then I reached
out and tapped the pole again. My finger struck solid metal.

"Now that," I said, "is the strange part."

Thomas's legs gave out and he thumped to the ground.

"What's going on?" he said. "You better not be
messing..." His voice trailed off.

I took a deep breath. "Don't know. I did it yesterday, but
it was hard to remember because I sort of passed out in slow
motion right after that. I wanted to be with someone when I
tried it again. You know, make sure I wasn't seeing things."

"It couldn't have happened. We just saw it wrong."

"It happened," I said. "I can't explain it, but we both saw
it, Thomas. My finger went through the pole. And the letter
kinda said that might happen. Like it was supposed to
happen. It's why we're here. To meet Mara."

"Bunk." He got to his feet. "I want to see you stick your
finger through the handlebars on my bike. I'm not going to

be messed with!"

I folded the letter back up in its envelope and put it in my back pocket as I stood up. We walked over to Thomas's bike and he held it upright.

"Now," he said, nodding toward the handlebars. "I want to see it again."

"Okay," I said, "but I'm telling the truth. You saw—"

"Shut up. The handlebars. Now."

I shut up and concentrated. It felt easier this time, like I knew it would work. I thought about the ghost finger, and held the image in my mind. I reached out and passed my finger through his handlebars. Then I reached under the seat and inserted my finger up through it so the fingertip stuck out on top. I wiggled it, and pulled it out.

"That's as far as I've gotten," I said. "I haven't even read the other six tests. You saw it, right? I'm not crazy?"

I looked up at him. Thomas looked pale and swayed back and forth. I punched him on the shoulder.

"Thomas! I'm not crazy, right? You saw it?"

He spoke, but it was too quiet to hear.

"What?"

"I saw it." Thomas shook his head and flared his eyes open for a moment. "This is insane."

"I know."

"What's the rest of the letter say?"

"I told you," I said, "I haven't read it yet. I got that far and thought I was losing my mind."

"Yeah. I get that. So what are you thinking?"

"I think we read the rest of the letter. And then we meet Mara."

Chapter 4

MEETING MARA

"WHAT ARE YOU getting me into?" Thomas asked.

I had no answer. We went back to the merry-go-round and sat down. As I reached for the letter in my back pocket, the faint sound of a car door closing caught my ear. I looked up and saw a woman walking toward us from the elementary school parking lot across the street. As she got closer, I realized she was coming right for us. Thomas and I sat up straight at the same time.

"Guessing that's Mara," Thomas said out of the corner of his mouth. "Way early."

She walked right up to us, though it wasn't just walking. She seemed to flow across the ground. I guessed she was in her twenties. Tall, with dark, wavy hair just past her shoulders. Jeans tucked into black boots and a dark T-shirt that said BOYS ARE BETTER ~~THAN~~ IN BOOKS. She was beautiful.

Mara smiled.

"Hey Joss," she said. "I'm Mara. Mah-rah"

The second time she said her name slowly, like we needed help saying it right. Which we did. I'd been pronouncing it May-rah.

"And you must be Thomas," she said.

"Yeah," I said, "that's us. So. Little freaky that you know all about me."

Mara smiled. "Oh, I doubt that's the freakiest thing that's happened if you actually did the tests I gave you."

"Good point," Thomas said.

"Joss, does Thomas know?"

"That I can stick my finger into solid steel?" I said. "Yeah, he knows."

Her breath caught when I spoke, and her eyes tightened up. She looked away for a moment, her mouth pulled into a line.

The moment passed. She looked back at me and smiled.

"Test one? You passed test one?"

"I guess."

"And the others?" she asked.

"I haven't even read them yet," I said.

"You didn't read the whole letter?"

I shook my head. "Stopped after test one. It was all so weird."

"Okay, I can work with that," she said. "But you need to read it. I'm not going to explain it all now, but you're in danger, and we don't have a lot of time. That's why I'm here. Now, Thomas, what do we do with you?"

She cocked her head to one side and folded her arms together, looking at him. Thomas stood and struck a tough-guy pose. He was eye to eye with her, even with the couple of inches of heel on her boots. Mara didn't seem to notice.

"What does that mean?" he asked.

She ignored him and kept thinking. Seconds tripped by.

"This is for the best," she said at last. "We'll need a class anyway. Thomas, you can help. You can be our inside man."

Thomas's eyebrows scrunched together in confusion. "Your inside man?"

She ignored him and turned to me. "Have your parents ever mentioned the Guild of Sevens?"

That wasn't what I'd expected. Had I expected anything? Thomas looked at me, his eyebrows still scrunched up.

"Uh, not really," I said.

"Nothing?" Mara asked. "No Guild? The Guild? The Guild of Sevens? The Sevens?"

Each word was spoken like a proper name. Each word meant nothing to me. Wait.

"Yeah, I've heard something like that."

"Good," Mara said. "What have you heard?"

I frowned. So now I was supposed to tell her about my family? "Not much. Something about a guild."

"Hey, you don't have to tell me anything. But I know you've got questions after passing that test, so you'll have to work with me a little if you want help wrapping your head around what's going on."

I did want to know. I wanted to know why she had given me the letter. How she'd known about my birthmark. What she meant when she said I was in danger. All of it.

"Well," I said, "It was like three years ago, and we were visiting my aunt and uncle for Christmas. I might have been up reading a bit later than my parents realized. Anyway, I got hungry, and headed toward the kitchen for a snack, only I heard all the adults talking. My parents, my aunt and uncle, and everyone sounded intense. My uncle said something like, he's got to get tested, I saw the birthmark, and the guild doesn't let sevens slip through the cracks. And then Dad got even more intense and said that wasn't going to happen."

"Idiot," Thomas said. "You heard that three years ago and never figured out your birthmark was important?"

I stood up and glared at him.

"Like I should have assumed it meant I had superpowers?"

"It's cute watching you two argue." Mara waved a hand between us. "However, this is serious business. Settle down."

"So who are you?" I asked, turning my irritation and fear on her. "How do you know all about me?"

"I'm a Seven," she said, "Like you. I know all that stuff because I work with the Guild, and we keep tabs on our Sevens. And we need you. We can't afford right now to have your parents keep you out of the action."

Again, not what I'd expected.

"I'm not gonna lie," Thomas said. "That sounded so cool, and made so little sense."

"I told you in the letter," she continued, "the butterfly is the symbol of Sharif, your family line."

"Sharif?" I said. "I'm so confused. My last name is Morgan."

"I know. The family names go back to the beginning. But names change through marriage and other shifts. Usually, there's only one Seven from each family at any time, born with the birthmark."

"Sharif," I said. "Sevens. The Guild. Does the crazy ever slow down?"

"You'll get there."

"And you're a Seven?" Thomas asked.

"Yes," Mara said.

"You can stick your finger into stuff?" he asked.

"Nope," she said. "I have other talents."

"What does that mean?" I asked. "Do you have a birthmark?"

"Sure. The owl. Goes with the Montuhotep family. But I don't show it to boys." Mara pulled a closed knife out of a pocket. "Now, as for my talent. Watch."

I took a quick step back at the sight of the knife, hit the merry-go-round with my calf, and sat down hard. Thomas stood his ground, but shifted between his feet, his hands balled in fists. Mara twitched her forefinger and the knife flicked open. She gritted her teeth and slashed the knife across the back of her forearm up near the elbow. A deep red line immediately started weeping blood.

I was shocked. Thomas sat down hard beside me.

"Just watch," Mara said. "I'm not a psycho. Just showing my talent."

She held up her arm across her body so we could see the blood drip to the ground. Then it stopped. The wound just closed up like a zipper, leaving blood smeared on her arm. She put the knife up, produced a tissue, and wiped away the blood.

There was nothing. No wound. No scar. Nothing. After a few seconds, I remembered to start breathing again.

"There are seven talents," Mara said, "but most of us only have two or three of them. That's one of mine. Look,

I've got to get back to the dojo... the, uh, martial arts training center. Here's what I'd like you guys to do." While she spoke, she pulled a folded piece of paper out of her back pocket. She handed it to me.

"Grab some lunch if you want, then come by our facility. It's called a dojo. It's close to here. I can answer your questions and we can figure out what comes next. We need to get you trained, Joss. Things are moving quickly. Read the rest of the letter, but you might as well wait to do the tests with me."

I unfolded the paper. It was a hand-drawn map. At the top was a squarish area labeled "Beckler Park." A set of arrows led from the park to a location marked with an X several blocks away near the railroad tracks.

"That's the dojo," Mara said and leaned forward to tap a finger on the X. "Come by this afternoon, okay? Joss? I'm serious."

"Yeah." I licked my lips. My mouth was parched. "The dojo-thing. Got it."

"See you then," Mara said.

With that, she glided back toward Franklin Elementary School. She went straight to the parking lot, got in a little silver Toyota, and zipped out of sight moments later.

"I think," Thomas said after a moment, "we may be in over our heads. What's our play?"

"Start with the letter, I guess."

I pulled the folded up envelope out of my pocket again and retrieved the letter. I read out loud starting with test two.

2. Relax your mind and body. Concentrate on your index finger (either hand). Concentrate hard. Pretend it is hard as rock. Pretend it is steel. Hold this image in your mind for a full minute. Then tap on something solid with that finger.

3. Relax your mind and body. Take a pin and prick your finger so it bleeds a little bit. Concentrate on the blood, the skin, the tiny hole. Imagine the hole closing up. See the skin knit back together. Feel it become whole.

"That's Mara," Thomas interjected. "It was unreal how the cut just disappeared."

I nodded in agreement and kept reading.

> 4. *Relax your mind and body. Sit at a table, and put a small, familiar object on the table in front of you. Use a pencil or a pen. Think about the object and nothing else. Imagine it rotating around on the table. Concentrate hard, and SEE it rotating.*

"That's like telekineptics, or, uh, telekinitis," Thomas said. "Tele-move-stuff-around!"

"Telekinesis," I said, "Like Jean Grey in the X-Men."

"Yes! That's the one. Joss, if this stuff is real... can you imagine?"

"You still think I was faking my finger going through metal?" I asked. "You think I faked sticking it through your bike seat? You think Mara faked that cut?"

"No," he said, "but it's a lot to process."

Yes, it was. I continued.

> 5. *Relax your mind and body. Stand near a plant. Hold your hand near the leaves and concentrate on your hand. Pretend your hand is transparent, and you can see the leaves through it. Hold this image in your mind for a full minute.*

"So, like, invisibility?" Thomas asked. "Or chameleon powers? Dude! I'm not saying you would do anything bad if you could do that, but imagine being able to sneak around without being seen!"

At that moment, I realized that I had been building up toward a complete panic all morning. It had been like the tide coming in, slow but relentless. Right then, I felt like my stomach was full of ice cubes. My chest felt tight. But Thomas was right. Why was I feeling so intense about this? It was incredible. I had superpowers. My panic ignored me and kept on panicking.

"Hey, settle down." Thomas elbowed me. "You're breathing fast."

I nodded, took a long, slow breath, and continued with the letter.

6. Relax your mind and body. Sit at a table with a sheet of paper and a pen. Draw 60 dots spread out on the paper in a grid. Tap each dot with your finger. See how fast you can do it. Now close your eyes and pretend you are touching all the dots four times as fast. Picture your hand moving with incredible speed. Open your eyes and see how fast you can touch the dots.

7. Relax your mind and body. Sit with a picture of a cat or dog in front of a mirror. Stare at the animal's ears. Concentrate on them fully. Now close your eyes and imagine your ears look the same. Hold this image firmly in mind for a minute, then open your eyes and look at yourself in the mirror.

END OF DIAGNOSTIC TESTS

Thomas gave long, low whistle. "That last one was super weird, but the implications. Wow."

"Yeah," I said, "but I'm still not seeing the danger part."

P.S. In case you still don't want to talk tomorrow in the park, you need to know that there is a Mocker setting up shop in town. Mockers are sort of like the mob, but they use Sevens. VERY BAD. He's looking for the person with the butterfly birthmark. You and your family are in grave danger.

"And there it is," Thomas said. "So, we've got Sevens, the Guild, and now the Mockers? Joss, this is crazy. What are you going to do? Are you going to do the tests?"

My stomach lurched like I was on a roller coaster. Too much to process. "Not right now. We need to figure out if we're going to the dojo."

"We've got to, right?" Thomas asked.

"But we don't really know who Mara is! She could be waiting there to, I don't know, kidnap us! We don't know what she wants. She could be making all this up."

"I don't think so," Thomas said. "She knew tons about you. If this Guild was trying to snatch you, would they talk to you first? Let you know they're on to you? Or would they just grab you?"

"Yeah, that sort of makes sense."

"And your parents did know about it, right?"

"I guess," I said. "But I don't think they like it."

"But it didn't sound like your uncle thought it was evil, right?"

"Probably not," I said, struggling to remember the words, the tone. "Alright. We go to the dojo."

"After I run home and grab some lunch," Thomas said. "I'm starved."

"Didn't I text you we should hit up Taco Bell?"

Thomas checked the messages on his phone.

"Yep," he said. "Totally forgot. I need to grab some cash and let my mom know. Hey, that's a great cover. Isn't Taco Bell close to where the map said the dojo was?"

I pictured the map in my mind. "Yeah, it would be. Okay, I forgot to get money anyway. Meet me at the corner by my house in five minutes?"

"Sure thing. And Joss, I know this probably isn't the case, but if you're playing me... if this whole thing is an elaborate prank, I will kill you and hide the body. Just sayin'."

Chapter 5

THE DOJO

"You WANT FIVE dollars?" Mom crossed her arms. "I told you I was fine if you ate there, but I didn't think I was signing up to pay for it."

"Mom, is it really a celebration of school being over if I have to pay?" I asked. "I'll bring back the change."

Mom gave me a flat look. I kept my face blank. I knew that if I appeared upset, she'd think I was acting entitled and shut it down.

She turned toward her purse. "Oh, you know what, sure. It's the first day of summer. My treat. But don't expect to do this every day."

A couple minutes later, I was sitting on my bike at the corner of Appleton and Chickadee Place. My house was at the end of the cul-de-sac, 3713 Chickadee Place. A cool five dollars rode along in the front pocket of my shorts, courtesy of Mom. I loved Taco Bell. Lunch was going to be epic.

In reality, though, I had trouble thinking about anything other than my finger sinking into a metal pole, and butterfly birthmarks, and Guilds, and Sevens. Even an upcoming lunch at Taco Bell couldn't distract me. I was going to have to figure things out, or go crazy. A couple minutes later, Thomas came into sight, riding his little bike.

He pulled up next to me. "You're breathing fast again."

"Right." I tried to take a normal breath. "This whole thing's got me freaked out."

"You're scared, aren't you?"

"What if I am? Wouldn't you be if you'd just found out you could, you know, do weird things?"

Thomas tilted his head. "I don't know. When I watch a superhero movie, I want to be the hero. Don't you?"

"Yeah, sure. Everyone wants to be a hero. But it's not the same."

"Maybe. Either way, I'm still hungry. Let's go eat."

Taco Bell wasn't a disappointment. Chalupas were incapable of disappointing me. But I still felt panicked, and the food sat heavy in my stomach.

"You're dawdling," Thomas said. "You think we shouldn't do this?"

I looked up from extracting each and every one of the tiny bits of leftovers in my chalupa papers. Dawdling? What was he talking about?

"Oh yeah," I said. "I'm good. Just making sure I don't waste anything."

"I guess," he said. "But I still say you're putting it off."

I grimaced and crumpled up my trash.

We cleaned up the table and headed out to our bikes. They were strapped together and locked to a parking sign using Thomas's super-long bike lock cable. He unlocked it and stashed it on his bike by winding it about thirty times around his seat stem. I pulled out the map and we looked it over one last time before heading out. It was a quick five-minute ride. We stopped at the corner of the last turn. The dojo was the third building on the left.

"We going in?" Thomas asked.

I glanced at him and nodded, but stayed put and studied the building. It looked like a worn-out, smallish warehouse. Three loading bay doors were closed, and there were stairs and an access ramp to a normal door to the left of them, about four feet above the parking lot. White paint had flecked off in places to expose concrete underneath. Mara's little Toyota sat out front, parked next to a black, two-door BMW.

"Let's do this," I said, and pushed off. Thomas was right behind me.

We pulled in next to the ramp, and Thomas locked our

bikes together to the ramp railing. I gave him a quick nod when he stood up from the bikes, and we headed up the stairs to the door. On it, small letters proclaimed it was the BATTLEHOOP SCHOOL OF MARTIAL ARTS. I pulled open the door, and Thomas and I stepped through.

The inside was a huge room with a couple offices along the left side and bathrooms toward the rear. The shades were drawn on the offices, hiding their interiors. The middle of the room was dominated by a raised, square platform covered with firm-looking blue mats. Nine large white circles were painted on the mats, like a giant game of tic-tac-toe, except everyone had played Os. The platform stood about waist high off the floor.

All sorts of gym equipment were scattered around the platform. Heavy bags, speed bags, stationary bikes, racks of free weights, yoga mats, medicine balls, and other stuff. Over to the right of the entrance, from this side, the loading bay doors looked like they had been sealed off. The whole place smelled of rubber and metal.

A very large man came out of the door to the office closest to the front wall. He was wearing a black tank top, black baggy pants that were cinched at his ankles, and white tennis shoes. His dark, shaved scalp reflected the lights hanging from the ceiling.

He wasn't just large. He was huge. Maybe six and a half feet tall and all muscle. Thomas and I shifted in place as he walked over to us. Then Mara stepped out from behind him and gave me a smile.

"Hey Joss," she said. "Glad you came by. Jordan, this is Joss."

The huge man nodded to me. "Joss, glad you decided to come by. You made the right choice." He spoke in a low, quiet voice.

"And this is Joss' friend, Thomas," Mara said. "I told you about him."

"Hey," Thomas said.

Jordan glanced at Thomas and nodded, then turned back to me. "Mara says you passed test one." He looked like my sister did when she was waiting to open her Christmas gifts. Excited and greedy. It looked gross on a grownup.

"Yeah, test one," I said. "I stuck my finger in a steel pole."

"Good." His face relaxed. "Joss, you did the right thing coming here today. I know this all seems, well, sudden, but I've been assigned by the Guild to get you trained fast. We believe a Mocker is on your trail, and we think you're just the person to take him down. We're going to turn the tables on him. Got it?"

"I think so," I said. "Well, not really."

Jordan smiled for a moment. "It'll be fine. Plenty of time for questions later." He turned to Mara. "Take him through the rest of the tests. I'm going to show Thomas the incredible program we are offering at Battlehoop this summer and see if we can sign up some of their friends."

"Sure thing," Mara said. "Joss? Let's just step over to one of these yoga mats. We can run through the rest of the tests in no time."

"I... uh..." I said.

Jordan laid a big hand on Thomas's shoulder and took him over to a small table stacked with papers along the front wall. Mara put a hand on my left elbow and guided me to the left side of the platform. A neat stack of papers, two pens, a hand mirror, and a pincushion sat on the floor beside a yoga mat. I could hear Jordan talking in a low rumble, but couldn't catch the words.

Well, Thomas and I were still in sight of each other. I'd roll with it. Mara and I sat on either end of the yoga mat facing each other. She had changed since the park. She was now barefoot and wearing leggings with a fitted T-shirt that said MY DAY STARTS WITH COFFEE.

"Let's start at the beginning. Can you show me?" She said. "Test one? Just use the floor."

"I... sure." I closed my eyes and concentrated. I felt the change. It happened almost immediately. I stuck my finger into the concrete floor. It went in all the way up to the last joint this time.

"Quick tip," Mara said. "Don't get in the habit of closing your eyes. Any little tic like that can become a habit."

"Okay. So my eyes should be open?"

"Open or closed. Doesn't matter. Just don't close them if they are open. Don't make a habit out of any specific approach to using your talent."

"Got it," I said, like we were just making small talk while I wiggled my finger in concrete. "Wait. No I don't. Why not?"

"As a Seven, you want to develop flexibility. Adaptability. You don't want needless habits hindering your use of your talents."

"I think that makes sense." I pulled my finger out of the concrete and let it return to normal. "I slept like 14 hours last night. That was after a two-hour nap."

"Totally expected," she said. "It's hard on the body when a Seven comes into his powers. I think I crashed for a full day and night. It's why I told you in the letter to do the tests right before bed."

"Oh. That makes sense. So you're a Seven. You can heal yourself."

"I am, and I can. I'm a shifty reggie," Mara said.

"A shifty reggie," I said.

"Yeah," Mara said. "Each of the seven talents has a nickname. You've read all seven tests?"

"Yes. I, uh, don't remember all the details."

"That's fine," she said. "You'll pick it up. A shifty reggie is test seven, shape shifting, and test three, regeneration. Those are my two talents. So I can take a lot of damage and keep going, and I can honestly say there's not a better shape shifter out there than me."

Shape shifting. Something clicked in my mind.

"The letter," I said. "Yesterday at school. Some teachers thought they saw a wolf or dog or something about the time your letter ended up in my locker."

"Guilty." Mara smiled. "I didn't go in as a wolf. I started much more discretely, but when I saw you go into the principal's office, I thought it might help you out if there was a distraction of some sort."

"You saw me? Going to the principal's office?" That motion I'd seen. "Were you, maybe, smaller at first?"

"I was. Like I said, I'm a very good shifter. Most can't really change their mass when shifting. I can. Lets me stay unnoticed."

"Huh." I glanced over at Thomas. He and Jordan were looking at some papers together. "I guess I owe you, 'cause I was going to get busted."

"Glad I could help."

"And you said Sevens don't have all seven talents?"

"Right," Mara said.

"And this?" I nodded at my finger and stuck it back into the concrete.

"You're a ghost. Doing that is called ghosting. The talent names get used lots of different ways."

"What's the point of sticking your finger in concrete," I asked. "I mean, if I play it right I'm sure I can win some bets, but what's the point?"

"Well, we're going to help you learn to pass your whole body through solids. We're going to teach you to control your movements when in solids, and to stay safe."

"Oh."

"Yeah," Mara said. "It's not a talent to be trifled with."

"And you said I'd learn to do it safely? It can be unsafe?"

"You don't want to run out of steam, say, when you are passing through a steel wall," she said. "But we'll get to all that. First, let's do the rest of the tests."

"Will it make me tired again?" I asked.

"Using talents is always an exertion, but it's like using muscle. You get stronger with practice, and it will never be as bad as that first time. Not even close."

"Why wouldn't my parents want me to know about the Guild? What is it?"

"You like asking questions." She smiled. "The Guild's an organization, a really old one, devoted to using the Sevens to keep the world sane. It's made of ranking members of the various families, the ones who still care. I don't really know why your parents didn't want you knowing about the Guild, but they aren't the only ones who feel that way. More and more Sevens go through life never knowing about their talents."

"But why?"

"Well, I guess some parents think it's a bunch of myths. Family legends. That sort of thing. They don't want their kids sucked in by an organization fronting a myth."

"Mara?" I asked.

"Yes, Joss?

"I'm pretty freaked out by all of this."

"I understand." Mara leaned forward and reached out to give my hand a quick squeeze. "That's the heart of it, isn't it? It doesn't matter how cool it is, or how amazing the talents. They aren't normal, and that makes it feel bad."

"Something like that."

"I get it. I've been there. You'll do great. Let's just take one step at a time. The tests?"

I felt like the whole world was holding its breath, waiting on my answer. Why was all this happening to me? I didn't have the answers. I could stick my finger into metal and concrete. That's what I knew. And I wanted to know more.

"Let's do the tests," I said.

Chapter 6

SEVENTY-SEVEN

"LET'S RUN THROUGH the tests in order," Mara said. "We'll start with bruising."

"Bruising?" I asked.

"Think of bruising others, not you. Makes sense? A bruiser can harden himself to the point where bullets bounce off him. Or, picture your hand hardened when you hit someone. It can be a real asset in a fight. Of course, bruisers tend to move a bit slower and more stiffly."

"Yeah, of course. I've heard they totally move slower."

Mara gave me a warm smile. It made me want to do something heroic. "Do you remember the test? Relax. Concentrate. Make your finger hard as rock."

I concentrated on my finger, picturing it harden into stone. My eyes started to close, but I forced them open this time, and after a few seconds I felt a change. I reached down and tapped the floor. My finger pinged against the floor as though two rocks were being tapped together.

"Wow." Mara's eyebrows lifted. "You're also a bruiser. I don't think that's common."

"What's not common?" I said. "Is any of this common?"

"I mean, the bruiser-ghost combo is uncommon. They're very yin-yang, so it's fantastic to have both. Just not common."

"Okay," I said. So I wasn't just a freak, but an uncommon freak.

"Onward!" Mara said.

She reached over to the pincushion and selected a pin.

"Your hand?" she said. "Need to check if you are a reggie like me."

"I meant to ask about reggie. What's up with that name?"

"Short for regeneration. Think, Wolverine."

I nodded in appreciation and held out my hand. Mara took it and jabbed the pin into my index finger.

"Ow! What the heck?" Blood welled up from the puncture in my fingertip. "Did you have to stick it in all the way to the bone?"

"Don't be a baby." Mara put the pin back. "Now concentrate. Try to heal it."

"How?" I asked.

"If you can do it, it'll feel natural, even the first time. Reggie is usually the most intuitive talent. In fact, it's the only talent that can be trained to run on auto-pilot. Over time your body just starts healing itself, usually before you even know there's a problem. But that can take years to acquire."

I concentrated, and I had the odd sensation of the pain just melting away. A gleaming droplet of blood still sat on my fingertip, but the pain was gone. Intrigued, I stuck my finger in my mouth and cleaned off the blood with one good lick.

"Ewwww," Mara said.

I held out my finger, awestruck by the seamless whole skin. I showed it to Mara. Her eyes widened.

"Ghost. Bruiser. Reggie. Three talents. And we've only done three tests. Let's keep going."

"Hold on," I said. "This whole auto-pilot thing. Why didn't your cut heal immediately? Back at Beckler Park?"

Mara nodded at me and smiled. "Good memory. I was actually concentrating on not healing for a minute there. I figured you'd think I'd faked the cut if it didn't bleed a little first."

"That's pretty intense." A wave of tiredness swept over me. "Whoa. Starting to feel like I need to rest."

"I told you it would be tiring." Mara picked up a pen

and set it on the mat between us. "Let's keep moving. Try to rotate it."

I reached out and flicked the pen on one end. It spun in place.

"I think I'm pretty good at this one." I smirked. "What's that talent called?"

"It's called being a smart aleck."

I looked back down at the pen. This whole thing was madness. I'd just healed myself. Now I was going to move a pen without touching it? I clamped down on my emotions. Just had to keep talking. Keep taking the tests.

"So what's this one really called?" I asked.

"Telly."

"Telly?"

"Yeah, like, telekinesis."

"I get it," I said, nodding.

I concentrated and pictured the pen moving. Nothing happened. I *reached* for the pen with my mind. For a moment, I was thrown off by the odd sensation that I could feel the pen. That I was somehow holding it. I concentrated harder.

The pen jerked around a quarter turn. It felt as though I had moved the pen with some invisible appendage, but the pen had felt more like a couch.

"Huh," I said. "That's pretty cool."

My body felt weak, and I couldn't hold back a yawn.

"I'm stunned," Mara said. "We're getting into pretty rare territory with four talents. Add telly to your list of talents. Three more to go, Joss. Do you think you have any more talents to show?"

How should I know? Mara's eyes looked past me over my shoulder, and I twisted around to see Thomas and Jordan walking over to us. I looked back at Mara. She raised an eyebrow in question, still looking at Jordan.

"We're good to go," Jordan said. "Thomas here is going to recruit our class for us. He's going to be rewarded for getting us at least three more students. And to keep his mouth shut about his friend."

I glanced over to Thomas, who gave me a quick thumbs up.

"Class?" I asked.

"Just finish the tests," Jordan said, "then we'll break it down for you. Any other passes?"

"He's a ghost, bruiser, reggie, and telly," Mara said. "Three tests to go."

Jordan's eyebrows climbed up his forehead and made a run for his bald scalp.

"That's unusual," Jordan said.

"Awesome." Thomas looked from me to Mara, and then Jordan. "That's good, right?"

Mara ignored Thomas and pulled a paper printed with a picture of a brick wall from the bottom of the stack of paper.

"Back to work." Mara lay the picture on the mat in front of me. "I know this is exhausting. You'll get through it, and it will make you stronger. Next up is blending."

"Like, blending into things?"

"That's about it. Now relax. Concentrate. Lay your hand on the paper. Imagine you can see the picture through your hand."

I relaxed. I concentrated. I put my hand on the paper. I concentrated some more. Nothing happened. Jordan grunted.

"So, not a blender," Mara said. Was there a hint of satisfaction in her voice?

I ignored them. It felt like my hand shouldn't still be visible, but there it was. I was doing something wrong. I had been trying to will the picture of the bricks to become visible through my hand. Instead I shifted my focus to the hand alone. The hand was opaque, but I thought of it just fading from sight. Not like with ghosting. Still solid, but invisible.

"Whoa!" Thomas yelled, just as Mara inhaled sharply.

"Yes!" Jordan's voice had an edge of abandon to it, like his team had just kicked a winning field goal in overtime.

My hand was still there. It looked normal.

"What? It isn't working," I said.

"Oh, it's working," Mara said. "You'ı was
blender." ble

If I hadn't known better, I would have tho\
mad. Her eyebrows were pulled together aı
sounded harsh.

"But..."
a
"Blenders can't see themselves blending." ı
words came out in a rush. "They have to be coached\
talents need coaching, but blenders more than other\
when you're more or less invisible to others, you'll
normal to yourself."

I looked at my hand. It was my hand. I looked up
Thomas.

"I think I may sort of see your fingers," Thomas said ɛ
he stepped closer. "Nope, they are pretty much gone. This
is awesome." He glanced at Jordan. "And totally top secret."

"Joss," Mara said. "Two more."

"Hold on," I said. "Do I have to be naked for this to
work? I mean, once I learn how to really do it with all of me?
How does it work?"

"No." Mara grimaced. What had gotten into her? "It's
not like that. Ghosts, bruisers, blenders, and shifters... it's
hard to explain. Basically, stuff close to you gets pulled
along by the talent. But it has to be really close. Like, within
an inch."

"So when I ghost?"

"Your clothes ghost with you as long as they're fairly
snug."

"And if they aren't?" I asked.

"Let's say you wore a cowboy hat while ghosting
through a wall. The main part of the hat would ghost with
you, but the brim would probably be destroyed if you took
it through something solid. It's why, when you meet other
Sevens, you're going to notice most of us wear tight
clothing."

"What did you call this?" I asked and pointed at the
brick wall picture.

"Blending," Mara said, her words still clipped. What

up with that? Had she wanted me to fail? "You're a ider. Any other questions?"

"Tons," I said.

"Tough luck," she said. "On to the next test."

She put a plain sheet of paper on the mat in front of me, id then handed me the pen I had moved a few minutes efore with my mind.

"Draw fifty or sixty dots on the paper. Spread them out."

Easy enough. I drew sixty dots. Six rows of ten. When I looked up, Mara was holding her phone with a stopwatch app ready to go.

"Okay, this is the test for the kinney talent. Touch all the dots as fast as you can with a finger."

Again, pretty straight forward stuff. I touched the dots.

"11.4 seconds," Mara said. "Now close your eyes and visualize touching them twice as fast, and then twice as fast as that, and then twice as fast a third time. Then open your eyes and touch the dots as fast as possible. And be ready. This one will leave you wrung out."

"So six seconds, then three seconds, then one and a half seconds?" I asked.

"It doesn't have to be that exact, but yes."

I closed my eyes. I relaxed. I concentrated. In my mind's eye, I was wearing a red Flash outfit, and my hand blazed across those dots. I took it one further than Mara had said, because Flash could totally get it done in less than a second.

My eyes popped open, and I touched those dots as fast as possible. When done, I looked up in time to see Mara's thumb slowly descending toward the stop button in the app. That was odd. The time on her app seemed to be ticking by in slow motion. Then everything clicked back to normal.

Thomas made a choking sound. Mara's eyes were huge. She held up her phone.

0.74s

A yawn cracked my jaws. Mara hadn't been joking. I was worn out.

Mara slapped a paper with a picture of a dog down on the mat in front of me. It was a close-up of its head. Probably a German shepherd. It had perky ears. She passed me the hand mirror.

"What was that last talent called again?" I asked.

"Kinney. You're a kinney. If you're also a shifter—"

"The Seventy-Seven," Jordan's voice cracked as he spoke.

"A seventy-seven?" I said.

"THE Seventy-Seven," Mara said. "I guess there could be more than one at a time, but it's very rare. The Seventy-Seven. All seven talents. There hasn't been a Seventy-Seven since the Italian died back in '83. We'll see. Take a good hard look at that picture, then close your eyes and picture your ears becoming like the dog's."

"This one is just so weird," I said.

"You think so?" Mara asked.

"Yeah," I said. "Don't get me wrong. It could make for a great Halloween costume."

Mara shook her head. "You're not thinking about the big picture again. You're just focusing on the test itself. Watch."

She shifted, blurred, and suddenly a brownish-golden eagle stood where Mara had sat.

"Whoa!" Thomas yelled as he scrambled backwards. His legs tangled and he sat down hard. If he wasn't careful he was going to make a habit of falling over. I remained perfectly still, but I may have lost bladder control for a split second. At least the fright woke me back up.

The eagle, Mara, leapt into the air and beat powerful wings as it circled the room twice before landing on the pad opposite me. There was another moment of eye-wrenching oddness, and Mara sat across from me once again.

"You see?" Mara said. "It's not like putting on a costume. It's about changing all of you."

"Joss," Thomas said in a quiet, awed voice from where he sat, "you've got to learn to do that."

"Yeah," I said. "Like you said, Mara, I guess I was just thinking about the dog ears, not the whole thing. So if I'm a kin… what was that word?"

"Kinney," Mara said. "As in, kinetic energy. The energy

of motion."

"Kinney," I repeated. "So if I'm a kinney, it isn't just about moving my hand really fast. I could be Flash for real."

"Where do you think the idea of Flash came from?" Jordan asked.

"It will take a lot of practice to move your entire body that fast," Mara said. "Or ghost your entire body. Or heal a huge wound. Or shift into an animal shape. Or whatever. But yes, that's what we're going to train you to do."

"Let's do this, then," I said. "Let's see if I'm the Seventy-Seven."

Mara tapped the picture of the dog. I concentrated on the picture and focused in on the ears. I took in every detail. I pictured myself with those ears. It was strange. It didn't feel like I was pretending. It felt like work. Hard work. I was so tired.

Thomas gasped.

"There will be no stopping us," Jordan said in a low rumble under his breath. How had I heard him? Mara held up the little mirror. I only saw a flash of the impossible before my concentration shattered and the image was the normal me.

Mara looked at me, her eyes wide. "The Seventy-Seven."

Chapter 7

THE PLAN

"COOL." I STRETCHED. "The Seventy-Seven. What comes next?"

I was so very tired. Not zombified like Friday, but bone weary. And I didn't feel like things were cool. When I was in fifth grade, someone had run a red light and hit our minivan. We'd all made it through okay, but I'd struggled with nightmares for a couple months. I kept seeing the car coming right for us. All this Seventy-Seven stuff made me feel like I was stuck in that moment right before impact.

"Thomas can break it down for you," Jordan said. "Short version is we're going to give a free class this summer. In return, you agree to spread the word next year in high school."

"It's sort of a cover," Thomas said. "Sure, we get trained to be like ninjas or something, but you get trained as a Seven. A class within the class." Thomas smiled and rubbed his hands. "And I score some serious money."

"You need to get home, Joss," Mara said as she gave Thomas a hard look. "All these tests wore you out. Like you just tried to sprint five miles. Sync up with Thomas tomorrow after you get home from church. If all goes well, we'll see you on Tuesday."

"Tuesday," I said. "Wait. How do you know I go to church?"

"Go!" Mara stood up. She pulled me to my feet and marched me to the door with Thomas, who held a large mailing envelope. When had he gotten that?

"Thomas," Mara said, "Get him home and make sure we

have a class to teach, okay?"

"You bet, Mara."

What, so now he was in tight with Mara? How did that happen? I didn't have time to sort it out, because I was shuffled out the door to my bike. A minute later we were on the way back to our neighborhood.

"So the sleep thing," Thomas said, "you getting tired all of a sudden, it's the Seven stuff?"

"Yeah," I said, "Mara said it has to do with the talents waking up. Something like that."

"So the talents wake up and you go to sleep," Thomas said.

I smirked. Then I swerved. How had I not seen that fire hydrant?

"Something like that," I said. "She said I'll get stronger with training. It's just that today… it's bad."

We turned into our neighborhood.

"You know the really weird thing?" Thomas asked. "We're riding our bikes talking about you being a freakin' superhero like it's normal."

"I guess." I grimaced. I felt overwhelmed, not heroic. "I'm pretty much clueless as to what comes next. What's the plan?"

"What happens next is I make some money," he said. "And I help provide a cover for you to receive training all summer long while learning some serious martial arts. It's a win-win-win."

"Break it down for me."

"Okay. You need training, right?"

"Pretty sure I do," I said. And a soda. Or maybe coffee.

"And your parents. They're not going to sign up with the Guild to train you?"

"I don't think so," I said. "And I don't want to ask to find out, 'cause once they've said no, it's game over."

"Exactly," Thomas said. "So Jordan and Mara are going to offer a free class this summer. It's supposedly to help them build the business next fall. They train a few of us with a crazy intense course. All morning, five days a week. We spread the word next fall at school. Show off what we've learned. That's the story."

"Who's in this class?"

"I'm recruiting Tyler, Deion, and Arjeet. Maybe Frankie and Julius. The dojo is totally legit, and our parents can tour it if they want, watch the training, whatever. There'll be some one-on-one time each day. That's when you'll get trained as a Seven. The rest of the time you'll be trained with the rest of us."

"And the money?" I asked.

"Right," Thomas said. "I'm their inside guy. I can get the students they need for a cover. I know all the secrets. So they pay me a hundred bucks a week. Cash."

"Wow!" I said.

"Like I said, it's a win-win-win. You get trained to be all freaky cool, I get money, and on top of that I learn how to be a tough guy. Should help in high school, right?"

"Yeah it should. So when do we start?"

"Tuesday, 8:00 sharp," he said. "Doesn't give me much time to recruit, but I'll get it done. I'll sell them on the idea. Then we let them sell their parents on this great chance to work out all summer. That's free. Once in a lifetime opportunity. Blah blah blah. Shouldn't be a problem."

We turned onto Appleton.

"So," I said, "you're going to tell the guys they should get up early every day to learn martial arts? That's it?"

"No," Thomas said. "I'm going to tell them they should get up early to learn martial arts from a hot chick. You can't leave out the hot chick part, Joss. Really. You need to learn how to sell."

"You are wise, Master," I said.

"Thank you, Grasshopper. I'll hand you a flyer when we stop. Tell your parents they should come with you the first day to check out the place. Seriously. Push to have them go with you. It will make it seem totally legit."

"Just that simple, huh?"

"Just that simple," Thomas said.

We pulled to a stop at the corner of Appleton and

Chickadee Place. Thomas opened the mailing envelope and pulled out a flyer printed on thick, glossy paper. BATTLEHOOP SCHOOL OF MARTIAL ARTS SUMMER STARTER PROGRAM. There was some text describing the program with a professional, clean look, and a picture of Jordan flying through the air kicking a board.

"All right," I said. "We'll see if it works."

When I got home, I snuck a cup of coffee and took a cat nap. I got my second wind in time for a family outing to Uncle Guido's Italian Restaurant. The flyer for Battlehoop was tucked away in my back pocket. Once my parents were each well into a glass of wine, I pulled the flyer out and showed it to them.

"Thomas handed this to me," I said, leaning forward so they'd hear me over the din of the restaurant. "Looks totally cool, and it's free."

"What is it?" Janey asked. She got up and walked over to stand behind my parents to look at the flyer.

"Huh," Dad said. "Where'd Thomas hear about this?"

I pretended not to hear him and barreled forward. "Thomas says parents are encouraged to visit. Honestly, I really want to give it a try, but I want you guys to check it out for me. Do you think one of you could go with me on Tuesday morning?"

That was all it took. Mom and Dad discussed the details for a moment, and decided Mom would go with me the first day to make sure it was a real opportunity and not a sales pitch or something. Shocking. Thomas had been right. It had been simple.

"I want to go!" Janey said.

Uh oh.

"Uh, Janey," I said, "I'm not sure it's designed for twelve year olds."

"I want to go!" she said. "Mom, say I can go with you."

Mom smiled. So did Dad. This was a disaster.

"Tell you what, sweetie," Mom said. "You'll go the first day and we'll see together if it's a good opportunity for you."

So much for simple.

We headed to the dollar theater after dinner. We split up because we couldn't all agree on which movie to watch. I had no idea why Mom and Janey didn't want to watch CROCOCANE, a riveting story about a hurricane full of crocodiles. They went to some movie about a little dog.

I managed to fit in ten hours of sleep between arriving home from the movie and getting up Sunday morning for church. I grabbed a shower, dressed, and headed downstairs. Breakfast felt incredibly weird, mainly because it was totally normal. How could life be so normal, when I could walk through walls? Well, at least poke my finger through walls. I looked down at my Fruity Circles and focused on one of the yellow rings of sugary goodness. I concentrated, and it slowly rotated in a circle. I cracked a smile.

The smile lasted up until the exact moment the toe of Janey's shoe met my shin under the table.

"What the heck?" I glared at her, then looked around. Of course. Janey had waited for Mom and Dad to go back to their room.

"What are you grinning about?" Janey glared right back at me. "And why did you try to stop me from coming to the class?"

I calmed my mind, and concentrated on the sharp pain in my shin. I imagined it dissipating. Just like that it was gone. Until Janey kicked me in the shin again. Then it was back. And I felt tired.

"Don't stare at me like a baboon," she said.

"Kick me in the shin again," I said, "and I will... OW!"

"Well, you said, kick me in the shin again. So I did."

I concentrated, and the pain dissipated again. It seemed to be getting easier. Or maybe my shin was toughening up. I took no risks, though, and kept my feet well under my chair.

Maybe if I reasoned with her, she'd drop the idea of going to Battlehoop with us. "Janey, would you want me hanging out with your friends? Like, going to a movie with all of you?"

"Of course not. But this is totally different, and you know it."

"No, I don't know it."

Janey's eyebrows came together in a frown. "This isn't like going to a movie. It's a chance to learn something. Like, if just because I had a chance to learn the guitar, you weren't allowed to."

"But all my friends are going to be there." I shook my head. All I needed was a repeat of the Christmas break incident when Janey had tagged along to the mall with me and Thomas. She'd spent the whole time telling Thomas embarrassing stories about me and trying to flirt with him. It had been both irritating and gross.

"So? It's a free class, Joss. Just because your friends are going doesn't mean you own the place."

I shook my head in frustration, but didn't bother answering her. She wasn't going to give in. Hopefully, the class would be too intense and Mom wouldn't let her stay. The last thing I needed was Janey hanging around while I was secretly trained as a Seven.

After church, I hid out in my room and called Thomas. He picked up immediately.

"You good?" Thomas asked.

"Yep," I said. "My mom's going with us Tuesday morning."

"Good. That's what I needed."

"What for?"

"I'll pass that along to the others so they can use it as ammo to help bring their parents around."

"What about you?"

"Oh," Thomas said. "I'm good. Mom just wanted to make sure at least one parent was going."

"That's great. One problem. Janey is going."

"Huh. What's the problem?"

"Janey?" I said. "My sister? She's coming with us."

"Yeah, I heard that," Thomas said. "What's the issue?"

"I don't know. Oh. Wait. Yes, I do. My little sister is going with us!"

"Whatever. That's actually pretty cool. Good for her."

Thomas didn't have any brothers or sisters. Just him and his mom. She did great. Some sort of big-shot lawyer. Thomas was never shy about mentioning he wished he had someone else in the home while his mom worked long hours. He didn't understand the burden of having a little sister.

"Just text me when you hear from the others," I said.

"Will do."

The first message came about an hour later.

```
Deion is in. His Mom is coming too
```

Unreal. Thomas was going to make it happen. We just needed a couple more. An hour later my phone buzzed. And buzzed again.

```
No go on Tyler. Doofus.
But we've got Arjeet. And Frankie
We are on!!!!!
I'm in the $$$
Deion's house Tues 7:45. We bike over
together
```

A tightness in my chest that I hadn't even noticed loosened. I was going to be trained as a Seven. The tightness gave way to a lump of ice in my stomach. What was I getting myself into? And how much time did I have before this Mocker caught up with me?

Chapter 8

BATTLEHOOP

Sunday afternoon crawled by like a slug on a hot road. The clocks seemed to slow down. The anticipation as I waited to begin my training Tuesday morning almost killed me.

My family ate big lunches together after church, so Sunday evening was every man for himself. I scrounged up some crackers, reheated a hotdog that had been grilled the previous weekend, and found an apple in the refrigerator. I wasn't sure why people always acted like cooking was such a big deal. I had no problems preparing my own meals.

After dinner, I decided to practice my talents. Mara had said practice would make me stronger, so I figured doing something, anything, was better than sitting around. I locked myself in my room and practiced ghosting. After an hour and a half, I headed to the bathroom to try it in the tile and glass of the shower stall, and to see what would happen if I ghosted in water. It was tiring work, but I improved fast. Within an hour, I could stick my arm into the wall between my bedroom and closet up to the elbow with a flicker of thought.

Ghosting didn't seem to depend on the material. The wall felt the same as a sink of water which felt the same as the tile and glass. If I didn't stick my hand in something solid or liquid my hand felt normal when ghosting. My ghost fingers could even feel each other. The craziest part was that when I snapped my fingers it made a sound. How was that possible?

After a couple hours of practice, I was done for the night.

I laid down on my bed, thinking I would read, and woke up ten hours later. I grabbed a shower and headed downstairs for breakfast. Dad zipped through the kitchen on the way to work, and Mom left a few minutes later for the doctor's office where she worked as a physician's assistant. Janey stayed in bed.

I went back up to my room to try out my telly talent. It proved way harder than ghosting, and it got harder if the object was further away or heavier. My big accomplishment was lifting one end of a sock an inch off the floor from about five feet away.

Kinneying was next on my list. It was different than ghosting. I couldn't speed up part of me. It was all or nothing. And it didn't feel like I was faster. Instead, it felt like the whole world slowed down. I also found that the more of me I moved when sped up, the more tiring it was.

After messing around with it for a little, I decided to try juggling three baseballs. I figured if I moved fast enough I should be able to keep three balls in the air. Because kinneying made it seem like the whole world had slowed down, I guess I lost track of how fast I was moving. When I tossed a baseball up in the air, I actually threw it super hard and ended up with a dent in my ceiling. Not good. And I was worn out.

I worked at it for a while longer, then took a rest before going down to eat lunch. After eating a few slices of leftover pizza, I went back to my room to practice more. Janey burst into the room just as I was closing the door.

"What are you doing in here?" She looked around the room, her eyebrows pulled together. "I know something's up."

I stepped in front of her and walked toward her, maneuvering her backwards out of the room. "Nothing. Now get out. You want me barging into your room?"

She gave me a hard look. "I'm not stupid. I know something's up."

"Whatever. Out!"

"I'm going to figure it out." Her eyes narrowed to hard

slits as she spoke. "And by the way, thanks again for trying to stop me from doing the martial arts training. What's your problem? Why can't you look out for your sister like a normal brother?"

"It's nothing personal. I just didn't want you tagging along with my friends."

"Drop the act, Joss," Janey said. "You're just selfish. Well, I'm not going to get even. I'm not like you. I look out for family."

"Okay, this conversation is over." I stepped forward, pushing her out of my room and closing the door. "Goodbye."

After another hour of practicing ghosting and kinneying, I was worn out. Mom and Dad got home a little later and we ate dinner together before watching an episode of our favorite family show, *LOL Videos*.

Afterwards, I had thought I would practice shifting, but I couldn't bring myself to do it. I needed to know more about it. What would happen if I actually transformed myself into an animal of some sort and then got too tired? Would I immediately transform back to normal, or could I get stuck? Did the change consume energy, or was the whole time you were transformed tiring? Did the size and weight of the animal matter? Could you change into a toaster?

Those questions led to the "Big Picture" questions I struggled with. How did the Sevens come to be? What would happen to me? What would my parents think if they found out I knew? Why hadn't they told me about any of this? What did they have against the Guild? What was the point?

I had no answers. I did know one thing. I was a Seven. Any doubt about weird magical abilities sort of disappeared once you stuck your hand through a wall.

My alarm went off at 6:45 Tuesday morning. I had set the alarm. Me. The first week of summer vacation, and I had intentionally told a machine to blare an angry noise at me early in the morning. On top of that, I actually got out of bed. That was like getting up at 4:00 on a normal school morning.

I'm not sure when it had happened, but at some point in the past two days Mom had talked to Deion's mom who had talked to Thomas's mom and Arjeet's mom who had talked to Frankie's mom. They had come up with a plan. Interestingly, the plan sounded exactly like what Thomas wanted to have happen. I made a mental note to consult Thomas the next time I needed something really important from my parents. That felt backwards—me asking Thomas for help.

All five of us were going to meet at Deion's house and bike over together. Deion's mom and my mom were going to drive over to Battlehoop to check out the place for the other parents. They'd stay with us until they felt comfortable and then head out.

Janey was part of the plan, too. I didn't want to think about it. Dad had put Janey's bike in Mom's minivan before he left for work so Mom could leave it at Battlehoop for her if they decided to let her stay.

I hopped on my bike at 7:30 sharp and got to Deion's house in a leisurely ten minutes. Arjeet and Deion were waiting on their bikes out front. Arjeet was second generation Indian, but he sounded like he was from Alabama, because he was. He could do an awesome Indian accent, though, and loved to mess with people. He'd lay on a thick accent and say, "The village of my youth had no talking screens." That sort of thing. He had a small head, and his hair was long enough to cover his eyes half the time.

Deion was a little taller than me, and a little bulkier. He lived for music. He played the trumpet and was determined to be the second coming of Louis Armstrong, whoever that was.

"You ready to learn to kick some..." Arjeet said.

I widened my eyes and cut him off with a frantic shake of my head as the front door opened. Mrs. Davies, Deion's mom, walked out and came down the sidewalk to us. She smiled.

Mrs. Davies was a happy person, but you did not mess with her. I had a vivid memory of her pinching Arjeet's ear, with him up on his tip toes, and smiling while she came down on him for trying to scare her when she came in from grocery shopping. She loved having the neighborhood kids over, but didn't put up with anything from us. Today she wore some jeans and a white whatever those shirts for women are called. Her hair was done in a million tiny braids hanging to her shoulders.

Just then Thomas came streaking around the turn toward the house on his tiny bike with Frankie in hot pursuit. Frankie was gaining, but Thomas skidded to a stop just before Frankie arrived. Frankie didn't really hang with us, but he lived two doors down from Thomas, so the two of them spent some time together. He was kinda weird and into all sorts of board games and stuff. He was about my size and had bushy red hair.

"You boys are really impressing me," Mrs. Davies said. "First week of summer break and here you are, bright and early, about to take advantage of an opportunity and do some hard work."

"Thanks, Mrs. Davies," Arjeet said, cutting in before anyone else could answer. He was probably trying to cover his tracks in case she had heard what he almost said. Mrs. Davies was still smiling, and it made me smile.

Mom's silver minivan swung around the corner into view and pulled up alongside us. The passenger front window rolled down as she arrived. Janey leaned out and waved. My smile vanished.

"Hey Janey," Thomas said. "Going to learn martial arts with us?"

"You bet!" Janey gave Thomas a big thumbs up.

"Lyla," Mom said from the driver side, "do you want to ride with me? I'll have Janey flip to a middle seat."

"Why, sure," Mrs. Davies said. "Let me run inside and grab my purse. Do you have the address?"

Mom flashed her phone. "Ready to go."

Mrs. Davies nodded and turned to us. "You boys want

to get a head start? Do you know where you are going?"

"Sure thing, Mrs. Davies," Arjeet said.

Thomas flashed her a thumbs up, and Frankie gave her a big grin.

"We're good, Mom," Deion said. "See you there?"

"All right, boys, but be safe and stick together." Mrs. Davies walked back up to her house to get her purse, and we took off.

"As I was saying," Arjeet said as we reached the end of the block, "let's go learn to kick some—"

Deion interrupted him. "So how'd you first hear about this, Thomas?"

"Mara met us in the park Saturday morning," Thomas said. "She and Jordan are establishing this new dojo—"

"Battlehoop," Frankie interjected.

"Yeah, Battlehoop," Thomas said.

"What kind of name is Battlehoop?" Deion asked.

"No idea. Joss, any ideas?"

"Nope," I said. "But Jordan is legit. He is huge. I'm betting he can teach us. And Mara..."

"I already told them, Joss," Thomas said. "Mara's hot, and supposedly a black belt in like three different martial arts."

"You had me at hot," Arjeet said.

"And we just have to talk it up next year at school?" Deion asked.

"Yep" Thomas said. "And make them look good by showing off our crazy skills so they can get more students. Paying students."

We had come to a stop at the edge of our neighborhood. The light changed, and we cut across the street.

"I'm a little sketchy on where we're going," Frankie said.

"Up ahead a few blocks," I said. "On that street by the train tracks. You'll see the sign on the door."

Mom's minivan passed us as we took the last turn. The black BMW and little silver Toyota were parked in front of the building. Mom pulled in and parked one space over from the Toyota. We caught up and took a minute to figure out how to chain all the bikes together using Thomas's ridiculous bike lock chain.

"You boys ready to go inside?" Mrs. Davies asked as she and Mom walked up with Janey.

"Wait. What's Janey doing?" Arjeet asked. "Wasn't she joking about coming with us?"

"No," Thomas said as he worked on the bike lock. "She's here to learn, same as you. You scared, Arjeet?"

"No, I just didn't know there was going to be a girl with us."

"Doofus," Deion said. "We're being taught by a girl. Why wouldn't a girl be in the class?"

Janey stepped up to Arjeet and glared at him. The poor guy was only about an inch taller than her. "I'm going to work harder than any of you, and then I'm going to pound you."

Thomas stood up from chaining the bikes together and saw the stare-down. He walked toward the door, cutting between Arjeet and Janey. "Okay, let's do this!"

He led the charge up the steps and opened the door. At the last second he stopped himself from dashing through the doorway and instead stepped back and held the door for the ladies. Mom and Mrs. Davies thanked him, and he gave an over-the-top bow in return, still holding the door with a foot.

"Gentlemen," Thomas said, gesturing grandly with a hand for us to enter.

I guess I'd be pretty excited too if I'd just roped several other kids into training all summer, and as a result was going to make a hundred bucks a week. Not too shabby. And not too fair, either. Wasn't I the one with the superpowers that made all this possible? Why should he be making all the money? I did feel excited, but it was borderline apprehensive. What was I getting myself into? I felt as though I hadn't stopped to think since I'd read Mara's letter. Which made no sense because I'd fretted constantly.

I gave Thomas my best smirk while bowing in return, and headed into the dojo. Mara and Jordan were walking toward us. Jordan was once again wearing all black with white tennis shoes. Mara was barefoot and wearing a snug, black T-shirt that said <SARCASM> along with purple yoga pants. Arjeet and Frankie were staring at her with wide eyes. Classy. Mrs. Davies and Mom stepped toward them.

"Ladies," Jordan said, "may I presume you are the mothers of a couple of our students?"

"Why, yes, we are," Mrs. Davies said. "I'm Lyla Davies."

"Jordan Johnson, ma'am," Jordan said. He nodded toward Mara. "My associate, Mara Torres."

"I'm Jennifer Morgan," Mom said. The adults did that awkward thing where they all shook each other's hands, trying not to get in each other's way.

"Looks like we've got a great group of students," Mara said.

"Yes we do," Jordan said. "So, ladies, I'm sure you have some questions. How can we put your minds at ease?"

Mom and Mrs. Davies proceeded to politely interrogate Jordan and Mara on everything under the sun. Safety. Certification. Standards. Techniques. I was terrified at first that my cover would be blown and Mom would find out this was really a front for the Guild.

It turns out, there wasn't even a sliver of a chance of that happening. Jordan brought out printed materials, showed them the corporate Battlehoop website on a laptop, discussed instructor training and certification, and last of all pulled out an Olympic bronze medal in judo. *His* Olympic bronze medal.

"Well, this is just tremendous," Mrs. Davies said. "Can we see a demonstration?"

"Sure," Mara said. "However, keep in mind what you'll see will be well beyond anything your sons can learn in a few weeks."

"I should hope so," Mom said with a smile.

"Students," Jordan said, "shoes off as you step onto the platform. Find a seat around battlehoop five. That's the center one. Stay off the white."

I slipped off my shoes and left them beside the platform.

Three sharp steps led up onto the padded surface. Each of the nine circles were defined by maybe a two-foot thick white line around a ten-foot or so circle of the blue padding. I walked over to the middle circle and sat down outside the white line. The other guys joined me. Janey sat beside Arjeet and gave him a hard look. The moms stood behind us.

Jordan and Mara stepped into the circle and bowed to each other. Jordan was barefoot now. They started. Mara and Jordan attacked each other with such speed and ferocity it was breathtaking. It only lasted a minute, which was a good thing, because I think I stopped breathing after about twenty seconds.

They threw fists, feet, and elbows at each other. Jordan was like a rock slide, crashing down with massive force, while Mara was the wind, elusive and everywhere at once. My eyes couldn't keep up, and what I did see my brain had trouble processing. There were hints, the tiniest cracks in the illusion of their sparring, that Jordan could crush her at any moment, but Mara evaded all his strikes.

And then it was over. Jordan leapt backward and stood straight. Mara straightened, they bowed to each other, and walked over to the moms.

"Dude," said Frankie.

That about summed it up. I looked over at Janey. Her eyes were wide and sparkled from the lights above as she stared at Mara.

"Well," said Mom. "That was... my goodness."

"Any other questions we can answer?" Jordan asked.

Mrs. Davies and Mom looked at each other for a moment.

"I think that about covers it," Mrs. Davies said. "Jen, are you going to leave Janey?"

"Yes!" Janey yelled from where she sat.

"I suppose so," Mom said. "Thomas, would you mind adding Janey's bike to your lock?"

"Sure thing, Mrs. Morgan," Thomas said. He hopped up and followed the moms out. A minute later he was back.

Jordan and Mara moved to the center of circle five.

"Scrunch in," Jordan said. "Sit in a tight semi-circle. Any questions before we start?"

Arjeet's hand shot up. Jordan nodded toward him.

"What does Battlehoop mean?"

Jordan waved his hand at the rings painted on the mats. "These are the battlehoops. You'll learn to fight in them. We aren't going to teach you to look pretty while jumping around and prancing. You're going to learn real martial arts suited for close quarters hand-to-hand combat."

"Cool," Arjeet said. I looked around. Frankie, Thomas, and Deion were nodding in agreement. Even Janey nodded.

"What Jordan means," Mara said, "is we'll teach you top-notch self-defense."

Jordan snorted. Mara gave Jordan a hard look, her eyes narrowed. "We're going to give you these abilities. Develop these talents. And we're going to train you to use them well and wisely."

She emphasized the word 'talent' and looked right at me when she said it. I gave a quick nod in response.

"We will begin your training," Jordan said, "by teaching you to fall."

Chapter 9

BOBBY FERRIS MUST PAY

BATMAN PUT AQUAMAN on the ground with one last kick to the face.

"That's five matches to two," Thomas said. He sat beside me on the couch, his XBOX controller in one hand, the other reaching behind him to scratch his back. He stifled a moan. "I think my arm may fall off. That medicine ball thing we did today almost killed me."

It was Friday night, and I was tired. Six weeks of training at Battlehoop had worn me out. We'd started with falling, and kept at it for weeks. While learning to fall, we were simultaneously taught other skills. Blocking. Punching. Gouging. Kicking. Elbowing. How to control someone by rotating and levering their limbs, or by pushing on nerve centers.

Around week three, Jordan had also introduced non-fighting skills that he called "useful." Janey had started calling them our ninja skills, and it had stuck. How to walk silently. How to hold perfectly still without getting muscle cramps. Something called tactical breathing, which involved breathing with a certain tempo to control your heart rate. Ninja skills.

On top of all that, we each had private instruction with Mara every day. It was all a cover, of course, for that twenty to thirty minutes I spent with her training as a Seven. Mara pushed me on ghosting and blending each and every day. If I wanted to talk about shifting, well, that was for another time. She kept saying it was important to build up one or two talents first, but I wasn't so sure.

Blending was straightforward. I was pretty much invisible, though Mara said a faint motion might show in someone's peripheral vision if I moved too fast. Ghosting was another matter. She had me start by learning to sink into the floor a few inches. I had to sort of push into solids when ghosting. Not physically, but with my will. It was like my body knew it was unnatural to sink into the floor or step through walls.

Once I ghosted down a couple inches into the floor, I could drift, a movement controlled by my will. The parts of me in a solid had no sensory input. No sights or sounds if my head was in a solid. I could drift in any direction, but going down all the way into the ground seemed scary. How would I know which way was up?

Mara also combined my Seven training with my martial arts training. This was the only time she had me practice something other than ghosting and blending. She'd throw a punch or kick at me, and I had to blend whatever part of my body she was about to strike. Then I was supposed to retaliate with a punch or kick, making my foot or hand rock hard to deliver a vicious blow, or trying to kinney to speed up. The flashing between talents, first bruising, then kinneying, was tiring and sometimes felt impossible.

For six weeks we'd all trained, and I'd practiced ghosting and blending each day when at home to the point of exhaustion. I was so tired. For all of Thomas's complaints, he only had the four hours at Battlehoop wearing him down. I did have one advantage. Every time I got sore or bruised I practiced my reggie talent.

Mara had worked with me on that one as well. She emphasized the importance of reggying for everything immediately to build up the reggie auto-pilot. I wasn't sure how long it would take, but it still took serious concentration to heal myself. Each day I recovered from any aches and pains at the cost of feeling even more tired. I'd never slept so much in my life. The other guys weren't as tired, but they were sore and bruised.

The other guys and Janey. I still couldn't believe she'd

stuck with it. And she hadn't just survived— she was a natural. Coordinated and super-fast, Janey held her own with us boys in spite of being smaller and lighter. I'd never admit it to anyone, but I was proud of her. What a strange feeling.

All of us guys would hang out after class sometimes. I was even getting used to hanging with Frankie. But we were always in a big group, or I was sneaking off by myself to practice ghosting and blending, and I hadn't had much of a chance to talk to Thomas about the whole Seven thing. The weeks kept slipping by, and living a secret life of trying to learn to be a superhero was driving me nuts. I needed an outlet. I needed to talk to someone. Thomas was my only option. I had finally gotten him to invite me over for a sleepover.

We were upstairs at his house. His mom had her bedroom and office downstairs and almost never came upstairs. Thomas had two bedrooms and a game room to himself.

"Man, I wish you could reggie my arms," Thomas said, stretching them one at a time across his chest. "Your talents are selfish, Joss. Just plain selfish."

"Six hundred dollars, and you're calling me selfish?" I said. "I saw Jordan slip you the envelope today. Six weeks. Six hundred dollars."

"Well, okay, that's true. There's been some upside for me."

"Not just the money. We're not going to have to take it next year. Any kids who mess with us are in for a surprise."

"That's the truth," Thomas said. "I mean, I know Jordan's just giving a cover for you to train with Mara, but he's good. I'm going to be good. Never thought I'd feel that way."

We sat for a moment, thinking. Thomas broke the silence. "Wish I'd felt this way in seventh grade. I hated seventh grade."

"Bobby Ferris," I said.

Thomas nodded. "Bobby Ferris."

Just thinking about Bobby made my head feel hot. I made a general rule of not saying his name.

"Jerk had no right," I said.

"Yeah, but I still don't think he meant to get your underwear when he pantsed you."

"Whatever. Doesn't matter," I said. "He did it, and he never paid. Shelly and her friends always looked at me funny after that."

Thomas nodded. "Big kid. He'll be a sophomore when we go to high school. I bet he won't look as big anymore."

"How could he?" I asked. "Spar with Jordan, everyone else looks smaller."

"Yeah, that's right."

I jerked to my feet, a thought captivating me.

"Bobby Ferris. Doesn't he live just north, past Estes Street?"

"Yeah," Thomas said.

"You know the house, right? Doesn't your Mom hang out with that family next door?"

"Yeah, the Walkers. We eat there sometimes. Mom and Mrs. Walker go way back. Dad was friends with Mr. Walker first, but, you know, not anymore. Not since..."

Thomas trailed off. He didn't like talking about his parents' divorce.

"Take me there," I said.

"Where? The Walkers'?"

"Yeah. No. Bobby's."

"What?" Thomas sat up straight. "Why?"

"Take me to Bobby's." I smiled. "It's payback time."

"It's 10:30," Thomas said. "10:30 is not payback time. It's XBOX time. And then sleep time. I'm exhausted."

"Tell your mom we're going to bed. And we will be, eventually. We shut down. Head out the window. Pay a visit to Bobby Ferris."

"Why? What are you going to do?"

Thomas knew about my talents, but he hadn't seen me using them recently. He didn't know what I could do. I blended. Thomas gasped. He stood up and looked right at me, then around the room. I ghosted down into the floor a few inches so I could drift, a slow, silent motion. I ghosted into the couch, then drifted up through the couch until I was standing on the back of it. I let go of the ghost and blend, and tapped Thomas's shoulder.

"Dang!" he said as he whirled toward me, his eyes wide. "That is some freaky stuff. Didn't realize you could do it that well."

"Yep." I stepped down to the floor. "Just ghosting and blending."

"Wow, that's scary."

"Yeah. They've had me focus everything on those two talents. I'm getting a little better at the other stuff 'cause I'm stronger overall, but Mara's all about the ghosting and blending."

"Why?" Thomas asked.

"Guess they need me to sneak somewhere, right?"

"Yeah, makes sense."

"I need some lipstick," I said. "Can you snag some when you talk to your mom? Red lipstick, okay?"

"Hold on. What's the plan?"

I smiled. "I'm going to leave Bobby a message on his bathroom mirror written in red lipstick. Something so crazy it's scary."

Thomas's eyes got wider. "That's insane. They'll call the cops, Joss. Or—"

"Or his parents will blame Bobby, even though he'll be freaking out because he knows he didn't do it."

"That's wrong. Just wrong."

"But it was right for him to show my stuff to half the seventh grade girls?"

"No," Thomas said. He sat back down on the couch and rubbed his forehead. "But I don't like it."

"Not asking you to like it," I said. "Just need you take me to his house. Come on! He humiliated me! Go tell your mom we're crashing. Snag some lipstick. She must have some in her purse."

"Alright," Thomas said, "but this is on you." He glared

at me as he headed downstairs.

Thomas and I stood in the deepest shadows of a large oak to the side of the Walkers' house. It had been effortless to climb out Thomas's bedroom window, cut across the roof, and drop ten feet to the ground. Maybe all that practice falling had been worth it. An easy fifteen-minute walk, and we were there.

I pulled the lipstick out of my pocket. Thomas had done me right. It was bright red. Not that I could see the color right then. There were no street lights in this neighborhood. "I'm going in. Back in ten."

I blended, and took off at a quick jog across the Walkers' yard over to the Ferris house. It was one-story, and the porch light wasn't on. Shadows clung to the eaves and shuttered windows along the front of the house. I faintly heard voices through the front door. What was that about? Sounded muffled, but loud. I ignored them.

Time for Bobby to pay. He should have never messed with the Seventy-Seven. Maintaining the blend, I ghosted through the front door.

Words assaulted me from up ahead. A deep, ugly voice yelled, "You good for nuttin' piece of trash! Gonna take my bottle? Huh, tough guy?"

My eyebrows came together. What was going on? I stepped forward with the careful ninja steps Jordan had taught us, past a living room to the left along the front side of the house. The entryway opened into a large family room.

A man stood, swaying on his feet, a bottle held in his left hand. I could smell him from ten feet away. He stank of alcohol. Bobby Ferris faced him, his hands balled into fists, tears streaming down his face. The man pushed Bobby with his free hand, and staggered backwards. Bobby hadn't moved.

"Dad, please," Bobby said. "Let's just save some for tomorrow."

Bobby's dad? My stomach lurched.

Mr. Ferris roared incoherently. He stepped forward and

took a wild swing at Bobby. Bobby took a quick step away from the blow, and Mr. Ferris overbalanced. He twisted around crashed down backwards onto the coffee table in front of the couch. The bottle fell from his hand to the floor, and a golden liquid leaked out onto the beige carpet.

Bobby swooped down, righted the bottle, and stood, looking down at his dad. Mr. Ferris was out cold. Bobby stood there, his body trembling, crying. I was frozen in the horror of the moment, a witness to something I wished I could wipe from my memory.

Bobby picked up his dad in a smooth motion and carried him toward a hall at the far end of the family room. Wow, Bobby was big. The kid had not stopped growing. His dad wasn't tiny, but Bobby carried him like a child.

I snuck along behind Bobby down the hall, still blending. Bobby nudged the last door on the right open with his shoulder and rotated his dad through the doorway. By the time I got to the door and looked in, Bobby was settling his dad on a large bed in the middle of a dark bedroom.

I had seen enough. I'd seen too much. I didn't bother with the hallway. I ghosted straight through the walls toward the front of the house, out the brick wall, and through the hedges. I ran back to the the tree where Thomas was waiting.

Thomas jumped when I stopped blending.

"Let's get out of here," I said.

"You do it?"

"No. I don't want to talk about it."

"Say what?" Thomas said. I ignored him and started walking. He caught up with me a moment later.

"What happened?" Thomas asked.

"I hate Bobby Ferris."

"Okay. I know. But what happened?"

"What happened was, I hate Bobby Ferris," I said. "I've hated him for so long I'm not sure I know how to not hate him." A tear leaked out of my eye. I was so angry. So upset. I jerked my hand across my face to wipe the tear, but another one replaced it.

Thomas walked beside me for a block without talking. It gave me a chance to pull myself together.

"You saw something," Thomas said.

"Yeah." We walked another block. "How do you not hate a guy who humiliated you in front of the whole school?"

"I don't know. Maybe you forgive them?"

I ignored his comment. "How do you hate a guy who's got a drunk, violent father?"

"Oh," Thomas said. "Was it bad?"

"I guess not," I said. "Only because Mr. Ferris passed out or something when he tried to punch Bobby."

"Yeah, that's bad."

"How can I just forget about what he did to me?" I asked.

"Because you want to be happier?"

"I'm serious!"

"I know," Thomas said. "Look, I don't think you just forget what he did. I think you start with forgiveness. I mean, I get it. You like your life. But you push. You've got stuff going on under the surface."

"So now I'm Shrek? I've got layers? Guess that makes you Donkey."

"Yeah, that's me. Donkey."

We walked in silence the rest of the way back to Thomas's house. There was a tree that had a branch right near the roofline. Thomas monkeyed up it with a practiced skill. I ghosted into the middle of the trunk and leaned forward so my head stuck out so I could see what I was doing. The few moments I had been completely in the trunk of the tree had been as bad as I had thought it would be. No sight. No sound. No sense of anything. Just a gentle, cool pressure.

I drifted up the trunk to the the limb that extended over the roof, my head sticking out the whole way. Even in the faint light of the moon, I could see the whites of Thomas's eyes as he stared at me from the roof.

"That just looks so wrong," he said. "I may hurl."

I drifted out of the trunk onto the branch, took two quick

steps, and jumped to the roof beside Thomas. "Seventy-Seven for the win," I said, and walked past him to the bedroom window. It didn't feel like a win, though. I was the one who felt like I might hurl.

I kept seeing Bobby crying as his dad swung a fist at him. Carrying his dad to the bedroom. Laying him, passed out, on his bed. Crying. His father yelling. I'd never seen anything like it before, and I felt violated. But I knew I wasn't the one being violated, Bobby was. I felt angry. Helpless. Disgusted.

I lay in my sleeping bag for a long time, alone with my thoughts. What was this all about? Who was I to try to take revenge on a kid who had a horrible life? What did that say about me? And why was I a Seven? So I could discover horrible facts about people I wanted to hate but pitied instead? What was the point?

On Monday, I learned the answer to one of the questions. I found out why I was being trained as a Seven.

Chapter 10

ROBIN HOOD

"WE NEED YOU to come online for your first mission."

Mara and I stood in the center room along the left side of the dojo. Unlike the room up front, which had office furniture, this room had only blue mats on the floor. All our individual training was done here.

Mara faced me wearing black yoga pants and a dark green T-shirt that said, IRON BOOTS, IF THEY GET TOO HEAVY STICK THEM IN YOUR POCKET. She looked solemn, and she held a black laptop.

"You like saying mysterious things, don't you?" I asked. "Are we finally going after that Mocker?"

She sat down cross-legged on the floor and held a hand out for me to do likewise. "We are. The Guild needs you to acquire some files from an office building downtown."

"Wait." I sat down hard. "You want me to steal something? That's what all this is about? You need a thief?"

"No!" Mara said. "Well, yeah, if you want to think about it that way. Remember I told you, the first time we met, the Guild needed you? That a Mocker was looking for the Seven with a butterfly birthmark?"

"Of course."

"Well, the Mockers are like a crime syndicate. But they've started turning Sevens, using them. It's bad news. We need info on the Mocker targeting you." Mara didn't look at me. Her eyes drifted toward the corners of the room.

I had daydreamed what I would one day do for the Guild. Mostly, it involved being heroic. Saving people. That sort of thing. Not stealing. When I had pictured myself ghosting and blending through buildings, it had been to rescue kidnapped people. Usually very pretty girls, who would catch a glimpse of my face as I struggled through overwhelming odds.

"Stealing," I said. "What hero steals?"

Mara sat back and bit her lower lip, her eyebrows pulled together. "Robin Hood?"

"I was thinking more of superhero heroes."

Mara nodded. "I get that. Sometimes, Joss, you get forced into tough situations to do what's right. Welcome to the real world."

That sounded weak, but maybe that's what it took to stop the bad guys. "So the Guild wants me to steal some files? From some criminal masterminds? You think I'm ready? To go up against these Mockers? I mean, I don't even really know anything about them."

"Oh, yeah, you'll do great." Mara's eyes locked onto mine. "The Mockers are bad news. Evil. We need to hit them when we can. Hit them hard." Her eyes narrowed as she spoke.

"And they are turning Sevens. What does that even mean?"

Mara sighed. "It means they're making Sevens commit crimes. Maybe they're convincing the Sevens to work with them. Maybe they're coercing them. But it's all bad news, and it's going to point back to the Guild."

"How can you point a finger at something nobody knows about?"

"Oh, the Dirty Dozen knows about us."

"What. The. Heck," I said. "The Dirty Dozen?"

"It's the Guild nickname for DOSN," Mara said. "The Department of Seven Normalization. Look, skip all that. There's tons for you still to learn. We haven't even talked about silver yet. We've got work to do. We need to focus on the Mockers right now."

My mind spun. Crime syndicates. DOSN. And silver? It was too much. I needed to zero in on something smaller, more manageable, before my head exploded. I took a deep breath, and focused on the mission.

"So do the Mockers have, I don't know, a hide-out here in town?"

"No, nothing like that," Mara said. "Each Mocker has their own operation. They pay a percent back to the central organization, and get access to shared intel in return. You can't really take the Mockers down. You take them down one Mocker at a time."

"So I steal some files, and it helps take down the Mocker looking for me. What's his name?"

"Honestly? I don't know."

I frowned. "You said there's a Mocker hunting me, right? Well, not me, but the butterfly birthmark."

Mara nodded.

"But you don't know his name. How do you know he's hunting me if you don't even know his name?"

Mara shrugged. "You sort of get used to it, Joss. The Guild holds information closely. I don't hear much beyond what I need to know, and you won't either. Sorry. Here's what I do know. He's supposedly getting closer. We need to start fighting back before he tracks you down."

I shook my head. What was I supposed to do? I didn't want some evil crime guy coming by the house looking for me. I had to do what I could to stop him. "So what's the plan? What exactly do you want me to do?"

"Should be straight forward. You'll ghost and blend through the building. Stay blended the whole time so you don't show up on security video. Then you grab a hard drive out of a laptop, and come back out."

"Ah. That kind of files, " I said. "Why not just take the whole laptop?"

"Too big," Mara said. "It would hamper your movements too much if you had to keep the laptop flattened against you while ghosting through a wall. But the hard drive shouldn't be a problem. We have some special clothes you'll wear to hold stuff right up against your body. We'll gear you up tomorrow night when we pick you up."

"Tomorrow night?"

"Yeah. We'll pick you up around 1:00 in the morning," Mara said. She frowned. "What's wrong? You worried?"

Betrayed by my face. I *was* worried. And scared. I've done some crazy pranks in my time, but I'd never just strolled in and stolen something. Not really. Not where the cops would get involved if I was caught.

"Hey," Mara said, "we get this hard drive, and we might be able to take down a real bad guy. This is what we've trained you for."

"Yeah, I'm good," I said, ignoring the ice in my stomach. "1:00. How long will this take?"

"Maybe a thirty minutes round trip drive to the location, and less than thirty minutes to grab the hard drive. I'd say we'll have you back in bed by 2:00."

"Alright. I can lose an hour of sleep."

Mara put the laptop on the mat between us. "Good. Today's lesson is going to focus on ripping hard drives out of laptops, as well as the mission ops plan."

I sat facing her. I learned.

At 12:53, I got out of bed and slipped on my shoes. I'd gone to bed dressed in jeans and a T-shirt after my shower. For two hours I'd lain there, adrenaline pumping through my veins and sleep an impossibility. Enough waiting and thinking. It was time for action. My first mission for the Guild.

Troublesome thoughts kept popping up. What did I know about the Guild? Was I just going to jump when they said jump? Did I really know who "they" were? And why did my parents want to keep me away from the Guild?

I yearned to know the answer to that last question, but feared that asking it might ruin everything. I loved training at Battlehoop. I had come to terms with my freaky powers over the past six weeks. I didn't want my parents to shut me off from all that, and yet, I needed something. Their understanding.

All were questions for another time. I stepped to the back wall of my room and ghosted into it. I drifted over and leaned my head forward out the far side of the brick exterior wall so I could keep myself oriented. I still had trouble drifting blind. I blended in case anyone was up and saw my backside sticking into the house, and drifted down to the ground level.

I kept the blend going as I stepped out of the wall and jogged around to the side yard. The side yard fence had a gate in it, but I kept jogging and ghosted right through it. I could snap into ghost mode now.

At the sidewalk in front of our house, I looked toward the mouth of the cul-de-sac and saw Jordan's BMW silhouetted in the moonlight. I jogged over to the car and released my blend. The passenger door swung open and Mara hopped out.

She pushed a black bundle toward me. "Your work clothes. Change quickly. We need to move."

I glanced around. "Where?"

"What have you been teaching him?" Jordan's voice came from the dark interior of the car.

Mara's eyes narrowed for a moment when Jordan spoke. "Just blend. We won't see you."

"But I thought the clothes had to be on me to blend with me."

"Correct. The clothes will come in and out of view, depending on how close they are to you, but you'll stay out of sight. Hurry."

That actually made sense. I blended and stripped my clothes off down to my underwear and socks. Mara picked up my clothing as I dropped it and stacked it in a neat pile with my shoes.

The 'work' clothes Mara had given me included a black shirt and pants made from a heavy, stretchy material. There was also a tight, stretchy pair of boots that zipped up the front, had a split between the big toe and other toes, and had rubberized soles. I was going to look ridiculous, or incredibly cool.

Something poked me as I pulled on the pants. I stretched open a pocket on the left pant leg and found a multi-head screwdriver and a multi tool with pliers. On the right side a pocket held a sheathed fixed-blade knife with a good five-inch blade. Was that supposed to be a tool, or a weapon?

Fully dressed, I let go of the blend. Mara gave me a quick once over and nodded. "That should do it. Into the car."

I scrambled into the back seat. It wasn't large, and the driver seat was set way back to give Jordan room. The interior of the car smelled like leather. I buckled in behind the passenger seat as Mara got back in. Jordan pushed a button, the engine hummed, and we were off.

"Stay low, Joss," Jordan said. "The windows are tinted dark enough it shouldn't matter, but you have to learn to not take risks. The front windshield is clear, and I don't want a traffic cam getting a look at you."

I hunched low behind Mara's seat. My stomach started clenching. What had I gotten myself into?

"Here," Mara said, and her hand thrust toward me holding something black. I took it and held it up in the flashes of light as we drove under street lights. It was a ski mask-looking hood made of the same material as the shirt and pants, with holes cut out for the eyes, nostrils, and mouth. "Go ahead and put it on."

I pulled it on, and struggled with it for a minute to get the holes lined up comfortably with the associated body parts. I noticed I wasn't seeing Jordan's bald scalp in the dark interior. He was wearing a mask, too.

"There's a couple pockets in the front of your shirt, and a couple in the back that can be used to stash the hard drive," Mara said. "When we get to the building, you're going to blend and then ghost out of the car. Security cameras will just see a BMW parked on a side street. You won't exist."

"And I blend the whole time, right?"

"Right," Mara said. Her voice sounded odd. Deeper.

I sat up to get a better look. From the silhouette of her head, it wasn't Mara anymore. "What the—"

"Quiet," Mara said. "And get back down. It's me, Mara. I shifted to a persona I use for work."

I took a hard look. She'd shifted her face to look like some little man. The rest of her that I could see looked the same. I hadn't known she could do that.

"Wow," I said, slouching once again. "Talk about getting your game face on."

"Cute," Mara said.

"So who are you supposed to be?" I asked.

"Nobody. That's the point. This is a man's face I made up and use for work."

"Shifters can do that?"

I caught the movement of Mara shaking her head as we passed under a street light. "No, most can't."

"And you only shift your head?"

"Yeah. If I shift all of me, the clothes would shift with me, right? So I'd look like a man, all right, and you'd see far more than you wanted to."

"That is so weird. And I don't get it," I said. "What's the point of all this if security camera gets a picture of your license plate, Jordan? Won't they know it's you?"

"What makes you think my plates are the ones on the car?" Jordan said.

Oh. I didn't have anything else to say, so I shut up. We drove in silence to the outskirts of downtown. The streets weren't empty, but it was close. A stray car or two shot by as though they had important places to go in the middle of the night. Jordan pulled to the curb and stopped next to a hulking building that was shrouded in darkness.

Mara turned to face me. "You've got this, Joss. What floor is the target?"

"Fourth floor," I said. "Polypotel Industries International."

"Good. What office number?"

"Is that a trick question? There's no office number. It's the office of the CEO."

"That's right," Mara said. "Remember, keep your blend going the whole time. Move as little as possible. We don't want security guards seeing a video feed of a laptop jumping around in an empty office."

"Right," I said. My heart beat a staccato rhythm against my ribs, and my mouth was dry.

"Don't screw up," Jordan said, still staring straight forward.

"Words to live by," I said, and blended.

"He's off," Mara said as I ghosted and stepped out of the locked car.

I walked toward the building, holding onto my blend. The building loomed a dozen stories or more in the dark above, but the street level was well lit near the main entrance on the corner of the building. I ghosted through the glass door, and walked with careful steps across the lobby.

A night guard sat at a desk to the side of the lobby. His feet were propped on a small desk, and he was reclined as far as the chair would allow, with a slack look on his face as he stared up at the ceiling. He wasn't asleep, but I didn't think he was fully awake either.

The shoes Mara had given me were amazing. They were comfortable and silent. The rubber soles gripped well but didn't squeak. I'd thought I would have to drift down into the floor a bit so I could silently ghost across the lobby. Instead, I ninja-stepped my way right past the guard.

I found the fire escape map posted on the wall near the elevators. It directed me around a couple of corners to a hallway with bathrooms. Opposite the bathrooms was a heavy, locked door with a STAIRS sign in red letters above it. I stepped through the door into the stairwell.

I had thought a lot about this lying in bed earlier. I could try to drift in a wall up to the fourth floor, but I didn't really know much about how buildings like this worked. Were the walls solid and thick? Were there gaps between floors? Did the walls align floor to floor? Much simpler to take the stairs.

The stairwell was lit with fluorescent bulbs above the door I'd just passed through and at the landing a dozen steps above me. I headed up the stairs, hit the switchback and went another dozen steps to a landing with a door labeled FLOOR 2.

On the landing in front of the fourth floor door, I stopped

to catch my breath. I was surprised to realize I wasn't winded. Blending was getting a lot easier for me, but still took real effort. And running up stairs used to exhaust me. All the training at Battlehoop was making a difference. I was getting tough. Strong. And I was stalling.

For weeks I'd felt like I was being pulled along by events. I had these talents, so I had to train, so I could become this bizarre ninja-magic-dude, so I could blah blah blah. But why should I care? If the Mockers were harming the Guild, why did that matter to me? My parents didn't even want me in the Guild. And why did my thoughts keep going in circles?

But as I'd trained, something had changed. I liked being part of a team, of feeling like I could do something bigger than me. Something good. And Bobby Ferris still haunted me. I felt bad for him. I'd been so angry at him for so long, I wasn't quite sure what to do about it. And I had used my powers selfishly. I hated thinking of myself that way. Time to do something good. Something for the team.

FLOOR 4. The sign on the door was to the point. I could do this. I could go through that door, and do my part to take down a Mocker.

Heart racing, I ghosted through the door.

Chapter 11

POLYPOTEL INDUSTRIES

I STEPPED INTO a poorly lit hallway. One in four light fixtures did night duty, emitting clinical fluorescent light along with a faint buzz. Vague colors and frigid AC completed what Dad called the office zombie garden.

I had to find the CEO's office. I could just start ghosting through walls, but I had this terrifying vision of accidentally ghosting right out of the building. I wasn't sure what would happen if I fell four stories while ghosting, and I had no intention of finding out.

Instead, I turned and followed the hall a short distance past some restrooms to the floor's elevator lobby. Six silver doors stood three to a side. Opposite me was a glass wall with POLYPOTEL INDUSTRIES INTERNATIONAL stenciled across two large glass doors. Behind the wall lay a barren office lobby. A badge reader with a red light stood on the wall beside the doors.

I ghosted through the glass and started looking. It didn't take long. The executives weren't subtle. One huge section at a corner of the building had its own reception area behind more glass walls and several offices framed with stained wood and etched glass doors.

I stepped through the glass and walked along the near wall, checking the office doors. Each door had a name and job title. It seemed like everyone had a three letter job that started with C and ended with O. The door closest to the corner had an E in the middle. The CEO.

I frowned. Was there a faint glow coming through the frosted glass of the door? I stretched my neck for a moment to loosen the tension, took a deep breath, and stepped through the door.

The office was large. Windows reached from the floor to the ceiling along the walls ahead of me and to the left. Lots of details assaulted me, but only one stood out. A man sat hunched over a laptop at the desk directly across the office from me, typing furiously.

I froze. What was he doing here in the middle of the night? His tie was loosened, and the top button on his white dress shirt was unbuttoned. A dark coat was neatly laid out to the side of the laptop on the large, wood desk. A lamp with a narrow, green shade sat on the corner of the desk and cast a pool of light. The glow of the laptop revealed a frown of concentration on the man's face. The only sound was the rapid clicking of keys as he typed.

He jerked upright in his chair and slapped the desk. I jumped, but he never looked at me. He rubbed his face with both hands and stared intently at the laptop's screen. The laptop that held the hard drive I was supposed to take. What was I going to do? I looked around for inspiration, but nothing came to mind. I stepped backward through the door behind me.

Back in the reception area, I took a deep breath. No problem. My blending was in full effect. He wasn't going to catch me. I just needed to get him out of that office. There were a couple of black leather chairs and a couch in the middle of the space, so I went over to them and flopped into the couch to think. The cushions made a whooshing sound as I hit them. I winced and held my breath, hoping the CEO hadn't heard the noise.

Or, maybe that was exactly what I wanted. I hopped up and pulled one of the chairs over to the glass door at the entrance to the executive area. I pushed open the door and then pulled the chair halfway through and left it holding the door open. Hopefully that would get his attention. Now I needed to draw him out of his office.

I glanced around the room. A coffee maker sat on a counter on the far wall opposite the offices. I ran over to it, grabbed the glass carafe, and headed back to the CEO's office door. I ghosted and leaned through the door. He was back to typing on the laptop. I pulled back out of the door and raised the carafe.

Once I threw it, there was no turning back. I could feel it in the fear coiled around my stomach like an icy spring, and in the prickles of heat in my scalp. No turning back.

The carafe hit the floor in the middle of the room with a satisfying crash, shattering into tiny shards of glass confetti. I turned and stepped through the office door. The CEO surged to his feet, his eyes wide, and raced toward me. My breath caught in my throat and I dove to the side, landing in a shoulder roll.

He never glanced my way. He grabbed the handle and yanked the door open. A moment later he was through the door and gone. I jumped to my feet and ran to the desk, where the laptop waited. Mara's advice came to mind as I reached for it. *Move stuff around as little as possible. We don't want security guards seeing a video feed of a laptop floating around in an empty office.*

I thought of the chair, the carafe. Well, that ship had sailed. I glanced through the open door, but didn't see the CEO in the narrow slice of the room beyond in view. I slammed the screen closed and flipped the laptop over. Multitool and screwdriver in hand, I located the hard drive.

When Mara and I had practiced, it had been so easy. Three or four screws and the hard drive was out. Now, the tiny screws swam in my vision as I tried to get the sharp tip of the screwdriver aligned. I looked up. Still no CEO. How long did I have? I looked back down at the laptop and frowned in concentration. What demented fool had thought little fairy screws were a good idea?

The first screw finally came out. Three to go. A drop of sweat dripped off the tip of my nose through the hole in my mask and landed on the desk beside the laptop. I glanced up again. Still nothing. I attacked the second screw. Seconds slipped by before the screwdriver grabbed the slots in the teeny screw and it came loose. The third screw behaved properly and came right out. One to go.

A voice drifted in through the open door. "... telling you, I want our head of security down here immediately!"

He was coming back. My hands wouldn't behave, and I couldn't get that last screw out. The hard drive moved a bit as I bumped it with the screwdriver. In desperation, I pulled my knife out of its pocket and jammed it into the crack on the side with both screws already out. I wiggled it deeper and leaned into it to lever the hard drive out.

For a moment, everything froze as I strained with the effort. Then a sharp crack of splintering plastic accompanied the hard drive popping out of the laptop. I stuck my tools and knife back into their pockets, picked up the hard drive, and dropped down behind the desk just as the CEO stormed back into the room. I was still blending, but I didn't want him to see parts of a laptop appearing to float around in the air.

I heard him gasp and run toward the desk. With hands that still shook, I stuffed the hard drive into the large, stretchy pocket just under my sternum. His feet came into view around the side of the desk, and I ghosted and rolled through the desk away from him.

On the far side of the desk, I stood and ran. The CEO cursed and slammed the laptop onto the desk, but I never looked back. I ran through the glass walls out into the main office, and through the branching hallways until I found the main lobby.

The security guard I'd seen downstairs stood just outside the glass walls by the elevators. He swept the beam from an enormous flashlight past me, and I instinctively recoiled, but the flashlight stayed in motion and didn't come to rest on me. I decided subtlety wasn't needed, and ran through the glass doors at the entrance. I almost ghosted through the guard, but something Mara had told me a few weeks ago came to mind. Something about ghosting through people being stupid because they could feel you, even gain a sense of who you were.

I dodged around him instead, maintaining only my

blend, and ran for the stairwell. He gasped and the flashlight beam spun around and shone through me as I cut past the elevators. So much for ninja-stepping silence. Speed was more important right now.

I didn't stop running until I was down the stairs, through the lobby, across the street, and ghosting into Jordan's car. The moment I was in the backseat, I released the ghost and shouted, "Go! Go! Go!"

To his credit, I don't think Jordan even flinched. He calmly hit the start button, revved the engine, and smoothly pulled out onto the street. Mara, on the other hand, almost jumped out of the car. She was still shifted into the form of a man.

"What the heck, Joss?" Mara turned around to glare at me, though she didn't quite look in the right spot. I was still blending, but was panting with exertion and stress, so she had a pretty good clue as to where to look. It was just too weird being glared at by an attractive woman whose face looked like a middle-aged, less-than-handsome man.

I released the blend, and slumped back in my seat. I couldn't seem to catch my breath, and my head felt hot. The hooded mask came off a lot easier than it had gone on, and the cool air of the car felt great. Mara's man-face softened a bit when she saw me.

"You look terrible," she said. "What happened?"

Before I could answer, Jordan cut in. "Did you get the drive?"

I nodded, not that Jordan could see me while looking forward and driving, and pulled the hard drive out of the pocket. My hand shook as I reached forward with it. Jordan glanced back, then turned and snatched it from my hand before returning his attention to the road.

"Joss," Mara said. "What happened?"

I told them. Somehow, talking it through helped. They asked a few questions, but mainly let me do the speaking. When I was done, I no longer felt like I was going to throw up. The exhaustion, though, was intense. At that moment, I didn't think I could have ghosted through a wall if my life had depended on it.

Jordan flipped his mask off and grunted. We were back in the suburbs, driving through well-lit streets. "I tried to pick a simple grab-and-go for this first mission, but stuff happens. You improvised. You got what we came for. You did well."

I smiled. Jordan didn't exactly heap the praise on us when training at Battlehoop. Unfortunately, he wasn't done.

"But next time, improvise in ways that won't seem inexplicable to anyone who watches it on a security feed."

"Got it," I said. "So that guy I saw…" I trailed off as Mara shifted back to herself. She was looking back at me, and cocked an eyebrow at me. She really looked better as a woman.

I tried again. "Was he the Mocker we're going after?"

"Him? A Mocker?" Jordan made a short barking sound. It took me a moment to realize he'd laughed. "No. He was just a guy with a hard drive we needed. But it's a step in the right direction."

"Oh," I said. "I'd thought maybe…" Did I really want to admit what I'd thought? That I had saved the day? Gotten the evidence to bury a bad guy?

Mara reached back and gave my hand a quick squeeze. "You did well. It'll just take a lot more. Sorry."

I nodded and gave her a smile. "So have I earned some time off? I don't think I could do that every night."

"Absolutely," Jordan said. "Next mission won't go down until this Saturday night."

Chapter 12

GUARDIAN ANGEL

"YOU JUST RAN?" Thomas asked.

"Like a scared rabbit." I put my foot back on the ground and nudged the merry-go-round into a slow orbit. "CEO dude was yelling and security was closing in."

Thomas sat on the opposite side of the merry-go-round facing me. It was Friday, a week and a half after my first mission. Early dusk lit the sky with pink, yellow, and red, and a cool breeze broke up the summer heat.

"But you were invisible, right?"

"Sure, but it's not like that." I frowned, struggling for the words. "Invisible isn't part of real life, you know? If someone looks at you, they see you, right?"

Thomas shrugged. "Okay. But not you. Not when you're blending."

"Yeah, but it's like my body, or my mind, or whatever, doesn't feel that yet. So when the security guard shone his light on me, I felt like I was caught. I was terrified."

"Huh," Thomas said. "I think I follow. So then what?"

"Like I said, I ran. Didn't stop running until I was back in Jordan's car."

"That's pretty intense," Thomas said.

"It was." I stuck a leg out and gave the merry-go-round another push. "And I felt sort of dirty. I mean, sure, a couple of our pranks haven't been totally in line with the rules, but none of it was go-to-jail illegal."

Thomas nodded slowly. It was like a tight cord around my chest loosened. It helped having a friend know what was going on. "But you're working for the good guys, right?"

"Sure, but..." I wasn't sure what to say. "Should the good guys be using me to steal stuff?"

"Good question." He looked off toward the setting sun for a moment, and then turned back to me. "So your first mission was a couple weeks ago. And you've done two more since?"

"Yeah. Last Saturday night, and then this past Tuesday night."

"How'd they go?" Thomas asked.

"Piece of cake. Just walk in, take a hard drive, walk out. Nothing like that first one, except for the part about stealing stuff not feeling right."

Thomas glanced toward the sun again. "We should start walking. I told Mom we'd get home before dark."

We got up and headed toward his house. "Hey, you know that message you sent me a couple days ago?" Thomas asked as we passed the elementary school.

"Yeah, the Mockers. The whole 'guy looking for the butterfly birthmark' thing. You get something on them?"

"I dropped it in when talking to my mom like you asked. The Mockers are real. And real bad."

"So she's heard of them?" I asked.

Thomas nodded. "Mom says they're some sort of major new force in organized crime. Pulling off stuff that shouldn't be possible. Stealing corporate secrets, then making money on stock trades. That sort of thing. Like, a mix of old school mob violence and high-tech theft."

We passed Beedle Junior High and turned onto Thomas's street. There were a few minutes of light left, so I slowed down. "Hey, wanted to ask you something else."

Thomas raised an eyebrow. "Okay."

I plunged ahead before I could chicken out. "Since I'm sleeping over again, it made me think about Bobby Ferris and..." Thomas stiffened. "Hold on, hear me out. I want to do something. I've got an idea."

"Dude," Thomas said, "leave him alone."

My head jerked back in surprise. "Not something bad! Something to help him. What kind of person do you think I am?"

Thomas frowned. "Is that a trick question?"

I punched him in the shoulder. At least, I tried to. He slipped my blow with an instinctive twisting motion. I laughed.

"Battlehoop!" we yelled together, and banged forearms to make an X. It was something we'd started doing whenever one of us did something cool that we'd learned from Jordan or Mara.

"Seriously, though," I said as we started walking again. "I think I can help him. I'm still mad at what he did, but I've been trying to forgive him. I... I want to try to do the right thing."

I looked over at Thomas. He gave me a quick smile.

"Good for you, Joss. What do you think you can do to help?"

"I was thinking I might pour his dad's liquor out. Make it all dramatic while blending, like some evil spirit was going to haunt him if he didn't cut it out."

We turned up the walk to Thomas's house. "Maybe you could put a more positive spin on it," he said. "Play it like you're Bobby's guardian angel."

Thomas unlocked the front door to his house and stepped in ahead of me. "Mom! We're home!" he yelled and headed up the stairs to the side of the entryway. I closed the door and flipped the deadbolt before following him.

"I like that," I said as we flopped down on the couch in the game room. "But isn't it, I don't know, sort of wrong to pretend to be an angel?"

Thomas laughed. "So you're stealing for the Guild, but worried about pretending to be an angel?"

I smiled. "Good point. Listen, I'm going to head into the bathroom, so if your mom checks on us, that's where I am as far as you know, okay?"

"I get it. You sure you want to do this?"

"They may not even be home, but, yeah, I'm going to try."

"Good luck, sir," he said. "I guess a Seven's safe

wandering around alone at night, right?"

"Pretty much." I stood and headed to the bathroom. I'd gotten in the habit of wearing snug clothing, but I still checked out my shorts and shirt in the mirror on the back of the bathroom door. I tucked in the shirt, just to be sure, and stuck the loose ends of my shoelaces under the knots.

That done, I blended, and ghosted through the locked bathroom door. I passed Thomas playing XBOX in the game room and headed downstairs and out the front door. It was dusk, a deep purple painting the western sky. I set out at a steady jog.

It was full dark when I arrived at Bobby's house. I took a moment to make sure my breathing was even, and ghosted through the front door. The entryway was dark, but flickering, colored lights painted the slice of family room I could see up ahead through the doorway, and the faint roar of a crowd roar swelled for a moment before subsiding. I stepped forward into the family room.

Mr. Ferris sat on the couch across the room, facing me. A bottle and glass stood on the coffee table in front of him. The room was lit by the TV on the wall beside me. The crowd cheered again. I glanced over. Baseball. If Bobby was home, this was the perfect setup.

I slowly stepped toward the hallway off to my left past the TV. Something Mara had told me leapt to mind as I started. *Don't blend between people and screens. They'll see a distortion.* I ducked low to get past the TV and continued down the hall.

The last time I'd been here, I'd fled the house by cutting straight through from the hall to the front yard. I was pretty sure the room I'd gone through was Bobby's. I remembered clothes on the floor, and junk covering a desk. Second door on the left. I ghosted into the room.

Bobby sat on his bed cradling a phone, his fingers twitching as he played some game. The room was lit by a solitary lamp on the dresser by his bed. The place was as bad as I remembered. Clothes, papers, books, and other junk covered the floor and every other surface. The room had a faint, sour smell.

I ghosted, and sank a couple inches into the floor. Even careful ninja-steps would probably disrupt the mess on the floor and catch Bobby's attention. I drifted over to the side of the bed, came up out of the floor, and released the ghost.

The next part of my plan put everything on the line. I pitched my voice high with my falsetto and spoke. "Bobby, do not be afraid."

Bobby didn't take my advice. I twisted out of the way of his fist as he surged off the bed and lashed out. He stumbled backwards away from me and fell across his desk and to the floor.

"I'm your, uh, guardian angel, Bobby. I'm here to help. I know you have trouble with your dad."

Bobby got his feet under him in a hurry and stood, his hands balled into fists. He looked terrified, but ready to put up a fight. For most of junior high I would have celebrated to have seen him scared, but now I was more proud of him for just standing there, fighting his fear.

"Stay calm, Bobby. I'm your guardian angel. Let's talk about helping your dad, okay?"

Bobby's eyes jerked around the room. "Where are you?" His voice had a wild edge to it.

"I'm here with you, Bobby, but you can't see me. 'Cause I'm an angel."

"I thought you could see angels."

"Only when we want to be seen, Bobby. We are normally invisible."

"Well, let me see you."

"I don't want to be seen, Bobby. My, uh, aspect is too terrible to behold."

Bobby took a small step forward and held his arms out, reaching toward me. "Put your arms down, Bobby. We should talk, first, about something bad you did. Once we clear the air, we'll help your dad."

He dropped his arms, and his shoulders sagged. "So you know about that?"

"I do," I said, still using my falsetto.

"Well, I'm not sorry," Bobby said, straightening back up. "I'll pound anyone who calls my dad a worthless drunk. Robert had it coming."

What the heck? "I'm not talking about that, Bobby."

"Oh. Okay, I admit it. I stole that pizza. But I was really hungry. My dad doesn't exactly look out for me."

"No, no, not that either. Eighth grade, Bobby, you pulled that seventh grader's pants down in front of those girls."

Bobby cocked his head to the side. "What are you talking about?"

"You pantsed Joss Morgan last year! You got his underwear!" My falsetto cracked when I yelled.

"I did? I don't remember doing that, but I remember him. He'd have had it coming. He was pulling pranks on other people all the time."

I took some deep, calming breaths. It wasn't about me. I was here to help.

"So angels keep track of that sort of thing?" Bobby asked, breaking up my thoughts. He was frowning. At least he no longer looked terrified.

"Let's just drop it and go help your dad. I want you to lead the way out to the family room and tell him an angel is here, and then point to where he keeps his liquor."

"Okay, I'll just..." Bobby nodded toward the door, and started walking, glancing back over his shoulder with every step. I decided to be dramatic and kicked the clothes lying on the ground as I followed. His eyes widened and he rushed through the door and down the hall.

"Dad! Listen, you've got to stop the drinking. There's an angel here who says she's going to make you stop."

I got to the family room as Mr. Ferris lifted bleary eyes to glare at his son. Bobby stood on the far side of the room toward the kitchen and pointed to a cabinet visible from where I stood.

"What the... Shut up, Bobby!" Mr. Ferris said. He lifted the bottle to pour more into the glass.

"Put the bottle down!" I yelled. Maybe it was a screech. After all, I was still trying to use my falsetto. I stepped toward Mr. Ferris and plucked the bottle out of his hand. I held it at the back, away from him, so that as little of the bottle as possible became invisible.

Mr. Ferris' eyes went huge, and he shook violently. I backed slowly toward the kitchen, his eyes riveted to the bottle, and upended it in the sink to drain. That done, I crossed the kitchen to open the cabinet Bobby had pointed out. There were at least two dozen bottles in there. It was going to take all night.

"Bobby," Mr. Ferris said, his voice trembling, "what's going on? Are you seein' this?"

I started carrying bottles to the sink as Bobby went over and sat on the couch near his dad.

"I really don't know, Dad, but I'm seeing it, too," Bobby said. "The angel just started talking to me in my bedroom. Said you needed to sober up."

Mr. Ferris hugged himself and sagged back into the couch, tears starting to well up in his eyes.

"Yeah," he said. "That's the honest truth." He looked Bobby in the eyes and nodded.

"We'll be okay, Dad," Bobby said, putting his hand on his dad's shoulder.

I put the last of the bottles in the sink. A mixture of clear and golden liquids flowed down the drain. I glanced up and saw Mr. Ferris embrace Bobby. This was about to get way too awkward.

"If you need help, Bobby, I'm going to tell you how to let me know."

Bobby pulled away from his dad and looked in my direction. "How?"

"Go to Beckler Park. The giant tree on one side of the park has a small hollow in it, about six feet off the ground. Leave me a note there. Maybe put it in a ziplock bag."

Bobby repeated the words under his breath. "A note in a tree? Why can't I just talk to you directly?"

"Bobby, don't question your guardian angel."

He nodded his head vigorously. "Okay. Got it."

I left him sitting by his dad. Mr. Ferris sat on the couch,

his feet pulled up and his head hanging between his knees. The televised crowd roared.

Chapter 13

THE 'GUILD'

SUNDAY AFTERNOON, THE doorbell rang. Dad jerked awake on his leather recliner and looked around, trying to figure out what had woken him. I tossed my comic book on the coffee table and sat up on the couch.

"Someone's at the door," I said. "I can get it."

Dad flared his eyes and shook his head. He had trouble waking up from naps. "Where's Jen, uh, Mom?"

"She and Janey took off after you fell asleep. I think they're shopping."

"Safe bet," Dad said as he stood and stretched. The doorbell rang a second time. "I'll get it."

He headed toward the entryway. I flopped back onto the couch and picked up my book. I heard him open the door. Hushed voices followed. Probably some fundraiser for a high school group getting a jump on start of school.

The voices got louder. Those were grown men arguing, not children. I couldn't quite make out the words. I stood and set the book on the table, and quietly stepped toward the entryway.

"… and we have nothing to talk about," Dad said. His voice had an edge to it.

"Mr. Morgan, the situation is very serious." A gruff male voice. Serious. Unhurried. Confident. "We know what you think of the Guild, but circumstances demand we find the rogue Seven."

My heart lurched up into my throat and I stumbled backwards. A rushing sound filled my ears. Heat prickled my scalp. The voices continued, but the words stumbled by unrecognized.

What was going on? How could the Guild be looking for a rogue Seven? How could they think I was rogue? The noise from the entryway rose, and I heard footsteps approaching the family room. Approaching me. I blended and ghosted.

Two men stepped into the room, Dad right behind them. His eyes, tightened in anger, darted around the room. Surprise registered on his face when he didn't see me. Then a faint smile lifted the corners of his mouth.

The two men glanced around, stepped over to the couch, and sat down, one on either end. Dad sat on the edge of his recliner and stared at the men from beneath lowered eyebrows. I stayed by the wall and tried to breathe with a slow, quiet rhythm.

They wore dark suits and were about the same height— a little shorter than Dad. The one on the left had blond hair and a scar that ran from his temple down to his chin. The other one had dark hair and dark eyes. Neither looked any happier than Dad.

"Let's first dispense with the talk of fairy tales so we can get down to business," the blond-haired man said. He turned to face the dark-haired man. "Luc?"

The dark-haired man gave a quick nod, and then stuck his hand into the coffee table. His hand passed through the table and was visible under it. Dad gasped and lurched out of his chair, which covered my own hiss of indrawn breath. Luc was a ghost! A Seven!

"So you see, we're not discussing fairy tales," Blondie said. "Now, the thefts that have taken place would require not only Luc's talent, but one more, which he doesn't have— the talent of invisibility."

Dad lurched forward, still staring at Luc's hand ghosting in the coffee table. He got down on his knees and knocked on the table, then crouched to look at Luc's hand sticking out the bottom. Luc waved. Dad sat back on his heels, his eyes wide with shock.

Blondie continued as Luc pulled his hand out of the

wood. "Luc's talent, when found in the same person as the talent of invisibility, is often called the Thief. I imagine you can see why, yes?"

Dad looked from Luc to Blondie, his eyes wide, but didn't answer. He looked pale. I'd gotten my own breathing back under control. My mind churned through what I had just heard. Luc wasn't a Thief. He couldn't blend. What other talent did he have?

And who were these people? It couldn't be the Guild. I worked for the Guild. Mara had said the Mockers had turned some Sevens. Was this the Mocker we were targeting? Maybe he'd come looking for whoever was harassing him. It had to be. A Mocker, in our home, and my dad talking to him, not knowing the danger.

"Now," Blondie said, "the house known for producing the most Thieves is house Sharif. So we have evidence of a Thief here in our own little city, and we have a family with children hidden from the Guild and untested, a family known for producing Thieves. Thus, here we are."

They were on to me. The Mocker must be closing in. I looked to my dad.

At the mention of children, Dad stood. Color returned to his face, and his eyes narrowed. "Get out."

Luc stood as Blondie rose to his feet and pointed a finger at Dad. "Do either of your children have the butterfly birthmark? We're going to find out. Understand?"

Dad balled his fists. "I'm not discussing my children with you. This conversation is over. Get out. Now."

"One of them has the birthmark," the man said, nodding. "Interesting. Do you really view us as the bad guys?"

Yes! I screamed in my mind.

Dad didn't answer. He just stood his ground.

"I see." Blondie stepped toward the entryway with Luc following. "We'll give you a few days to process it, but we'll be talking to you again. Soon. We will get to the bottom of this."

With that, the two men strode out. I heard the front door

open and close. Dad stood still and closed his eyes, breathing deeply. In that momentary pause, it hit me. I couldn't just reappear in the room with him. Dad's eyes snapped open and he strode toward the front door. I ghosted through the wall into the entryway ahead of him and hurried up the stairs as quietly as possible.

Halfway up the steps, I heard the deadbolt snap into place, so I released the blend and started back down. As the entryway came into view at the bottom, Dad saw me just before he went back into the family room. He stopped and turned toward me, frowning. He looked at me, looked at the family room, and back at me.

I breezed by him into the family room and flopped back onto the couch. "Hey. That sounded sort of intense."

"You listened in?" Dad asked as he sat back down on his recliner.

"Well, I... Yeah. What's with the Guild and all that?"

"Until today, I would have said it was a myth."

I had to play this carefully. I'd wanted to have this conversation with him ever since I met Mara, but now it was all messed up, because it hadn't really been the Guild. It had been a Mocker. I was sure of it. Pretty sure.

"And after today?" I asked.

"Even worse. It means... it means I have to rethink some really tough stuff."

"Worse than a myth? I don't understand. Can you start from the beginning?"

He pushed the leg rest of the recliner down and sat up facing me. "I'm not sure I can. Joss, there's this family secret that your mother and I decided to keep from you kids. But now..."

I sat up as well. "Dad, what's going on?"

He held up a hand. "Wait. Just give me a sec. There's this story. A family story. I don't want to go into the details. But the story claimed that your great-great-grandmother was... well, I always assumed it was, uh, just a crazy family story. But now, now I don't know."

"What did the story say?"

"That your great-great-grandmother was killed. Mauled to death. Fighting werewolves."

My mind lurched to a stop. "Werewolves?"

"Well, yeah," Dad said, and shrugged. "I know it sounds crazy. It is crazy."

But why not? In a world with Sevens, why couldn't there be monsters, too? It would make so much sense. It would be a real use for a Seven. Moving with blinding speed. Hitting with hardened fists. Dodging, blending, ghosting. My great-great-grandmother had been a Seven, and she'd fought monsters. It had to be true.

"Did she, uh, have a butterfly birthmark?" I asked.

"You heard them ask about that?" I nodded, and Dad grimaced. "Yeah. Yeah, she did. Or so my grandfather told me. It was his mother. She died when he was a kid, and Grandfather went to the grave swearing she was some kind of hero. I just thought he was nuts."

"A birthmark like mine?"

He looked at his feet and nodded.

"So my great-great-grandmother fighting, uh, werewolves. What happened? Why do you believe it now? And what's the Guild?"

He looked up at me and rubbed his temples. "I'm not saying I believe it now. I'm not sure what I believe. The, uh, Guild is supposedly this ancient association of people with powers. Special powers that run in families."

"And something changed. What happened?"

"I just saw a man stick his hand through the coffee table like it was thin air. Passing through things is one of the, uh, special powers, supposedly."

I felt this rush, this overwhelming need, to show him I could do it, too. But I was scared. What if it freaked him out? What if he was scared of me? Would he let me keep training? And what about the guys who were just here, these fake Guild-members? Would I have to explain everything to him if he found out I was a Seven? I decided to let it play out.

"That's pretty crazy sounding, Dad. I'm not saying you're crazy, it just... What will you do?"

"I saw it. His hand passed through wood like it wasn't there." He sat still for a moment, his eyes distant, and then shook his head. "What am I talking about? Joss, I'm sorry. I'm running my mouth."

"I'm glad you're talking," I said.

"No, your mother and I decided together to discuss certain things, and to not discuss other things. I can't just wave that all away. I know you probably have a lot of questions, but I need to talk to your mother first. We'll need to decide together how we handle all this."

"Yeah, of course, Dad."

After that, Dad shut down, and when Mom and Janey got home, Mom and Dad holed up in their bedroom for a couple hours. I heard raised voices now and then, but resisted the temptation to spy on them. It would have been so easy. Just ghost and blend. The Thief.

Had my great-great-grandmother been a Thief? It didn't seem like the best talents for fighting by themselves, but armed with the right weapon, one that could be held up against your body when blending, it would probably work.

More importantly, who were those men? Had it been the Mocker we were hunting getting close to me? Did he already have a Seven? Or was I totally wrong? Were they from the Guild, and people in the Guild didn't talk to each other? Whatever the case, someone was after me, and they knew where I lived.

Chapter 14

MISSION TO MARS (STREET)

"Mara, the Mocker or the Guild or someone was at my house!"

Mara sat cross-legged in the center of the personal training room. The words had burst from my mouth the moment the door had closed behind me. She wore a T-shirt that said FORTUNE FAVORS THE BOLD... MOUSE TRAPS DON'T. Her eyes had snapped open at my words, but she didn't speak. Instead, she motioned for me to sit across from her. I plopped down on the mat.

"Tell me," Mara said. "All of it."

I told her. She sat without moving, her hands resting lightly on her knees as I spoke. When I finished, she nodded.

"They're fishing." Mara stuck a leg out straight and grabbed her foot with both hands in a stretch that made me wince. "I mean, obviously they're getting closer, but they haven't pinned down the butterfly birthmark to your family, even if they acted like they had. They were bluffing. They're trying to shake out the Seven."

"Who?" I asked. "Who is shaking out the Seven? Am I the Seven? I thought we were the Guild. I'm a little freaked out. Give me something to work with."

She switched to the other leg and did the same stretch. It looked no less painful on that side. "The Mocker we've been tagging."

"Oh, good," I said. "You know, for a second there I thought some ancient organization I was supposed to be part of was actually hunting me. Glad to hear it's just some master criminal-underworld evil guy."

She sat back up and gave me a crooked smile.

"I'm serious, Mara!" I was too agitated to sit. I hopped to my feet and started pacing. "How did they know about my family? Are we in danger? I mean, I know you told me a Mocker was gunning for me and all, but now he knows where I live. He was in my house."

Her smile faded. "No, I doubt you're in any immediate danger. Or, not a lot more than before. First off, it was probably not the Mocker. Just henchmen. And yeah, he's getting closer, but so are we. And it's not like he wants to harm you. Most likely, he's going to approach it more slowly to recruit you. But I'll look into it, though, okay? For now, let's just keep it between the two of us."

I cocked my head to the side. "Versus between you, me, and...?"

"Jordan."

I stopped pacing. "You don't want Jordan to know?"

"I don't. He can be intense. I'd hate for him to overreact. It might tip off your parents."

"Weren't my parents tipped off when a Mocker came by our house?"

She waved off my concern. "They were reminded of the Guild. They learned nothing of your actual training. Here, sit back down. Let's talk your next mission. It's the best way to stop him. We're getting closer to having what we need."

I hated this. So many secrets. Secrets from my parents, my sister, my friends. And now Jordan. Not just secrets, but layers of secrets.

It hit me then. All these secrets were like a web, and Mara was the spider. It all came back to her. My knowledge of the Guild, the Mockers, being a Seven, Jordan, everything. I needed time to think about it. Could I really trust her? What did I know? What had I seen?

For now, I needed to play along. Buy time to figure it out. I sat down.

"The next job's on a high security floor of a building," Mara said. "Same as the other jobs, but you've got to hold both the ghost and the blend the whole time once you get to the sixth floor to avoid security. Grab a hard drive, then get out."

"Wait, " I said. "Ghost the whole time to avoid security? Not just blend?"

"Yeah, they're probably going to have IR cameras and laser sensors along with the regular cameras. Ghosting will suppress your heat signature."

"So I give off a 'heat signature' when blending? That makes about as much sense as being able to make noise when I'm ghosting. Speaking of which, how does that work? How can I make noise while ghosting?"

Mara shook her head. "No idea. But is that really the part of ghosting that seems odd? Not the part where you walk through walls?"

"Whatever. So how do I grab something while ghosting?"

"You don't. You'll have to assess the situation and pick how and when to stop ghosting so you can make the grab."

I thought back over the the missions I'd done already. Could I have held a ghost the whole time as well as blending? I didn't think I could've done it two weeks ago, but figured I might be able to pull it off now. It would be close.

"When?" I asked. "Wait. Let me guess. Tomorrow night."

She shook her head. "Hope you're well rested. You go in tonight. Normal time."

"You guys are pushing hard. It's not easy to ghost and blend for that long. I could use a couple more weeks to build up my strength."

"You can't have it both ways," Mara said. "We can't wait for you to get stronger and take down the Mocker faster. It's one or the other. And Jordan got some intel, said we had to move fast. Like I said, a high security floor. It's in a building over on Mars Street."

I closed my eyes and took a deep breath. My stomach felt fine. Sure, I felt a bit of tightness, but that was it. Maybe I was getting used to it. Besides, compared to having evil henchmen in your home, this was nothing.

I opened my eyes. Mara was studying my face. I nodded. "I'll be ready."

After Battlehoop, Janey and I peeled off from the others near Deion's house and headed for home. On Appleton, a fancy looking black car pulled up even with us, driving very slowly. The windows were tinted super dark. It was creepy. I felt exposed on my bike.

"Joss," Janey hissed. "I saw that car back by the Taco Bell."

She was right. It'd been in the parking lot near the corner. Like someone had parked there, watching for us.

"Pull over," I said, and came to a stop. "I don't like this."

She stopped beside me. So did the car. Not good.

"Joss?" Janey's voice had a slight tremor to it.

I slowly got off my bike and laid it down. I wanted to have both feet on the ground. Janey followed my lead. "Get behind me," I said. I figured anyone trying to nab us was in for a surprise when I went all Seven on them.

Janey stepped close beside me, but elbowed me in the ribs when I tried to push her behind me. I glared at her. She glared back. "I'm not hiding behind you."

The passenger and driver doors opened, and two men stepped out of the car. It was Blondie and his Seven sidekick, Luc. Janey glanced at me, the whites of her eyes showing. I put a hand on her shoulder as the Mocker stepped around the front of the car to stand by Luc, about ten feet away.

"Is it Joss?" he asked. "And Janey?"

I had trouble hearing him over my heart thundering in my chest. I leaned over to Janey and whispered in her ear. "They were at our house. Dad threw them out. Thought they were bad or something. We need to escape. Be ready."

Janey gave me a quick nod, her eyes narrowing. "Leave us alone." Her voice was steady. Very impressive.

The Mocker smiled. "Circumstances don't really allow for that. Now, we need to know if either of you has the butterfly birthmark."

Janey's eyes flared wide again, and she glanced at me. It was enough.

"So, you've got the birthmark, Joss," Blondie said. He leaned forward with his hands on his knees so his eyes were down closer to our height. "We're going to need to..."

That was as far as he got. Janey took three quick steps forward and leapt. Had I mentioned Janey was freaky fast, and that she'd thrived at Battlehoop? She jumped right at Blondie and lashed her foot up and out like a cracking whip.

Her foot met his nose. It was like she'd popped a water balloon. Blood sprayed from his face as his head snapped back. He stumbled backwards and fell across the hood of the car.

I stared in stunned silence as Janey landed on her other foot and pivoted to face Luc. He was more shocked than I was, which was a good thing. It gave me time to get moving. Janey had gotten in a great surprise attack, but I didn't think she was up to fighting a Seven. I rushed forward and used my bruiser talent to harden my foot and leg as I kicked him with everything I had. In the crotch.

He hadn't trained with Mara like I had. I think I would have instinctively ghosted given his talents, but he just sat there staring at Janey in shock as my foot hit him like a sledgehammer. Luc toppled over, made some weird choking sounds, and vomited.

"Go!" I yelled, and grabbed my bike. Janey ran to her bike and jumped on it. I hesitated to let her get ahead of me, then pedaled hard in pursuit. I glanced back. Black car. Luc curled in a ball on the ground. Blondie leaning against the car clutching his nose. Eyes boring holes into me. I turned away and pedaled harder.

We swung into the alley behind our house and stopped at the gate. Janey punched in the code and the gate rolled open. I repeated the code on the keypad inside the gate to close it.

"What's going on? Who were those men?" Janey didn't look angry or scared. She looked determined. Her mouth was pulled in a firm line, eyes narrowed. Her hands shook, though, and her face was pasty.

"They came by the house yesterday," I said. I stuck my bike in the shed before continuing. "You and Mom were out shopping. It got pretty intense between them and Dad. They wanted to meet us. Inspect us for the, uh, birthmark."

"Your birthmark? Why? Do we call the cops? They were going to grab us!"

I held up my hands to slow her down. She glared at me, and then flung her bike into the shed. "I think we let Mom and Dad decide if they call the cops."

"But what did they want, Joss? How did they know about your birthmark?"

The last thing I wanted was Janey getting into this tangled mess of Mockers, the Guild, and me. "Dad told me he needed to talk stuff through with Mom, okay? He needs to tell you about them. He's the one who talked to them."

"So you're blowing me off? I just helped rescue you, and you blow me off?"

"No! I'm serious! You need to talk to Dad. How's that blowing you off?"

Janey didn't answer. She just stood there, glaring at me. I needed to distract her. I held up my forearm at an angle. "Battlehoop!"

She'd seen me do it with my buds. She knew what it meant. At first her eyes narrowed further, then a small smile turned up the corner of her mouth. She banged her forearm against mine. "Battlehoop." She didn't yell it proper-like, but it would do.

"Seriously, that was incredible," I said. "I mean, I've seen you jump kick tons of times at Battlehoop. But in real life? Like, putting a man on his back?"

Her smile broadened. "I thought I was going to throw up I was so scared."

"Yeah, well, you weren't the one who threw chunks."

"I know!" she said. "Joss, you kicked him so hard in the privates I felt sorry for him."

I smiled back at her. "You don't mess with the Morgans."

Her smile faded. "But you're still not going to tell me what's going on?"

"Janey, please. I don't think it's unfair to ask you to talk to Dad."

"We'll see." She turned and headed for the house. I followed, grimacing.

Mom had pulled a Monday shift, so she and Dad arrived home about the same time. I expected Janey to rush them and tell everything. She didn't. It was just a normal evening. It freaked me out.

I cornered Janey as soon as possible. "What's up? You going to talk to Dad?"

"Yeah," Janey answered. "But there's more to this, and I want to hear it from you. I'm going to give you one day to tell me everything or I talk to them." She jabbed a finger into my chest. "One day."

That was not what I expected, but I was glad. One less variable before my big mission that night. The rest of the evening was a blur. Dad pulled me aside after dinner and told me that he and Mom were still in a tangled mess of figuring out how to talk through everything as a family. He told me they expected to have it sorted out within a day.

I managed to get in a solid two and a half hours of sleep before my alarm went off at 12:45. I had a pillow over it so it would wake me, but not everyone else. Ten minutes later, I was dressed in my work clothes and jogging down the street. I blended the whole way to make sure no one mistook me for a ninja. In the suburbs, people called the cops on ninjas.

I didn't stop when I reached Jordan's parked car, but ghosted right into the backseat and dropped the ghost and blend. "Here," I said.

"Two minutes early," Mara said from the seat in front of me. "Impressive."

Mars Street was near downtown in an area with lots of older buildings. Jordan stopped in front of a brick-clad building that was seven or eight stories tall, situated in the middle of a street with several other buildings of about the same height.

Mara had shifted her face to the man personae, and pointed to the building one over. "Give me the details," she said.

"Sixth floor," I said. "Grab the hard drive out of the laptop in office 678. Lots of security. Blend and ghost the whole time once I'm up there."

We talked it through for a few minutes, and I headed in. There wasn't much of a lobby, but I noticed card readers everywhere. The doors to the outside, the elevators, the hall doors off the little lobby. Cameras were mounted in every corner. That freaked me out. I ghosted just in case one of them was the kind that could see my heat signature.

There was no fire escape map, but I found the stairwell in less than a minute. Running up the stairs while ghosting took a little practice. If I went too hard, my feet punched into the steps, which would yank me to a stop. While ghosting, my body seemed to respect physical boundaries, but only to a point. By the time I passed the door to the third floor, I had found the rhythm.

A minute later, I was on the sixth floor landing. There were no cameras here, so I let go of the ghosting. I stretched, giving myself a moment to catch my breath. I was already feeling the strain of blending and ghosting together while running up stairs.

The utter madness of the past two days felt like a dream. Maybe if I succeeded tonight, we'd take down the Mocker. Maybe he was the guy stalking me and my family. Either way, I needed to move. I only had so much more energy to ghost and blend. I took one more deep breath, ghosted, and plunged through the door to the sixth floor.

Chapter 15

THE SIXTH FLOOR

WOOD PANELING. THAT was my first impression as I stepped through the stairwell door into the offices. It was my second impression, too. There was a lot of wood. I stood in a hallway with dark wood paneled walls, dark wood floors, and a light wood paneled ceiling. Maybe one in four lights were on, so the light was dim but sufficient.

Office 678. I wanted to get in, grab the drive, and get out. I glanced each way. The hallway went a short distance to my left and then turned to the left. To my right, the hallway stretched much farther before turned to the right. Wood paneled doors stood at regular intervals in the wall I faced.

I spotted four security cameras. They were small, dark globes hung at even intervals from the ceiling that contained regular or IR cameras. Or both.

I strode to the closest door on my left and was relieved to see it was numbered. A small bronze placard beside the door said OFFICE 672. I had gotten lucky. I continued down the left end of the hall to the next door. OFFICE 670. Well, I'd had a fifty-fifty chance. I jogged back the other way. Four offices later I arrived. OFFICE 678. I ghosted through the door.

A wave of dizziness swept over me. Keeping up the ghosting and blending was proving harder than I had thought.

I glanced around. The office was not what I'd expected. First, it was huge. Like, as big as my house's living room, family room, and dining room combined. I guess I hadn't noticed how far apart the office doors were off the hallway.

Second, there was no wood. The floor looked like tiled marble, and the walls had been dressed with some sort of rough stone.

The corner to my right was a mini kitchen. Stainless steel appliances. Marble counters on what looked like smoked glass cabinets. Glass shelving holding bottles of all shapes and sizes. A security camera globe mounted in the corner. To my left, was a living room with leather, more leather, and, oh yeah, leather. And another security camera. Was this an office or an apartment?

I looked to the far end of the office. A giant, dark wood desk hulked in front of windows that stretched floor to ceiling and overlooked the nighttime city. A tall maroon leather chair stood like a sentinel behind the desk, and a lone laptop was the only item on the desk's massive surface. Two more security cameras were mounted in the far corners.

I hurried over to the desk. The chair was pushed under the desk, but there was plenty of extra room under there for me to hide. I ghosted through the chair into the leg space, then arranged myself so no part of my body was overlapping with the chair or desk. It was a tight fit, but I managed.

Tucked in under the desk, I was completely hidden from the security cameras. I let go of my ghosting. There were no alarms. No shouted warning. I released the blend as well, and sagged back against the wood. The relief from the strain was immediate.

While I rested, I pondered my next steps. The laptop was directly above me with several inches of wood between. I could try to do something fancy with ghosting, where I made my fingertips solid while reaching through the desk to push the laptop to the edge. It sounded like a cool idea, and totally ridiculous. Even if I could pull it off, it made me tired just thinking about it. No, I was just going to have to reach up and around to grab it while blending. If my hand was going to set off some IR motion alarm, so would moving the laptop.

I took a deep breath and blended again. After shifting

onto my knees in a tight crouch, I reached up past the edge of the desk. The laptop was a couple inches further back from the edge than I'd thought, but after shifting up onto the chair a bit, I managed to reach it. Once I got a good grip, I took one last breath and pulled the laptop under the desk.

No time to wait. I dropped my blending and got to work with the screwdriver and multitool. The hard drive cooperated and came out of the laptop in two minutes flat. I lay my head back against the desk and closed my eyes. So tired.

"I'm going to need that hard drive."

My stomach shot up into my throat as my eyes popped open. The chair was gone, and a man wearing jeans and a snug fitting T-shirt knelt in its place. His dark hair was short and parted on the side, and his short beard had a few white hairs on the chin. The laptop and hard drive fell from my numb fingers. He reached in and picked up the hard drive.

"Good. Listen, you're not in trouble, okay? Can we talk?" He looked concerned.

How had I let this guy sneak up on me? I must have been focusing on the hard drive when he arrived. My training kicked in, and I began tactical breathing. In for four counts. Hold for four counts. Out for four counts.

"I get that you're scared. Why don't you step out with me?" The man stood, his legs remaining visible as I sat under the desk.

Escape. That one thought moved me to action. I ghosted and blended. Standing up, I drifted back out of the desk away from the man and toward the office door. The man stood with his arms crossed, tapping one finger on an arm. His eyes looked in my direction, but through me. He was about Thomas's height, with a lean build.

I started backing toward the door. His eyebrows came together in a frown, and he crouched for a moment to look under the desk. He stood back up and shifted. I didn't know what I was seeing. He didn't change, but it felt different. His eyes focused on me.

"You don't want to run. What hold do they have on

you?" He stepped toward me through the desk as he spoke.

My eyes widened in shock. How could he... another Seven!

My thoughts must have been written on my forehead, because he started smiling, still walking toward me while I walked backwards toward the door.

"That's right. I can see you. They didn't teach you that, did they? That someone blending can see others blending?"

I shook my head no, still walking backwards. He was blending and ghosting. A Thief.

"They sent you in here, and haven't even taught you the basics." He shook his head. He looked angry. "They sent you into a trap, you know. We had motion sensors under the laptop. It was all a setup to draw them out. Look, we're going to find you. There are only so many families that produce Thieves and aren't established in the Guild."

My back hit the door, and I pushed through it into the hall. A moment later the man burst through the door and I instinctively lashed out with a kick. Which was a waste of time, since I was ghosting.

My foot connected with his chest and threw him back through the door. I was so shocked that I overbalanced and fell through the wall on the opposite side of the hallway into a pitch black room.

He could blend and ghost, which must allow him to see me and touch me. The hard drive was lost, but that meant nothing to me. What had he been talking about? The Mockers wanted to help me? It made no sense. I had to escape. What were my options?

I could fight him, ghost to ghost, but that sounded idiotic. He was a grown man. A Seven.

Wait. A Seven. But I was the Seventy-Seven. It came to me. I knew what to do. Mara had said this was a high security floor. Hopefully that meant the other floors were low security. I needed to take the fight to another floor, away from all the security cameras. I didn't want to advertise myself any more than I already had.

I aimed for the hall at a forty-five-degree angle, and

entered it a few feet from where I'd left. The man was stepping through the opposite wall into the hallway several feet away.

"Nice kick. Caught me off guard. Not gonna happen again. What hold do they have on you? Why are you working for them?" His blue eyes shone in the dim light of the hallway. He didn't look angry, or scared. He looked confident.

I drifted down into the floor and dropped ten feet to the floor below. I stopped ghosting as I fell and landed in a forward roll. I stood in the middle of a room that looked like the break room at Dad's office. I only had a moment to glance around, and the man dropped through the ceiling to land beside me.

I could see it now. He looked off, like he wasn't fully there. He was still ghosting. He grabbed me, and I didn't resist. His arms passed through my body. I'd been right. Ghosts could touch other Sevens ghosting, but not Sevens who weren't ghosting. What I hadn't guessed was the jolt of recognition that hit me as his arms went through me. I had a sense of him, like we'd known each other for a long time. He seemed honest. How could some Mocker hireling feel honest?

"Nice trick," the man said, and his body firmed up. He had stopped ghosting. Nice kick. Nice trick. I was sick of his compliments.

He reached for me again. I kinneyed as best I could on short notice and used my bruiser talent to harden my fist. My body was spent, and kinneying wore me out. I had one shot at this. It had better work.

As I kinneyed and sped up, the other Seven seemed to slow down, his arms spread wide, reaching for me. I punched him on the side of the head, hard and fast. His eyes snapped up into his head and he dropped to the floor unconscious.

I pumped a fist in the air. "Seventy-Seven, baby! Bet you didn't see that coming!"

Then I ran.

I flipped back to ghosting and blending, and cut through walls, looking for the stairwell. It didn't take long. I ran down those steps and into the lobby like my life depended on it. For all I knew, it did.

Outside, the BMW was parked in the same place. I ran to it and ghosted into the back seat. Once inside, I lay down out of sight and released my talents.

"And he's back!" Mara disguised as a man said. "How'd it go?"

Jordan gunned the BMW forward as Mara spoke. "Where's the drive? Do you have it?"

"It was a trap," I said. "They knew I was coming, and had a motion sensor on the laptop."

The car lurched a bit as I spoke. Jordan whipped his masked head around to look at me for a moment, then looked forward and kept driving. Mara looked away from Jordan toward her window. I was lying across the back seat, panting, trying to catch my breath. My head was toward Mara's side, and I saw a smile split her man-face.

It was there for a moment, and gone. She turned back toward Jordan, and I sat up so I could buckle up in the middle seat.

"What happened?" Mara asked.

"I got it. Found the office. Really amazing place. Leather, stone, big wood desk, security cameras everywhere…"

"Joss, cut to the chase. What happened?" Jordan said over my description.

"I went under the desk, grabbed the laptop, then ripped the hard drive out of it. That's when the Seven showed up."

The car swerved again.

"A Seven?" Mara said.

"Yeah. Blendy ghost. A Thief. He could see me even when I blended, and when we both ghosted, it was like it cancelled each other out."

"I know how it works, Joss," she said.

"Well I didn't! And I didn't expect them to be waiting for me. You almost got me caught by the Mockers!"

"Keep calm," Jordan said. "Stuff happens. How'd you

get away?"

"I ghosted down a floor, away from the security cameras. He followed. I dropped the ghost so he couldn't grab me. When he dropped his ghosting, I punched him hard. Like, kinney-bruiser hard. Not that I'm good at either, but it worked."

"Smart move," Mara said.

"Not bad," Jordan said, nodding in agreement. "We'll sort all this out. For now, let's just keep your training going."

Oh, yeah. What was there to worry about? I wanted to scream, but I kept my mouth shut. I had too many questions. Why had the man said I wasn't Guild-trained? And why had he wanted to train me and not simply stop me? Did he know that other Seven, Luc?

Most importantly, why had Mara smiled when she'd learned it had been a trap? Whose side was she on? Had she been part of setting me up?

Everything was spinning out of control. The guys at the house who tried to grab Janey and me. Mara wanting me to fail. Janey holding information over me. And now yet another Seven, this Thief, waiting for me.

It felt like I was underwater breathing air from an overturned bucket. Time was running out, and I had no clue what was going on. I was not going to stand around and watch anymore. Tomorrow, I was going to sort out the biggest puzzle—Mara.

Chapter 16

MASKS

I'VE HEARD OF this thing called insomnia. I don't have it. I can stay up thinking, but not when I'm dead tired. My mind was on fire with questions, adrenaline pumped through my veins, and three minutes after my head hit the pillow I was asleep. I woke to my alarm five hours later.

My stretchy black work clothes and shoes from the previous night were scattered on the floor. I took a moment to fold them up and tuck them in the back of my bottom dresser drawer. I put on a slim fitting T-shirt and my tightest pair of athletic shorts.

I'd seen some weirdness from Mara starting the very first time I'd met her. I was convinced she'd been frustrated when she'd heard I was a ghost. And I'd swear she'd been happy when she'd thought I had failed test five. Ghost and blender. The two talents I most needed for that mission last night. The talents that made me a Thief.

And then there was that smile last night in the car. I'd told her about the trap, and for just one moment, she'd smiled.

I grabbed my phone and messaged Thomas.

Can you talk?

I waited. My phone rang.

"Thomas," I said. "I need some cover this afternoon."

"Okay. What sort of cover?" Thomas asked.

"Can you make sure your mom knows I'm coming over? I'll tell my parents I'm going to your house after Battlehoop. And I will. Just not immediately."

"Where are you going?"

"I had another mission last night," I said.

"Okay. And…"

"Well, I did it. And it went bad. Another Seven tried to take me down."

"*What?*" Thomas said.

"Exactly. The whole thing was a trap. I need to find out what's going on. What Mara is up to."

"Mara? Why Mara?"

"I've seen things." I started pacing my room. "Like she wasn't happy when I ended up being a ghosty blender. And last night, I swear she smiled when my mission failed."

"And you're going to…?"

"I'm going to follow her. See what there is to see. I'll give it a couple hours, then snag a bus back to our neighborhood. Shouldn't be a problem for the Seventy-Seven."

"Traps. Sevens. What the heck." There was a long pause. "I'll talk to Mom. Set things up."

"Thanks, Thomas," I said. "I'll catch you up at your place this afternoon. There's a lot more to it. Oh. Can you get my bike to your house?"

"Dude, now you're asking a lot. Yeah, I can manage it."

"Thanks. I'm out."

I headed downstairs and grabbed some breakfast. Both Mom and Dad had left early. I pulled my phone out and texted Mom to let her know I wanted to hang out at Thomas's house that afternoon. Janey sat across from me eating her cereal and giving me the eye.

"What?" I said, after being stared at for like three minutes.

"What did you do last night?"

My jaw froze mid-chew. A fist clenched around my heart.

"What do you mean?" I got my mouth moving again. "What did *you* do last night?"

"I had to go to the bathroom last night. A little after 2:00 a.m."

I froze.

"I heard you banging around in your room." Janey

pointed her spoon at me as she spoke.

Not good. I would have been changing out of my work clothes.

"I waited a couple minutes," she said, "and it got quiet."

"Yeah, 'cause I was asleep."

"Oh, I know."

"What does that mean?" I asked.

"I snuck in your room to see what you were doing." Janey whipped a hand from under the table. She was holding my mask. "Look what I found."

I was stunned. My jaw dropped open and some milk dribbled out. How had I missed the mask when I'd put up the outfit this morning? I just wasn't used to masks being part of my clothing.

"One more time. What were you doing last night? What's going on? Does this have to do with the men who tried to grab us?"

How could I play this? Sure, we had issues, but I wasn't going to put her in danger. She was family. And we had sort of bonded the previous day. I couldn't tell her what was going on. It didn't feel safe. At least, not more than Dad knew.

"Janey, please, I can't tell you. Let me have that back."

"Oh, you can tell me." She waved the mask back and forth just out of reach. "Or I show this to Mom and Dad." Janey stood and waved the mask closer to me. "Someone tried to kidnap us yesterday. You're sneaking around at night or something. What's going on?"

I slammed my fist on the table. "I'm trying to keep you safe!"

"Liar."

Stupid, stupid girl. I took a deep breath, closed my eyes, and kinneyed. My eyes snapped open. I leaned forward and snatched the mask out of Janey's hand as she slowly pulled away from me. I tried to move slowly so that I was just fast enough to get the mask. The last thing I needed was Janey wondering about my Seven talents. I released the kinney and slumped back into my chair. Boy, that was tiring.

"How did you do that?" Janey looked from her empty hand to me. "I'm faster than you!"

"I guess I got lucky." I stood and headed for the stairs.

"This isn't over, Joss," Janey called to me. "I'm going to find out what's going on. And I'm going to talk to Dad. Today!"

I went upstairs and got my work clothes out of the drawer. I stuffed them with the mask under my mattress. I'd need a safer place to store them, but for now I had to get to Battlehoop. I was running out of time. I had to find answers fast.

After a quick trip through the bathroom, I headed downstairs and went out back to get my bike. Janey was just getting on her bike and heading down the alley toward the meet up at Deion's house. I ran back and locked the door, then got on my bike and gave chase. When I got within a hundred feet, she heard me.

"It's not over!" she said, looking back over her shoulder, and started pedaling hard.

We raced. She won. But I had easily gained ten feet on her. Not bad, if you ignored the fact that she was two years younger than me and a girl. We rode as a group over to Battlehoop. Thomas still looked ridiculous on his bike. Frankie was still weird, but I was getting used to him. Arjeet was talkative. Deion had gotten leaner, and talked about music less. If we kept this up, we'd end up being a gang or something.

"Today," Arjeet said, "is the day Janey falls to my masculine prowess."

Janey laughed and steered her bike over to him. "Did you just say I'd fall for your masculine princess?"

I looked down and kept pedaling, tuning out the laughter. Too much to figure out. And I was out of time. Once Janey talked to Dad, I knew the whole thing would just blow up and slip out of my control. Not that I felt in control now, but it would get worse. And after yesterday, and last night, I feared for my family's safety. What could I do?

I needed to know who I could trust, other than Thomas. I had to pin down what Mara was up to. Mara. It all centered on her. Was she even a good guy? And were Luc and that guy really working for the Mockers? Did I really even know who the Mockers were, or the Guild?

We arrived at Battlehoop. We trained. When I went to take my turn with Mara one on one, she came out of the room and stopped me. "I've got to take care of a couple errands today, so I'll need to skip your lesson. Sorry."

My eyes narrowed as I watched her walk out of the dojo. Jordan jerked my attention away from her with a sharp word. I climbed back onto the platform and continued training. Jordan put Janey and me in a hoop together to spar a short time later. It struck me that in all the weeks we'd been coming to the dojo, I'd never been in a hoop with her.

"Gonna kick your tail," she said as we pulled on the safety gear. "We'll see who's faster."

Mara had a strict rule for me. I was never to use my talents when training with the other students. She had told me it would both put my identity at risk and hinder my ability to learn fighting skills.

In the ring with Janey, I was tempted to break that rule. Janey was just so fast. I had a longer reach and a lot more weight, but Janey had taken to fighting like a fish to water. She knew she weighed less. She knew we all had longer reaches. So she fought within her limits, letting her speed make the difference.

Every time I closed with her to beat her out of the hoop, she'd just disappear and I'd hit air. I knew one good hit would do it, but I couldn't land anything solid. In the meantime, she peppered me with punches and kicks. I felt like I was being tenderized.

And then it was over. I had her near the edge of the hoop, faked a left punch, and kicked hard with my right foot. I'd thought she'd dodge my fist and go right into my kick. Instead, she dropped, caught my foot in both her hands as I kicked, and yanked me forward. She hit my butt with a vicious kick of her own as I stumbled over her, sending me out of the hoop.

I'd been beaten by a twelve-year-old girl. And my backside was on fire. The indignity was almost too much for me.

"Way to go, Janey." Thomas strode over and offered her a hand. He effortlessly pulled her up from the mat. "I've told you over and over, Joss. You don't mess with Janey."

Janey walked over to where I was rubbing my butt. She looked me in the eye, her eyebrows raised. "And the faster Morgan is…?"

I looked away and dropped my hand after one last massage. "You are."

She nodded. "This isn't over. The 'masks' are coming off."

I grimaced. Now she was threatening me with puns. The rest of the day was hard, but didn't involve any new humiliations. Mara returned in about an hour. I edged over to Thomas when I saw her. "Got me covered?"

He nodded, avoiding eye contact. It was just as well that he didn't speak, because Mara stepped onto the platform and trained with us for the remaining hour. She seemed determined to avoid eye contact with me. Something was definitely up. At the end of the session, we all headed out on our bikes.

As we rounded the first corner, I stopped. "Hey, Thomas, can you hang back. I, uh, forgot something. Need to head back."

"You want us to wait?" Arjeet called back.

"No, I'll just be a few minutes. I'll see you guys tomorrow, okay?"

Arjeet nodded. Deion waved. Janey glared at me. Frankie looked at Janey. Then they all rode out of sight. Wait a second. What was Frankie doing looking at my sister? I'd have to deal with that later.

"Here," I said and handed my bike to Thomas. "Get going so Mara doesn't see you with my bike."

"You sure about all this?" Thomas asked.

"Yeah. I need answers. Need to see what's behind

Mara's mask. I'll see you this afternoon."

"Mara's mask?"

"She's got secrets. I need to uncover them."

"Ah," Thomas said. "You gonna be okay?"

I gave him a firm nod, and he nodded in return.

"I'm out of here," Thomas said. He grabbed my bike by the handlebar grip and slowly started riding away, holding my bike next to his.

I watched for a moment longer to make sure he wasn't going to crash, then glanced around. No one was in sight. I blended and jogged toward Mara's car. There'd have to be a way to deal with my mask and Janey. And my parents. And the Mocker. But for now, Mara.

Chapter 17

ISABELLA

MARA CAME OUT of Battlehoop a few minutes later and headed to her car. As she got in, I ghosted into the back seats. Maybe I should have checked out the car while I'd waited for her. The rear seats were folded down, making the back of the car one big trunk.

I scrunched myself toward the hatchback at the rear. It made sense to keep ghosting so I would make less noise, but I had this crazy vision of Mara accelerating and me popping out the back of the car, so I released it. She started the car and dropped it into gear.

Insanely loud, bouncy Latin music crashed into me. I jerked in surprise and suppressed a yell, and we were off. Mara drove for about fifteen minutes. I tried to keep track of where we were going, but I didn't recognize any of the neighborhoods. Mara added little head and shoulder dances with the music while driving, and busted out with loud singing here and there. She had a solid voice.

She turned off a two-lane road into a neighborhood. The whole place looked tired. Like the houses had given up. Gutters hung loose. Shutters were crooked or missing. The yards were overgrown. Most of them big and symmetric, and had two front doors. Duplexes or something.

About ten houses into the neighborhood, Mara turned into a driveway. It led behind one of the larger buildings. In the back was a mini-parking lot with several other cars. They were all new and high-end. Very different from the ones that had been parked along the street as we drove in.

Mara pulled into a parking spot and got out of the car. I ghosted out and followed her to a door in the back of the building. She pulled out a key and went in. The door had one of those metal arms at the top that made it close automatically, but I was still ghosting and followed her in as the door closed behind her.

A dim hallway with peeling wall paper and a musty smell led straight through the middle of the building to the front door. Two pairs of doors faced each other, spaced evenly along the hallway. An opening immediately to my right led to a flight of stairs. I glanced up them. The stairs ran parallel to the hallway I was in up to a second level.

A small camera sat near the ceiling by the front door facing down the hall toward me, and another one was about ten feet closer facing the front door. I glanced up. The same arrangement was at the back door. A camera just above where I stood, and one about ten feet down the hall facing the door I'd just entered.

Mara headed down the hall to the second door on the right and raised her hand to knock. The door opened before she could rap it. A large, blond-haired man stepped forward and stood in the doorway. He was wearing a black, long sleeved shirt with one of those collars that goes up really high.

"Checking in," Mara said. "Back from Battlehoop."

The man made a show of looking her over and nodded.

"Hey," Mara said as the man stepped back and started to close the door. "Isabella and I are going out this afternoon, right? Jordan promised."

I heard a grunt, which Mara seemed to think was a yes, because she nodded in response. She turned back toward me as the door closed. I stepped partially into the wall to my left to get out of the way as she hurried by me and turned into the stairwell. By the time I got to the stairs, she was almost to the top. Cameras were mounted near the ceiling at the top and bottom of the stairs. I followed as quickly as I dared while remaining silent.

At the top was a short hallway with a door on either side.

Another camera was mounted at the dead end of the hallway looking back toward where I stood at the top of the stairs. I realized these must be apartments or something. Smaller ones on the first floor, and two larger ones up here. Mara inserted a key into the door on the left and went in. I let the door close behind her before stepping forward.

I needed to be careful. I ghosted and sunk a couple inches into the floor so I could drift and ensure absolute silence. Then I entered the apartment. I skipped the door and went through the wall by the head of the stairs.

The living room I entered was cheerful, in sharp contrast to what I'd seen of the rest of the building, not to mention the neighborhood. Bright cushions decorated a cloth couch, and patterned curtains were pulled aside to let sunlight in through a couple windows. Mara stood near the front door hugging a girl who looked like her though a lot younger. Maybe my age. Was this Isabella?

They parted, and I got a better look at the girl. Yeah, she was definitely around my age, and looked an awful lot like Mara, including the part where Mara was really hot. The girl was wearing jeans and a plaid, button-down short-sleeved shirt. She spoke.

It was Spanish, and I didn't understand any of it. She and Mara started talking, and Mara headed past me to a little kitchen. The girl flopped down onto the couch while they continued talking.

I looked from Mara to the girl and back. They had to be sisters. If not for the age difference, they could have been twins. Mara was talking, and I heard something like, "Blah blah blah, Isabella, blah blah blah." Mara had said something closer to Ees-ah-bay-lah, but I recognized it. Isabella. This girl was Isabella, and she had to be Mara's younger sister.

That's when I noticed the cameras. It was the same type that I'd seen in the halls and stairs. From where I stood, I could see three of them positioned to give views of every angle in the apartment. This whole setup was unexpected and frightening.

There was just too much security, and the conversation with that blond-haired guy had been odd. Why was Mara checking in with him? And why had Jordan promised she could go out with Isabella?

Mara came back into the living room carrying a sandwich on a small paper plate and a glass of water. She sat down cross-legged on an overstuffed chair next to the couch, took a bite, and set her stuff down on the coffee table. Still talking in Spanish and chewing, Mara picked up a small notepad and pen from the table and started writing.

I drifted over behind the chair to see what she wrote. Maybe it would offer some clues. As I got closer, I saw a couple words. *Eggs. Bread.* That was helpful, but odd. It was written in English.

I got close enough to take a good look. It was a grocery list. That wasn't going to help. And then, right below *3 tomatoes*, Mara wrote, *Joss, tap my shoulder when you read this.* She didn't stop there. No, she went right on to *6 apples* and *1 banana bunch*, but at that moment my eyes were locked onto my name.

Mara knew I was there. How? And why was she keeping it a secret? I glanced around and saw the cameras again. Was she being watched? Could I trust her? What would she do if I tapped her shoulder? How had she seen me? *What was going on?*

I'd followed her here because I thought she'd been out to get me, but none of this made any sense. She didn't act like a bad guy. She acted more like a prisoner. Time to roll the dice.

I maintained my blend, but drifted up until my feet were on the floor and released my ghosting. I reached out, hesitated, and tapped her shoulder with a finger. Mara didn't acknowledge it. She kept on eating the sandwich, talking to Isabella, and writing her grocery list. Below *2 lbs ground beef* she wrote, *meet me in the bathroom, we need to talk.*

Mara finished her list and tore it off the notepad. She folded the paper and stuck it in her pocket, then finished eating her sandwich. The whole time she chatted with

Isabella in Spanish.

My mind churned. Nothing made sense. Nothing. I must have been wrong. Or was Mara playing me? Would it be dangerous? I was starting to get tired, but I knew I could blend and ghost a while longer, so not even a gun could hurt me.

Mara got up and headed toward a hallway off the living room opposite the kitchen. I guessed it went toward the front of the building. No time to think. There never was. I followed her.

Three doors stood off the hallway, two on the left side, and one at the end. All three were open. A quick glance said the rooms were a bedroom, bathroom, and then another bedroom at the end. Mara breezed past the bathroom and went in the far bedroom. Now what was she up to? I slunk forward and looked in.

Mara stood in front of a dresser on the near wall and pulled out a set of clothes. Jeans, shirt, the rest. Then she turned and came back toward me. I wasn't ghosting, and didn't really want to yet. It felt safer to save what energy I had for the unknown, so I stepped back down the hall as quickly and quietly as possible.

I got past the bathroom door just before Mara was going to run into me. She turned into the bathroom and closed the door behind her. A moment later, I heard the shower start. It all clicked. Bathroom. Fresh clothes. Shower.

What the heck. But she'd told me to meet her in the bathroom. I ghosted through the door. Mara was barefoot in front of the shower and rolling her yoga pants up to her knees. The shower curtain was pulled back, and the shower head was aimed at the tiled wall so the tub itself was only being hit with a light mist.

Mara stood up and and tilted her head up. Her nostrils flared, like she was trying to smell something. After a moment she looked in my direction, nodded toward the shower, and stepped in.

Fact number one. Mara knew I was there, even though I was invisible. Fact number two. She wanted to stand in a running shower with me. Fully dressed. My life was so weird.

I stepped into the tub. I had let go of the ghosting, and didn't try to step lightly. My shoes made some noise as I stepped, and the tub creaked under my added weight. Mara pulled the shower curtain closed.

"You can let go of the blend," she whispered. "It's safe here."

Chapter 18

BEHIND THE CURTAIN

EACH DECISION, EACH small step, had made sense. The end result, though, was insane. I stood fully clothed in a shower with Mara, the shower head blasting water into the tile wall to the side.

I took a slow breath and released my blend. Mara's eyes immediately locked onto mine. "How'd you know I was following you?" I asked.

"Shhh… keep it down," Mara said. "Look, when a teenage boy works out for four hours and then hides in a small car, I don't need my eyes to know he's there."

I kept my voice low. "I smelled bad? That's how you knew?" I couldn't believe it. There had to be a Seven talent to suppress funky body odors.

Mara shrugged. "I figured you were in the car. I mean, there's only one guy at Battlehoop who can make himself invisible, so when I smelled that lovely teen-boy aroma…"

I shook my head. I'd put so much effort into walking silently, when what I'd really needed to do was take a shower. Which was ironic, given I was standing in a shower. "So what's going on? Why should I trust you? And what's with all the cameras?" Mara held up a hand to stop me, but I kept going. "And who's Isabella? Or that big blond dude downstairs?"

"Joss, slow down. Take a breath."

No way. I was just getting started. I tried to stay quiet, but I was feeling intense. "Why are you glad when I fail? And why are we standing in a running shower to talk? Who are the bad guys?" I looked away from her for a moment, but there was nowhere else to look. "Where do you stand?"

Mara frowned and looked down at her feet. We stood there, the shower running, steam rising, for a full minute. When she looked back up, she seemed more confident, like she'd made a decision.

"What I'm about to tell you may make a bad situation worse, but I don't know what else to do."

"Okay." What else could I say?

"No mystery here, Joss, just brutal reality. Jordan's a Mocker. He's using you to make a ton of money. Just like he's using me. It's what Mockers do."

It was like the words entered my ears and just bounced around in my skull. Jordan. Mocker. Money. Using me. I took a slow breath in to the count of four, held it, and then released it to another count of four. Then did it again. The words stopped bouncing around and came to a rest.

"If Jordan's a Mocker, what does that make you? And why are we talking about this in a shower?"

"I think it may be one of the only spots in the house not under surveillance. I'm pretty sure my car is bugged. My phone is tapped. I don't have many options for a secret conversation."

Mara sounded sincere. And she was going to ridiculous lengths to have this conversation with me. Maybe she was telling the truth. "All right. Can you start at the beginning?"

"The beginning? No, but I'll give you the highlights. Two years ago, I was in my junior year of college. I was in the US on a student visa. My parents... I was told by relatives back home that they were killed in a car wreck."

Mara's eyes looked heavy with moisture. I looked away. "I'm sorry," I said. It sounded lame.

"Before I could grieve, or get on a flight home to Mexico, Jordan found me. He had Isabella. There's no way he could have moved that fast. He must have been involved before their deaths."

"You think he was involved, like, he planned the whole thing?"

"I do," Mara said. "He's evil, Joss. All the Mockers are.

I've met a few. Hard men. Deadly."

"So what's he doing with Isabella?"

"Leverage. He's held her for the past two years to control me. He knows I could escape easily. I mean, I'm a shifter. But I can't leave her. I've tried to get us out. Early on, we almost made it, or so I thought. He caught us. He beat Isabella. To make sure I didn't try again."

"I don't even know what to say," I said. "And this whole setup? The cameras? The guys downstairs?"

Mara nodded. "Isabella's prison. And mine. Oh, it's a nice prison. They don't want us desperate to escape. That would make their job harder. Heck, the apartment next-door is like a mini-gym, and we're given cash when we need it, but it's a prison. We don't go anywhere without Jordan's thugs on point. Well, I do sometimes, but they hold Isabella closely."

"So what about me?"

"I'm getting there," Mara said. "I think Jordan targets Sevens that aren't in the Guild. My family was all about me learning to be a Seven, but it was all based on family traditions and stories based on my birthmark. I sort of found my own way and learned, but I was hidden from the Guild. I'm not totally sure, but I think a lot of families with Sevens don't really trust the Guild. Anyway, once Jordan got me, he had me stealing stuff. Spying. That sort of thing. It's all about data he can sell. The Mockers have this network that provides a marketplace for illegal data. I did all right, but ever since I met Jordan, it was obvious I wasn't what he wanted."

It made sense. "He wanted a Thief."

"Yeah, and Jordan's good at piecing things together. He somehow figured out me, and he had me steal bits of information from the Guild. Eventually, he knew what he was looking for. The butterfly birthmark of the Sharif family. I was traveling the country for a few months, spying on your extended family, trying to find the butterfly birthmark. Jordan was still looking for other families that might have a Thief, but then I found you."

I slowly connected the dots in my head. My butterfly birthmark, which no one ever saw because I always kept a shirt on in public. Mara spying on my extended family. Mara discovering my butterfly birthmark. I could feel the heat of my cheeks turning red.

"You saw me…" I couldn't continue.

"I saw enough to know you were the one."

Anger replace my embarrassment. "So you violated my privacy, then sold me out to Jordan. Then you came along and lied to me to get me to steal stuff for Jordan. What have I been stealing, Mara?"

"Corporate secrets. That sort of thing. I don't know what Jordan makes off one of your thefts, but it's got to be large six figures. Probably more."

"And that last office?" I asked. "The one with the Seven?"

"A local office of the Guild."

Holy cow. I'd been tricked into working for some mobster to steal from an ancient organization of people with super-powers.

"This is so bad." I shook my head. "I'm screwed. What about those two who came to my house? They were pretty scary."

"The Guild. Joss, the Guild is ancient. It has weight behind it. It *is* scary, but I don't think it's evil. Look, you asked me why I smiled when you failed. Why I was happy when I thought you weren't a thief. Now you know."

I frowned, then nodded. "You didn't want me to be the Thief. You didn't want me to fail. You wanted Jordan to fail."

"That's about it. I'm sorry, Joss."

"Save your apologies," I said. I still felt a burning anger in my chest. "You didn't have to sell me out. You made the choice."

Mara's shoulders sagged. "Joss, Isabella is all I have. I have to protect her."

"So that's it? Just sell people out to Jordan? Let him control you?"

"It's not like that. There are four highly-trained men downstairs. There's four others. They work in shifts. How am I supposed to get Isabella out of here? They never let her out of their sight. We've lived like this for two years now."

I'd heard enough. I ghosted and stepped through the tub and shower curtain. Mara pulled the curtain back and tried to grab my shoulder. Her hand passed through me, and I felt a jolt. I think I would have known it had been Mara even if I hadn't seen her reach for me. From her startled expression, I could tell she'd felt the same type of thing. It was just like she'd said it would be. Overlapping another person gave you an awareness. A sense of them. Just like that other Seven who had tried to grab me.

"Wait," Mara whispered. She pulled the shopping list out of her pocket and held it toward me. "Take this. The numbers. It's my phone number. Jordan will know if you call or text, so it's only for emergencies. And be cryptic."

I remembered. *3 tomatoes. 6 apples.* Very clever. But I was still angry. I glared at her, but stopped ghosting long enough to swipe the folded piece of paper from her and jam it in my pocket before turning away.

I blended and ghosted through the bathroom door. I'd gotten the answers I wanted. I almost wished I hadn't.

It turned out a smartphone with GPS, a map, and access to a bus route website made getting home by bus pretty easy. I picked up the first bus about a quarter mile from Mara's apartment, or prison, or whatever it was. I ghosted and blended, stepped onto the bus, and made my way to the back. There were five empty rows in back, so I laid down in the final row, released the blend and ghost, and sat up. I had to hop another bus a few miles later, but that's all it took. The final stop was about half a mile from Thomas's house. I checked my phone. It was 3:13. I had time left to talk to Thomas before I needed to head home.

The whole time I was on the buses, my mind churned. I'd been stealing for the mafia, or something like the mafia. Making money for a mobster. Being used. And the good guys didn't seem all that nice to me. Luc had been threatening and arrogant. If that was what the Guild was like, I didn't think I wanted to be part of it.

But everyone wanted a piece of me. Guild. Mockers. They were all the same. I knew that probably wasn't true, but it felt true at that moment. I was glad I'd been wrong about Mara, but in reality, I'd only been a little wrong. She'd been using me, too, or at least helping Jordan use me.

I walked slowly to Thomas's house, giving myself time to chew on the facts. I had thought it all came back to Mara, but I'd been wrong. Jordan was at the middle, and there were people involved that I didn't even know. Isabella, for one. Talk about a bum deal. She'd been a prisoner for two years just because her sister had super-powers.

What were my options? I could try to get in touch with Luc, but I didn't like the guy, and he probably wasn't too happy with his rearranged nose. I could go back to Mars Street and see if that other Thief was there. Now that I knew he was with the Guild, what he'd said to me made a lot more sense. Maybe he wanted to actually help me, and not just use me like everyone else.

No, it was too risky. The last time I had seen him, he'd been laying on the floor unconscious. I doubted he was very happy with me. Besides, for all I knew, Luc kept an office in that building. That left my friends and my family. But how could I endanger them?

I arrived at Thomas's house and rang the doorbell. The door swung open and Thomas waved me in. "Well? What happened?"

I stepped in and looked around, then closed the door and bolted it. "Your mom home?"

"No, she's at some big meeting and then going to some corporate dinner. What happened?"

"Can I make a sandwich and eat while we talk? I'm starved. Never ate lunch."

"Yeah, yeah," Thomas said and led me toward the kitchen, "but start talking."

I told him everything, except the part about Janey

finding my mask and threatening to tell my parents everything tonight. That was Morgan business, and I figured I needed to deal with it on my own. Thomas's face made about twelve different expressions as I talked, from shock to anger to sadness. And I ate a ham and cheese sandwich. I'm not sure which did it, but I felt better when I was done talking and eating.

"I can't figure out what to do. I mean, every option has risks, and I can't tell who I should even be trying to help."

"What about Isabella?" Thomas asked.

"What about her?"

"Parents murdered? Held prisoner?"

"Yeah, she needs help," I said. "Even if I'm still pissed at Mara, that's not on Isabella. I get it. It's just a big mess. I can't figure out how to untangle it."

Thomas frowned in concentration. "Just pretend it's like the biggest prank you've ever pulled."

I sat up. A prank. Yeah, I could prank Jordan so hard he'd never showed his face again.

"We need to get Isabella clear," I said. "Get her away with Mara. Then we need Jordan on the run, or pinned down, or something."

"Okay," Thomas said. "How? You've got some freaky talents, but Jordan's scary. And you said he's got a bunch of toughs working for him. How do we go up against them?"

I sat back and thought about it. An idea popped into my head. "We need to bring in more firepower."

Thomas raised an eyebrow. "Meaning?"

I leaned in toward him. "Here's what we do."

Thomas and I schemed for the next hour. My idea was gradually hammered out into workable plan. There were too many unknowns, but it seemed like it might work.

"So tomorrow morning," I said, "you send the text, right?"

Thomas scowled. "Sure, I send the text, and then I sit on the sidelines while you kick butt."

"No, you send the text and then cover for me at Battlehoop."

"I get it. You're the superhero. I'm not even the sidekick. More like the butler."

I shook my head. "It's nothing like that, Thomas. You're a friend. It's what I need."

Chapter 19

THE MORGANS

THOMAS HAD MY bike waiting for me in his garage. The ride home was easy, except for the part where I thought I was going to throw up from the stress. We'd come up with a good plan. A simple plan. But it had steps in it like *deal with bad guys* that left me terrified.

When I got home, Janey and Mom were watching some show about remodeling a house. What was next? A show about plants growing? I chatted with Mom for a minute but broke off when I noticed Janey giving me a hard look. The last thing I needed was for Janey to start talking about Luc and the Seven. The next twenty-four hours were going to be complex. I needed her to keep her mouth shut.

I avoided eye contact with Janey and headed upstairs to grab a shower. Afterwards, I headed back downstairs to talk to her. I had to get her to keep quiet about the mask for one more night. She was still in the family room, reading a novel. Mom had moved on to the kitchen.

"Can we talk?" I asked, sitting on the couch beside her.

Janey ignored me and kept reading. I had thought about this while upstairs. The only thing I'd come up with was to let her in on some of my secrets. Not all of them, but enough to hold her interest.

I glanced around. Mom was still banging around in the kitchen. "I'll tell you about the mask."

The book snapped shut, and Janey looked at me through narrowed eyes. "I'm listening."

"Here's what I'm thinking," I said. "I think Dad plans to talk to us tonight, okay? You keep quiet for one more day about those two guys and the mask, and I'll fill you in after he's talked to us."

"Why wait? Tell me now."

"I want you to hear it from him first. That way you don't have to lie or anything if he asks us questions. You won't know anything, see? But after that, I'll tell you."

Janey started tapping her chin with a finger. Good. She was thinking about it. "What if he doesn't tell us anything?"

"Then I'll tell you anyway, but not until we're supposed to be in bed, okay?"

She went back to tapping her chin. She had to take my offer. I needed to keep everyone from talking things through until tomorrow. After tomorrow, everything would be better.

Her hand dropped to her side. "All right," Janey said. "You tell me what's going on tonight. After we head upstairs."

"Shake on it?" I stuck my hand out.

Janey shook my hand, but didn't let go when we were done. "Joss, you're gonna keep your promise, or I'll come right back down here and tell Mom and Dad everything, even if I have to wake them up. Understand?"

"I get it," I said. Janey released my hand and opened her book again. "Janey. I wasn't kidding the other day. I really am trying to protect you. After we talk tonight, you're going to have trouble sleeping. You can still let this go."

She shook her head. "Not a chance."

Dinner was quiet. Mom and Dad kept giving each other looks. Yeah, they were planning to talk to us. I just had to keep everyone off me until tomorrow. After eating, we cleaned up together, and Dad gave the inevitable clearing of the throat.

"Joss, Janey, your mother and I would like to talk to you. Let's go sit in the family room."

Janey looked at me, and I gave her a tiny nod. We all went to the family room and sat, Mom and Dad on their recliners, and Janey and I on the couch. Everyone looked back and forth at each other for a moment.

Dad broke the silence. "Janey, Joss and I had an odd experience this past Sunday. Well, I had the experience, but Joss was in the house when it happened. I asked him to keep quiet while Mom and I sorted some things out before we talked to both of you together."

"Okay," Janey said. Her face was blank. No expression. I hadn't realized Janey could play it so well.

"Janey," Mom said, and then paused. Wow. This was serious. Mom and Dad were tag-teaming us. "Janey, Dad already spoke to Joss about a couple things based on what happened Sunday, so we thought it would be best to bring you up to speed."

They took turns talking, but everything Dad and I had talked about came out. The Seven who stuck his hand through the table. House Sharif and the butterfly birthmark. The Guild. And great-great-grandmother fighting werewolves. The whole thing.

Dad sounded more confident this time around, like he believed it all now. Mom didn't, but she wasn't denying it either. Janey just sat there, stock still, and listened.

"So that's what we discussed on Sunday," Dad said.

Janey looked from Dad to me, and then back to Dad. "You saw a man just..." She made a motion like she was sticking her hand into the coffee table in front of us.

Dad nodded.

"What your father saw," Mom said, "is hard to believe. I struggled with it. But we've been making calls. Tracking down information. There are a lot of older people in our extended family who seem to believe in the Guild, Sevens, and all of it."

"And my great-great-grandmother?" Janey asked.

"Turns out," Mom said, "that your father's grandfather wasn't the only person who believed she died fighting werewolves."

"Now," Dad said, "the question that's been weighing on us, ah, your mother and I, well..." He looked at me. Mom looked at me. Janey's eyes swung around to me.

"Your birthmark," Janey said. "You have the butterfly birthmark. Can you stick your hand through stuff?"

I tried to laugh it off, but all three of them kept looking at me.

"That was the question on our mind," Mom said.

Dad nodded. "Joss, we have to figure out what to do, but we feel like we've ignored something that demands attention. Can you do, uh, stuff?"

All I had to do was lie, but I couldn't. "I... yes."

They kept looking at me, and Janey's eyes slowly narrowed. "Is this a big joke? Are you messing with us? If you are, I'm..."

She was going to rat me out in spite of our agreement. I had to stop her. In desperation, I ghosted my hand through the coffee table.

I wouldn't have gotten a stronger reaction if I'd danced naked in front of them. For all of Mom's talk, it was pretty clear she hadn't truly believed that the Sevens were real. She leapt to her feet and gasped, and then sat back down hard.

Dad's eyes popped open wide, and he did a little repeat of Sunday's performance. He jumped to his feet and staggered toward me, then knelt and looked at my hand coming out the bottom of the table top.

Janey just stared at my arm, and then made a grab for me. She went for my arm just above where it entered the table. The part of my arm that I was ghosting. Her hands passed through me, and I felt the jolt. Two times in one day.

I felt that "essence of Janey" along with part of her confusion and shock. I had expected the sensation, but it was still startling. Janey hadn't known it was coming. I'm not sure what my essence felt like, but she yelped and leapt back so hard that she tumbled over the arm of the sofa and disappeared from sight.

I pulled my hand out of the table and sat back on the couch. My family slowly pulled themselves together. Janey popped up and sat back down on the couch, though I noticed she had scrunched over as far as possible away from me. Dad got up and went back to his recliner, and Mom sat forward on hers, staring at me.

"So, this is awkward," I said.

"You're a... one of those..." Dad said.

"A Seven. Pretty much, I guess."

"A Seven." Dad's eyebrows pulled together. "Why didn't you tell me? We talked. It was just this Sunday. Why'd you keep this a secret?"

"I didn't think you were very happy about the Guild," I said. "I didn't know what you'd think. I guess I panicked and kept my mouth shut."

"All this time," Dad said, "we've thought we were protecting you kids from some crazy organization, when, really, they may have been able to help."

"I don't know, Dad," I said. "If those two guys on Sunday are what the Guild is about, I'm not sure it's for me."

I glanced at Janey, worried she might think this was the right moment to break our agreement and tell Mom and Dad what happened with Luc. Sure enough, she was just opening her mouth to speak. I gave her a hard look, and she snapped it shut.

"Oh, Joss," Mom said. "Does it hurt to do that? How long have you kept this a secret?"

Questions. Once they got going, they weren't going to stop, and eventually they'd go somewhere that might mess up the plan for tomorrow. I needed to get myself out of there.

"No, Mom," I said, "it doesn't hurt. And I found out I could do this at the start of summer break." I could see another question forming on my Mom's lips. I talked right over it. "Can we talk about this some other time? I know we need to figure out some stuff, but right now I just want to go to bed. It's been a long day."

Mom and Dad looked at each other. Dad frowned, but Mom gave him a small nod. His frown deepened for a moment and was gone. He turned to me. "We have a *lot* to talk about, but, yeah, we understand. You can go to bed."

I stood and headed for the stairs. "Thanks, Mom, Dad."

"All right, Joss," Dad said. "We'll talk more tomorrow,

understand?"

Before leaving the room, I turned and said, "Hey, Janey beat me at sparring today."

As I left the room, I heard Mom say, "Really? You beat him? I think I'd like to hear about something normal. You want to tell us about it?" It sounded forced, but Mom obviously wanted to think about something other than her son sticking his hand in a table.

I headed up the stairs as Janey started to describe my humiliation in great detail. For the next hour and a half, I heard faint noises through my bedroom door of my parents downstairs, and at one point Janey stomped up the stairs and must have gone to her bedroom. Finally, it quieted down.

A few minutes later, there was a faint knock on the door, and Janey slipped in. I still had my bedside light on, so I could see how she looked at me. It was like I was a dangerous animal. She stopped at the foot of my bed.

"So you're some kind of superhero," Janey said.

"I don't know about that, but, yeah, I can do some stuff that's not normal."

"And you wear a mask. At night."

"Right. About the mask. Something happened today. I'm going to tell you what I can, but I need to wait until tomorrow or the next day to tell you the rest."

Janey took a step closer and balled her hands into fists. "Are you going back on your word?"

"No, Janey, I'm not." I sat up on my bed and put my back to the wall. "Look. I told you I was trying to keep you safe. I wasn't lying. But it's bigger than that now. It's about Mara."

That caught her off guard. Janey's hands relaxed, and she sat on the foot of my bed. "What about Mara?"

"She has a sister, okay? I didn't know this before today. Her sister's in trouble. It turns out my, uh, talents may be needed. I may be able to help. But if I'm going to help, it all goes down tomorrow."

"And you don't want to fill me in ahead of time?"

I shook my head. "It's not about you. I don't want to fill anyone in."

"So no one knows what you're up to?"

"Thomas does. Heck, he helped me come up with it."

Janey sat back further on my bed and frowned in concentration. She looked away for a few moments, and turned back to me. "How do you know all of this? What's going on?"

"That's the part I can't tell you quite yet."

"Okay," Janey said. "Then why didn't you want me to tell Mom and Dad about those two guys that tried to grab us?"

"Because I thought they were bad guys. Really bad. And I was scared that if Mom and Dad freaked out about it and went after them, or got the cops involved or something, it would get dangerous. But I was wrong. I don't think they are good guys, but they weren't who I thought they were. Feel free to tell Mom and Dad whatever you want tomorrow."

That caught her off guard. She slowly nodded. "Okay, I'll play along."

"Thanks, Janey. Seriously. I've been so scared, and I thought if you told Mom and Dad…" I didn't have words for my worry. For how scared I was that things were out of control.

Janey nodded, and didn't push. I'd been sure she'd blow up my plans.

"There's a small price for my silence."

Huh? That couldn't be good. "What's that?" I asked.

"Show me the hand thing again."

My heart came back down out of my throat. That was a price I could pay. I ghosted my arm into the wall alongside my bed. "Like this?"

Janey stared at my arm where it met the wall, and her hand slowly reached up toward it, but then jerked back down to her side. "Does it feel as weird as it looks?" she asked.

"Not anymore. Hey, listen, about the thing I have to do

tomorrow. I'm not going to Battlehoop in the morning. Thomas is going to cover for me. Play along, okay? And watch out for Jordan. I don't think he's who he pretends to be. He's, like, a bad guy or something. But act normal."

I pulled my arm out of the wall while Janey slowly shook her head. "Act normal. Cover for you. Watch out for Jordan. This is the, oh yeah, I forgot to mention something thing you say to me?"

I shrugged. "Sorry?"

Janey shook her head, but she had a small smile pulling on the corners of her mouth. She stood and headed for the door.

"Janey," I said. I had this sudden, crazy urge to tell her everything. But more than that, I felt a strange rush of affection for her. She turned back toward me at the door. "Listen, tomorrow is, uh, scary. I'm scared. No, I'm terrified. Pray for me, okay? I'm trying to do the right thing."

"Shouldn't you be saying this to Mom and Dad?"

"Yeah, but I don't think they'd let me do it. I've got to see it through, Janey."

"I got your back, Joss. We're family."

Janey turned and left, closing the door behind her. I turned my light off and experimented with insomnia for about ten minutes before sleep overwhelmed me.

Chapter 20

BACK TO THE BEGINNING

THE NEXT MORNING, Janey and I set out together on our bikes toward Battlehoop. I broke off from her at the first turn and headed to Beckler Park. My black work clothes were in my backpack. The first big question mark in the plan was about to be settled. Would the text message from Thomas get Mara to come to the park before Battlehoop?

The park and school parking lot came into view as I rode down Milken Street. There it was. Mara's little silver car. I could see her sitting in the driver's seat. I pulled over to the side of the school and leaned my bike against the brick wall. Hopefully it would still be there when all this was over.

Mara got out of the car and walked over to me. She seemed tense and kept glancing around. "What's this about, Joss?"

"Oh, hey Mara," I said. "Good to see you."

"Cut it out. What's going on?"

"So you figured it out? The text? Pretty cool, huh?"

Mara pulled her phone out of the tiny brown leather purse she was carrying and read the text to me. "*Go back to the beginning before Battlehoop.* It's clever. Easy to miss, but I'd told you to be cryptic. Here we are, back at the beginning. Where we met before Battlehoop, and it's right before Battlehoop starts today."

I smiled. "Yeah, that's just so cool."

"If you're done gloating, why are we here?"

"Because that's not the only smart thing I worked up with Thomas. We are going to pull the ultimate prank today."

I broke it down for her. She listened, and about twenty seconds into it started nodding her head as I spoke.

"That could work, Joss." Mara looked away into the distance and tapped her front teeth with a fingernail for about half a minute before continuing. "It's pretty simple, really. No way I could pull that off on my own."

"That's why I'm here."

"Joss, if we did this, we… I can't control things." Mara's lips tightened into a line. "I mean, It's a good plan. It's simple. To the point. But it pretty much assumes we can fight our way through a bunch of killers. You understand? These guys have been trained by Jordan to manage Sevens. And they know about you. They know your talents."

"But together, we could do it, right?"

"Maybe. I mean, even if we got through, I'll probably be busted for child endangerment. But that's not what I'm worried about."

"I get it," I said. "I'm young. It's dangerous. My parents will probably freak out when it's all said and done. I'll get restricted for just about forever. Oh yeah, maybe I'll die. But I guess all that was true when you first dragged me into this, right?"

Her eyes dropped to her feet. "Yeah, I guess so."

"I mean, you knew Jordan was evil when you lied to me and suckered me into working for him."

Mara looked back up. Her eyes glistened with moisture, but I wasn't done. "Yeah, so don't suddenly start acting like my welfare was your top priority, 'cause that's bunk. But here I am. Ready to help."

A tear broke free and traced down her cheek. I looked away and grimaced. I didn't want her to start crying. Sure, I'd felt a burning anger ever since she'd told me what was going on, but I also understood. Her sister had been in real danger. I looked back, searching for a way to change topics. She was wearing a T-shirt that said KEEP CALM AND… OH, THAT'S A PROBLEM.

"So where do you get all these T-shirts?" It was a lame question, but I was under pressure.

She wiped her face as she pulled her hands away and glanced down at her T-shirt. "A website."

"Great. A T-shirt website. Oh, hey, that reminds me. Let's go rescue your sister so we can take down Jordan."

Mara looked at me for a moment, and then nodded. She looked caught between anger and resolve. Anything was better than crying.

"Phase one," I said. "Ditch your car. You think its bugged, right? We looked it up yesterday. There's a rental agency nearby. Here." I held out my phone with a map centered on a rental car place. "In case Jordan's tapped into your phone."

Mara took a deep breath and closed her eyes. She slowly exhaled. Her eyes opened and gave me a firm nod. "Game on."

She took my phone and we headed to her car. We got in and she turned the key. The little engine revved to life. She drove with the speedometer pegged on the speed limit. It made sense. The last thing we needed right then was to be stopped by a cop.

We pulled into the parking lot of a store across the street from the rental car place about five minutes later. Mara shifted to a female head that I hadn't seen before. Another one of her 'game faces.' I had blended as we pulled in, and thrashed around invisibly in the front seat to put on my work clothes while Mara went across the street and got a rental car. Ten minutes later, Mara pulled into the parking lot in a little red four-door car. I ghosted out of her car and into the passenger seat of the rental.

"You're in here, right?" she asked.

"Here," I said.

"And you're sure about this, right? From here on out, there's no turning back."

"I'm sure. Let's do this."

Mara nodded and cranked the car. Once we were out of the parking lot, I let go of my blend. We drove for what felt like a long time. I'd only been there once, so I didn't remember the way, but I didn't recognize any of the streets we were on.

"Where are we?" I asked.

"Taking a different route." She flipped a blinker on, and pulled into a store parking lot. "We're here. We'll walk the final two blocks. I don't want the rental car seen at what may be a crime scene shortly. But we need to plan."

"Okay, so how do we play this?" I asked. "We're not trying to, like, kill anyone, are we? I didn't sign up for that."

"No. Absolutely no killing if it can be helped. If you were fully trained, Jordan's four guys wouldn't stand a chance." She grimaced. "I see three options. I go in normal and attack first, or I go in normal and you do a surprise attack, or we both go in stealth mode and coordinate a surprise attack."

"So which is it?" I asked.

"I like the first option. Gives me a chance to assess and change the plan if needed without worrying about you making a move before me."

"Got it. So I'll blend and follow you in, then flip to bruising once you let loose on them."

"That sounds right." She turned and faced me. "They're armed with guns, but they'll go for the tasers if they know you're there. Remember, these guys know their stuff, and I'm sure Jordan's prepped them about you. He's cautious. Covers all possibilities."

"Tasers, not guns. Got it. Wait. Why?"

"Bruising can stop a bullet, but a taser will light you up like a Christmas tree."

"Okay," I said. "Note to self. Avoid tasers."

"These guys can fight, too. Even with option one, I'll have to shift. It could get ugly. Tooth and claw ugly."

That did sound ugly. "What, uh, are you going to shift to?"

"Depends on the situation, but probably a bear. A big one. The fur and fat make tasers and handguns less effective. Gives me time to reggie if I take gunfire."

I took a deep, calming breath. What had I gotten myself into?

"Okay, so once you shift, I'll bruise and start beating

goons. If I can manage it, I'll stay blended."

"And if it goes sideways," Mara said, "try to meet back here at the car."

"Got it." I pulled the mask on and blended. "I'm going to stay out of sight the whole time. Let's do this."

"Joss!" Mara's voice sounded urgent. Her eyes skimmed over me. "Joss, thank you. And I'm sorry. I got swept along. I blew it. I just kept making one more compromise to try to keep my sister safe. But I'm sorry."

Would I have done anything different? Probably. I'd have made an even bigger mess of it. "We're good. Let's go kick some bad guy butt."

She gave a quick nod, opened her door, and stepped out. I ghosted out of the car and followed Mara as she walked down the street. No one else was in sight, so I walked loudly. Mara glanced in my direction and gave a quick smile.

We turned onto a street that looked familiar. The sidewalk was broken in places and the houses looked sad. The small apartment house was just up ahead.

"Here we go," Mara said under her breath. "Hey, can you put a hand on my shoulder? Lightly. Don't want it to show. But it will be good to know where you are. Give me a couple taps when you're going to move away."

I rested my fingers on her shoulder as we strode up the walk to the apartment. She pulled a key out of her purse and unlocked the door. I had to briefly ghost to keep the door from hitting me as it closed behind us. We were in the dim hallway between the apartments. The big blonde goon I'd seen the first time stood a few feet ahead by the open door to the first apartment on the left.

"Where's your car?" Blondie asked. A real conversationalist.

"Not sure what happened," Mara said. She hooked a thumb back the way we had come. "It stalled out. Left it in a parking lot."

Blondie's eyes narrowed. That didn't seem good. I tapped Mara's shoulder and ghosted through the wall into the apartment behind Blondie. He started yelling something, but I didn't catch the words as I came through the wall. Two more goons were in the apartment, surging to their feet as I entered. They rushed the door toward Blondie, so I did too.

A primal roar shook the building and Blondie flew back through the doorway. The goon in the lead dove and caught Blondie, taking him to the floor in a smooth roll. Blondie shook his head. "Thanks, Sticks."

I didn't see Sticks' response. I was too busy trying to bruise while rushing the door, still blending. I got there just as the third goon did and sucker punched him. He must have heard me. Just before I connected my rock-hard fist to his pink, fleshy face, he dropped down and threw himself to his left away from me, rolling to his feet on the far side of the doorway. Then Sticks hit me.

I'm not sure how he'd gotten up so fast, or where he'd gotten the two-foot wooden batons from, but now I knew how he'd gotten his name. He wielded a baton in each hand. I couldn't tell much about them, because he was moving them with blinding speed. The first strike glanced off me and barely made contact, but it was like those sticks were antenna that he used to figure out where I was.

It turned out a glancing blow from a well swung piece of lumber felt like a train politely pushing you out of the way. I staggered back into the wall, which saved me from his next few swings. My ribs burned with pain. I bruised all of me just as he made contact again and reggied my ribs.

He bounced blows off me at a stunning rate, and it was all I could do to keep bruising so I wasn't knocked out or worse. Behind Sticks, I saw Blondie had recovered and pulled out a large handgun with a silencer. On the other side of the doorway, the guy I'd tried to hit held a taser and was lining up a shot at me. It was over before we'd really started. I was going down.

Mara surged through the doorway in an explosion of wood and plaster. She was a huge brown bear, all fangs and claws and muscle. She'd told me most Sevens couldn't change their weight much when shifting like her. What she hadn't said was just how much she could change when shifting. The bear was massive. Maybe there was hope.

The pop-pop-pop of silenced gunfire registered in my mind as blood sprayed from Mara's bear legs. She stood tall for a moment, roaring defiance, and then tottered forward and collapsed.

Game over.

Chapter 21

THREE BAD GUYS AND A BEAR

STICKS WAS BEATING me into submission, pinning me against the wall in spite of my invisibility. I wasn't used to bruising for more than a few seconds at a time, and I'd never tried to harden my whole body before. It was killing me. I was running out of time. And Mara had shifted to a bear to help protect against gunfire, but they'd known to aim for the bear's joints. Mara had just had her knees ripped apart.

I've read lots of comics, and no superhero ever falls to three normal guys, even if they were well armed. Yet three of Jordan's goons were going to take us down? Just like that? Was it really that easy to stop two Sevens?

Well, no. Mara the bear fell forward as she collapsed and rolled onto Blondie. She enveloped him, all claws and teeth and fur and muscle. I heard a couple more shots fired, but couldn't see what they hit. And right then, I asked myself why I was standing there being punished by Sticks. Being the Seventy-Seven was all about options and adaptation.

I switched from bruising to ghosting. Sticks' clubs passed through me, but he kept swinging. I went for the guy across the doorway from me. His spent taser trailed behind Mara, and he reached for a handgun like Blondie's that sat in a shoulder harness. I kinneyed and leapt. His draw slowed as time slowed down and I floated through the air toward him.

Ghosting, blending, and kinneying was too much. I dropped the ghost and blend. I hoped I was moving too fast for them to react. I switched back to bruising as I flew through the air and tucked into a cannonball. The goon's eyes slowly flared open and swung toward me as I closed the distance. I released the kinney and everything snapped back to a normal speed as I put all I had into my bruising.

I guess I was getting better at kinneying. I was going way faster than I'd planned. I hit the goon like an actual cannonball and kept going. I heard bones snap as I sailed by. I didn't slow down until I crashed through the wall to the adjoining apartment, slammed through a few pieces of furniture, and hit the far wall.

I stood and glanced around. The apartment looked similar to the one that I'd first entered. The only light came from the hole I'd just made in the wall between the apartments. A shadow swept across the light. Sticks was the only guy left standing. It had to be him.

Gunfire filled my ears again as bullets slammed into my weary body. Sticks had switched to his gun. I hadn't let go of my bruising, so I survived, but it was a close thing. I was thrown back into the wall behind me and twitched this way and that as bullets hit me. Pain seared through every part of my body. My concentration on the bruising wavered and the pain got worse.

I was done. End of the line. I knew I needed to switch to ghosting, but it was all I could do to keep my body hardened against those bullets. If I released the bruising and failed to ghost, I'd be shredded by the gunfire. But the strain was too much.

Dark fur flashed by the hole and Sticks disappeared. Mara. She was back in the game. It was my last coherent thought before I fell to the floor, helpless. Pain flared in my stomach and I struggled to roll over onto my back. I took a deep breath and lifted my head. A bullet stood a quarter inch out of my abdomen, a wet mass of blood flowering from it, soaking my black shirt.

I lay there with blood oozing out my my stomach and a bullet protruding for what felt like hours. The pain kept breaking up my thoughts. There was something I had to do, but I couldn't pin it down.

Instead, I thought of my family. Mom, Dad, and Janey. I

loved my parents, and Janey was all right. We had it pretty good. I was getting used to Janey being at Battlehoop, even if she could beat me at sparring.

I thought of Thomas. Here I was, in the middle of a plan we'd come up with. It had seemed like a good plan. There had just been that one little challenge at the beginning of the plan. Something about rescuing Isabella by taking on four of Jordan's henchmen. Or three. I was sure it had been four bad guys, but the number three kept coming back.

My thoughts splintered. Drifted. Time passed. Then focused on Isabella. She'd been awfully cute. I wondered if I'd ever meet her again. Did she know how to speak English, or were we trapped in a love that couldn't be spoken. What was I talking about? I didn't love Isabella. Who was Isabella?

"Joss!" My eyes cracked open. I saw Mara leaning over me. She slapped me again. It stung. Wait. Slapped me again? How long had she been slapping me? "Joss! You've got to reggie!"

Reggie. Seven-speak for regeneration. Cool. The pain kept me from speaking, but I slowly lifted up my thumb to let her know I understood. I knew the lingo. I passed the test. It was all good. Now what had I been thinking about? Something about Isabella. Oh, yeah. That cute chick I was in love with. The one who couldn't speak. No, that didn't sound right.

Mara slapped me again. Dang it! What the heck? I cracked an eye open. She was miming something. Pretending to yell, but I couldn't seem to hear her. What had she said before? She wanted me to reggie. Oh! I grabbed hold of my fractured thoughts and pretended to concentrate. It was enough. My body knit back together in all the right places. The bullet popped out and sat on my stomach, centered on a large circle of dark wetness.

I looked around. Mara sat on her knees looking ragged and bloody but whole. Furniture was scattered everywhere, and a large hole was torn out of the wall opposite me in the apartment. My mask lay on the floor beside me. It all came back. I tried to surge to my feet, but my head spun and I fell over on my side.

Mara put a hand on my shoulder. "Take it easy."

"Bad guys." I looked around and located the hole in the wall. "We've got to clear that room."

"It's cleared," she said. "Don't go back in there. Don't look through that hole."

Bile stung my throat. "Did we kill anyone?"

"No, but I wasn't gentle with Sticks and Joey, and you almost knocked Dirk's arm off."

"Dirk? The guy by the door?"

"That's him," Mara said. "Take some deep breaths. We don't have much time."

I breathed in and out, and my thoughts pulled together. What had I been thinking about Mara's sister? I didn't even know the girl. The room stopped spinning and I gingerly sat up. "I'm good. You reggied, right? You're not bleeding?"

Mara patted my shoulder and stood. "I'm fine now. Just weary. That was rough. You still get to feel the pain before you reggie."

"I know all about that." I hauled myself to my feet and stretched. I was feeling wiped out. "You said we don't have much time. What's going on? I mean, other than having to stay one step ahead of Jordan?"

"I used Sticks' cell phone to call 911. Asked for police and paramedics. They take a while to get to this neighborhood, but they'll get here eventually." She nodded toward the hole to the other apartment. "They need help. I'm not sure I'd mind if they died, but I told you I'd do what I could."

"Thanks. Okay, I'm fine. Just tired. So we grab Isabella and go."

"Jordan's got two crews of four men who watch us, Joss. Four. This was Joey's crew. The fourth guy, Gary, wasn't with them. I fear he's got Isabella."

My heart clenched. I didn't know Isabella, and I had every right to be angry at Mara, but all I could think was that Isabella was my age. Right then, some mobster named Gary was likely holding her hostage. My anger redirected. I came to terms with what Mara had done.

Mara didn't need my anger. Jordan did. Jordan and his thugs.

I glanced around. "Are we on camera? Is he watching us right now?"

She shook her head. "Cameras in the hall and upstairs, but not down here in their apartments."

"Okay," I said. "So Gary may have her. One guy versus both of us. I feel like I haven't slept in three days, but it'll be enough. We can do it. And Gary? Really? What kind of self-respecting bad guy calls himself Gary?"

Mara shook her head. "Thanks for trying, but the humor's not helping." She looked up toward the ceiling. Up there was the apartment she and Isabella shared. Her eyes blazed. "This is no smash and grab. We have to go in there and extract her. Carefully. The paramedics and cops aren't the real problem. If Gary's got her, he's notified Jordan. Either Jordan's inbound, or the other crew is. Probably the other crew, as Jordan wouldn't want to get his hands dirty with this. Gary knows he just has to wait. We've got to do whatever we're going to do fast. I'm going to go grab Joey's gun."

"Whoa!" I grabbed her arm as she turned toward the hole. "Mara, we can do this. But if you fire that gun, you may be on the run from now on no matter what happens."

"And?"

"And… and how does that help Isabella?"

"So what do you suggest?" she asked.

I took stock. Sure, I felt like death warmed over, but I could fall back on my main talents. "I'll blend and ghost. Head straight in. You go into the apartment, act like you're in a blind rage. Like, I've been killed or something. I'll be there with you. We're just going to have to figure out what makes sense once we're in there. I'll make the first move to catch him off guard, okay?"

Mara's eyes closed for a moment, and she took a ragged breath. "Okay, we'll try it that way. I'll go in as me. Get going. I'll give you a ten second head start."

I didn't wait for her to reconsider. I grabbed my mask, pulled it back on, and blended. "Here I go."

I ghosted straight through the wall into the hall and ninja-stepped down the hall toward the stairs. Though tired, I held the ghost. What if Gary surprised me and took a shot? I didn't think I would live long enough to reggie again.

As I turned into the stairwell, I looked back down the hall and saw Mara step through the doorway into the hall. She looked like a goddess of war. A scuffed up, bloody goddess of war, but still. Rage and power radiated from her. Gary was going to regret it if Isabella was hurt. I needed to get in there and figure out how to save Isabella before Mara did something really violent.

I scooted up the stairs and stopped. This was the very piece of wall I'd ghosted through yesterday. Had it really been less than twenty-four hours? I glanced back down the stairs and saw Mara turn the corner into the stairwell.

It was time to get moving. Time to be a hero.

Chapter 22

GARY THE GOON

I GHOSTED THROUGH the wall. At least, that's what I meant to do. The wall felt thick, and I had trouble pushing through it. I was running out of steam right when it mattered most. With effort, I pushed through and maintained my blend.

I took in the apartment at a glance. Isabella sat on the couch looking straight ahead. A large man sat beside her, but I didn't really see him. My vision was consumed by the gun he held pointed across his body at Isabella. It had a silencer on it which rested on his opposite forearm. The end of the barrel nestled against Isabella's ribs.

Even the gun could only hold my attention for so long. I was pretty sure the large, pasty blocks strapped to a vest Gary was wearing were major-league explosives. Wires ran from the vest to a handle with a large trigger held in his hand. He held the trigger squeezed against the handle. I'd seen this in a movie. A dead man's switch. If he released the trigger, the explosives would detonate, effectively making Gary *very important*. If he was knocked out or killed, everyone died.

So. Gary had a gun and a bomb wired to a dead man's switch. And all he had to do was wait until reinforcements showed up in a few minutes. On the flip side, Mara and I were spent. We couldn't take on four more guys, so we couldn't wait, but we couldn't just go head-to-head with Gary.

Isabella sat perfectly still. She was as beautiful as I'd remembered. I hated seeing her terrified, but there was nothing I could do. I needed to get back out in the hall and warn Mara. We needed a plan. We needed to—

The door frame splintered as the door crashed open and slammed into the wall. My eye caught a flicker of twisting motion, and Mara strode into the apartment. She must have hit the door as a bear and shifted back. Girl knew how to make an entrance.

Mara took in the situation at a glance. Gary might as well have slapped her. She looked stunned. It had taken me a lot longer to think it through, but I guessed Mara had come to the same conclusion. We were hosed.

"Hello, Mara." Gary's voice was as bland as his name. "Why don't you have a seat beside us? Is your little friend here with us?"

Mara stood tall for a moment, and then slumped, tears falling from her eyes. She shook her head and went to the seat she'd sat in yesterday when talking to Isabella.

"Dirk tasered him. Sticks beat him. They took it too far." She put her head in her hands and wept.

How did girls do that? She seemed to really be crying. And Gary looked shocked. But this was our plan, which meant Mara still expected me to do something. To take control of the situation and make the first move.

"That's not good," Gary said. "Jordan's not going to be happy about losing his Thief. Not my problem though."

While Gary spoke, I started edging forward. I saw my one and only one chance. I had to grab that hand and hold the detonator down long enough for Mara to disarm him. But it was impossible. I could grab his hand, but I had nothing left. There was no way I could bruise well enough right now to protect my body from gunfire. And what if he shot Isabella, not me?

Gary kept talking. Something about Mara having screwed up, big time. I tuned him out. I was standing across the coffee table from where Gary sat. Across from Isabella, who still stared straight ahead. She looked so scared.

One side of the gun was in plain view. An idea popped into my head. It was an impossible long shot, but we were out of options. I leaned closer to study the gun. There it was. Just above the base of Gary's index finger, where he reached forward to cradle the gun's trigger. A little switch that was pulled down, showing a tiny red dot that would be covered if it was flipped back up. The safety.

One chance, and failure meant one or all of us died. For a moment, I just stood there and made sure I didn't pee myself. Right then, I realized that being a hero sucked. It was too much.

I had once asked my dad what it meant to be a man. He'd looked at me for a moment, and said, "Being a man is being able to stand up under it."

"Under what?" I'd asked.

"Whatever needs standing under. Could be special, or spectacularly mundane. Whatever would crush you or those you love. We don't bear it in our own strength, but we bear it all the same."

At the time, I'd had no idea what he was talking about, but now I knew I needed to man up and bear it. To bear the weight of responsibility if I failed. To bear the weight of acting, of taking charge, of trying. It terrified me.

I closed my eyes for a moment, then snapped them open and stared at the safety. I reached out with my mind and felt it. Dizziness washed over me. I honestly thought I could have done it if I was fresh off ten hours of sleep, but now, it felt out of reach. I dug deeper.

There it was. A tickle in my mind. The safety. I could feel it. I didn't hesitate, but pushed with all my might. Nothing. I tried again, and failed. I couldn't do it. I was barely hanging on to my blend, and I didn't have enough left to move that safety.

It was too much to ask. I couldn't stay invisible while moving the safety. My telly talent was just terrible and untrained, and I was worn out. If I grabbed the gun while invisible, I couldn't be sure he wouldn't shoot me or Isabella or both of us, not to mention he might release the dead man's switch. To do all of it, I had to telly that safety and grab the detonator, all the while staying invisible.

And that was the answer. I couldn't do all of it. But maybe I could do enough. I took one slow breath, and released my blend. As I did so, I pushed again, calling on all my energy to move that safety. It felt like fifteen different things happened at once.

Gary's head whipped around and he stared at me in shock. I'm sure I looked weird, all in black and wearing a mask. I felt the mountain shift slightly, then break free. It wasn't really a mountain, just a tiny steel switch, but it felt like one. The safety moved over with a satisfying click to its safe position. As it moved, so did I.

I dove over the coffee table and grabbed Gary's hand holding the bomb detonator in both of mine. I landed awkwardly sprawled across Isabella, but I locked onto that hand like a spider monkey and made sure he did not release the switch.

I felt a steel tube poke me in the ribs. Two shallow clicks were followed by a curse from Gary. The safety had worked. That meant I had about two seconds to live before he flipped it off and tried to shoot me again.

Mara roared. It was an inhuman, savage sound. I caught a blur of motion in the corner of my eye and looked over in time to see Gary's gun punch into the wall by the front door where Mara had flung it. She towered over us in the form of a gorilla. Gary looked from her to me and back. Her gorilla fist came down on the top of his head like a sledgehammer, and his body went limp and sagged away from me onto the arm of the couch.

Isabella sobbed loudly, a sound filled with pent up terror and relief. She struggled to get up, but I was half on her lap, still clutching Gary's hand in both of mine. There was another blur, and Mara was back again. No longer a gorilla, and no longer a goddess of war. She looked more like a refugee of war.

"Sorry," I said to Isabella. "I think we may blow up if I let go of his hand."

Isabella sobbed again and ripped my mask off. She held my head in her hands and gave me a long look. Then she hugged me so hard I thought she'd cut off the oxygen to my brain. Mara ran from the room, yelling something to Isabella in Spanish.

"What was that about?" I asked, then reconsidered. "Do you, uh, speak English?"

"She gets the tape." Isabella nodded toward my hands clutching Gary's hand which held the detonator. "You will let go soon."

I was still half on the coffee table and half on Isabella's lap. Her arms encircled my neck. I was almost disappointed when Mara ran back into view a few seconds later holding a big roll of duct tape. A minute later, Gary's hand was thoroughly taped in place holding the trigger detonator, and Gary himself was taped to a dining room chair. I'd even remembered to retrieve my mask and tuck it into a pocket.

Mara turned from the chair, set the tape down, and grabbed her sister in a fierce hug. When they pulled apart, each still clutched the other's hand.

"Isabella," Mara said, "may I introduce you to Joss Morgan?"

Isabella smiled and nodded to me. "It is good to meet you, Joss the Seven. Mara has told me you are rare? Even for a Seven?"

My face burned and I looked at my feet. "I, uh, think we're all going to be a lot rarer if we don't get out of here right now."

"He's right," Mara said. "I'll fill you in on the way, Isabella, but we have to move right now. But first, I'm hitting the safe downstairs."

"The safe?" I said, but Mara was already on the move.

She turned to Gary and fished around in his pockets until she pulled out a wallet. Mara held it up with a smile and waved us toward the door. On the way out, she pulled Gary's gun from where it was lodged in the wall. Outside in the hall, she retrieved three other wallets from the floor. We headed downstairs and followed Mara back into the first apartment we'd entered. I noticed all the cameras were twisted around and broken. Mara had been busy on her way upstairs.

In the apartment, Mara cut to a back bedroom and yanked a painting off the wall. A small safe sat behind it. Mara spun its black combination knob this way and that for a few seconds, then yanked down on a small handle. The little silver door popped open.

"I couldn't do anything with the information," Mara said as she pulled tightly bound bundles of bills out of the safe and tucked them in various pockets, "but I learned what I could the past couple years. Including the combo. Criminals deal in a lot of cash, you know?"

"Yeah, sure," I said while giving Isabella my best puzzled look and shrugging. She smiled.

Mara grabbed one last stack of bills and waved us after her as she headed back the way we'd come. Outside, Mara led us on a roundabout tour of the alleys and back ways in the neighborhood, until we finally arrived at the parking lot. We piled into the little rental car, with me stuck in the tight back seat. Mara stuffed Gary's gun in the glovebox and piled the cash in after it.

Isabella rotated in her seat to look at me as we pulled out of the parking lot. "*Gracias*, Joss the Seven. You were very brave. I was too frightened to move."

I would not let my cheeks turn red again. Perhaps just a light pink. "Uh, you can call me Joss, okay?"

She smiled. "Thank you, Joss Okay."

Maybe there was more of a language barrier than I had realized. Isabella laughed.

"I joke," she said. "Thank you, Joss." She turned toward her sister. "What do we do next? Are we trying to escape?"

"Ask him," Mara said. "His plan. But yes, we are going to escape."

Isabella looked back at me and raised her eyebrows in question.

"Well," I said. "My friend Thomas helped me come up with it. Getting you out of there was just phase two of the plan, and that was just about a disaster. Phase three is shopping. Mara's got to buy some clothes, and I need to rest.

Then we hit phase four."

"And what is this phase of four?"

"The ultimate prank. We rob a bank."

Chapter 23

300MINUTE

IT TURNED OUT that during her two years with Jordan, Mara had managed to steal the ATM PIN codes for most of his thugs. She'd tailed them as a bird when possible, which was rarely, and watched as they retrieved cash.

Mara pulled the car into a parking lot across the street from a bank with a drive-through ATM. "Isabella, you need to get in the back seat with Joss. They've got cameras at the ATM. You both need to get down low."

Isabella nodded as she climbed over the center console between the front seats and we scrunched down. It was a cozy arrangement. Isabella smiled at me from her spot on the floor behind the front seat, but her eyes looked bigger than when I'd first seen her yesterday. She was scared.

Mara shifted. She looked the same from the shoulders down, but had that man's head she'd used on my missions. Isabella's eyes got even bigger. Apparently, she'd never seen that particular shift before.

It took fifteen minutes and three banks for Mara to empty a large stack of bills from the ATMs courtesy of Sticks and company. I spent the time with my eyes closed and my head resting against the car door at my back. We had so much more to do today, and I had hit my limits already.

It was 10:30. Hopefully Gary had been waiting for Jordan's other crew of four guys, and not Jordan himself. I hadn't thought Jordan would want to blow his cover unless it was absolutely necessary, and Thomas had agreed. If that was the case, we had an hour and a half until Jordan finished at Battlehoop. Not much time to shop for clothes and rob a bank.

After the ATMs, Mara made two quick stops before pulling into the parking lot of BIGGUN'S FASHION MART - CLOTHES FOR REAL BIG MEN. First, she grabbed some meal deals for all of us at a fast food joint. Second, she picked up several energy drinks at a convenience store.

Isabella and I ate in silence while Mara shopped at BIGGUN'S. She'd gone in with a female game face on that I hadn't seen before. After eating my burger and fries, I popped open a 300MINUTE ENERGY DRINK and downed it all at once. It tasted like sweetened cough syrup with a hint of lemonade. Nasty.

I hated to suffer through that flavor and not get the benefit. It was such a tiny bottle. I decided to play it safe and drank a second one. I hoped that would give me twice the energy for three hundred minutes instead of the same energy for six hundred minutes.

"I will never return to my apartment, yes?" Isabella said.

I looked up from the empty little bottle and frowned. She was looking intently at me with her big brown eyes. Were they brown? They had hints of that golden-amber color of Dad's bourbon. Then I remembered to speak. "Did you want to?"

"No, no, it is not the place. Mara never allowed me to be personal there. Nothing to tell of me. But my clothes are there. Other things too."

"Yeah, I don't think you'll be going back to get your stuff. I bet Mara picked up enough money from the ATMs to replace a lot of it."

"Maybe it is so."

"Here's the thing," I said. "We have a rough plan, but Mara didn't know about any of it before today. And I doubt she's got anything for tomorrow yet. But she'll think of something."

"Yes," Isabella said. "Mara is strong."

"Yeah, she is. Ever sparred with her?"

"Yes, many times. She taught me for past two years. But not strong with her arms. Strong with her heart."

"Ah." Strong with her heart. I hoped someone would think that about me one day. Except for the *her* part. "Do you think you'll go home after this? To Mexico?"

"What is home? My parents are dead." She paused and stared off in thought. "It would be good to go back. To see my aunts and uncles. Let them know we live."

"It's been a hard day, hasn't it? Did Gary just burst in and grab you?"

Isabella shuddered as she nodded yes. On instinct, I reached out and gave her hand a squeeze. She squeezed back, and then held onto my hand. My head started buzzing. I couldn't tell if it was the energy drinks, or her hand in mine.

"You'll get there," I said. "We've just got to take care of Jordan first."

Mara opened the driver door and got in, dumping a big bag on the empty seat beside her. I pulled my hand free and tried to act natural. Thankfully, I was directly behind Mara so she couldn't really see me. Acting normal was hard.

"Okay, we're good to go," Mara said. "I tried the shift out in the changing room. I think it'll work. How are you two doing?"

Now that I wasn't staring into Isabella's eyes, I noticed I felt weird. "Should I be hearing, like, a buzzing in my ears?"

"You drink a 300MINUTE?"

"Two of them."

"Good Lord, Joss." She twisted around in her seat and stared at me. "What were you thinking?"

"It was such a tiny drink." Was my hand shaking? Was it still attached to my body? I felt weird. Like my body was made up of a bunch of different parts that happened to be next to each other but weren't really connected.

Mara shook her head and mumbled something in Spanish as she turned back to the front and started the car. Isabella smiled. "*Mi hermana*, she says you have left your brains behind when ghosting."

I smiled and shrugged. At least, I tried to. My shoulders felt all twitchy. My shrug probably looked more like a spasm.

"We've got about forty-five minutes to set things in motion," Mara said, steering the car out onto the road. "Let's head back to that second bank we hit up for the ATM. I'll shift and dress up there. Isabella, here's what happens next."

Mara had put off her sister's occasional question ever since we'd gotten her away from Gary. Now she laid it out for her in detail. It turned out there wasn't much left to tell. We'd be more or less free of Jordan in the next hour, or things would have gone terribly wrong.

"It is, how do you say, devious?" Isabella said when Mara finished.

Mara pulled into a parking lot at a strip mall. "Bank's just around that corner. Joss, you need to blend. Your little black get-up's going to stand out too much. Follow me, you two."

Mara flipped open the glove compartment and retrieved the gun. She put it in the clothing bag and took the bag with her as she opened her door and stepped out. I gave Isabella a quick smile, which she returned, and blended.

"*Increíble*," Isabella said, and reached toward me from where she still sat. Her hand found my knee.

"Time to go," I said, and ghosted. It was a mistake. Isabella's hand was still on my knee, and I got a strong jolt as her fingers passed through my leg. What I sensed didn't make me like Isabella less. She gave a start, and then nodded, like she was thinking.

I ghosted out of the car, and was relieved to find it was easy once again. On the flip side, I still felt like my body was assembled from mismatched parts, and my ears were ringing. Two energy drinks had definitely been a mistake.

Isabella got out of the other side of the car, and Mara led us around to an alley between two rows of stores. It smelled like leftover things rotting in the sun and pizza. Several dark-green dumpsters stood nearby. I released my blend, and Isabella started.

"Be right back," Mara said. "And nobody freak out when

you see me."

She took the bag of clothes behind the dumpsters. Four minutes later, Jordan stepped out from behind them carrying the now empty bag.

"*No manches!*" Isabella cried, as I let out a low whistle.

Mara really looked like Jordan, huge and bald. She had on a dark sports coat over a plain, black shirt tucked into black slacks. Black leather shoes and sunglasses completed the look.

"How do I look?" Mara as Jordan asked in his deep voice. She casually pulled open the jacket to reveal the gun she'd lifted off Gary tucked into an inside pocket.

"It's him," I said. I didn't mention that I'd almost run away when I first saw her. "This is actually going to work."

"It better," she said.

"I still do not understand," Isabella said. "Why a bank? Why not the store? Banks have guards, yes?"

"It gets the Feds involved," I said. "The FBI leads on bank robberies, at least for most banks. FBI, local police, everyone comes down on bank robbers."

"Ah. You know so much, Joss."

"Well…" I had to give credit where credit was due. "My friend Thomas actually knew about all that stuff. His mom's like a big-time lawyer."

Mara-who-looked-like-Jordan had narrowed her eyes while we talked and looked from me to Isabella and back. I'm not sure what she saw that she didn't like, but it freaked me out to have Jordan look at me like that, even if it wasn't really him.

"Shall we, uh, get going?" I asked.

Mara stepped forward and handed her small purse to her sister. "The car keys are in there. Wait in the car. Keep it running." She kept the bag the clothes had come in.

Isabella took the purse and gave Mara a big hug. Then she turned to me and I swear I could feel heat coming from Mara's eyes. Maybe the caffeine in the energy drinks had given me super sensitive skin. I ducked in for a quick hug and broke away.

We waited until Isabella disappeared around the corner back the way we'd entered the alley, and then walked the other way. At the far end of the alley we'd turn left, cut across the street, and be at the bank.

"You up to this?" Mara asked as we walked. "You may need to stop bullets."

I checked things out. I still felt spacey, but I wasn't tired anymore. "I feel okay. Maybe a little fragile. Just make it fast, and I'll manage."

"I always rob banks fast." Mara looked at me and cracked a smile. I had to keep reminding myself it really was Mara, since she looked almost exactly like Jordan, and Jordan's smiles were not reassuring.

I smiled back. Mara was in a better place if she was joking with me. Then she stopped smiling and she put a hand on my shoulder. A big Jordan-hand. It felt heavy. We came to a stop near the end of the alley.

"What'd you and my sister talk about while I was shopping?"

"Just, you know, what comes next, if we take care of Jordan. Stuff like that."

Mara held me with a hard look on her fake-Jordan face. I think I'd have confessed to stuff I hadn't done if she'd kept it up.

"All right," Mara said and released my shoulder. "Get the mask and blend. We'll talk more later."

I pulled my mask on in a smooth motion. I was getting better at getting it aligned and in place. Just then, a youngish couple with a small boy in tow walked by the wide mouth of the alley up ahead. I blended immediately, but the little boy looked over toward me just before I winked out of sight.

His eyes went wide and he stopped, staring. His parents turned to see him apparently staring into the alley at a very large, well-dressed man. They each grabbed one of his hands and hustled him off past the alley.

"So, that kid's gonna need therapy," I said.

"Focus," Mara said. "We've got a bank to rob."

"Right. Got to focus on the important stuff in life."

Mara strode forward and I followed a step behind. We turned the corner and the bank came into view. It was a big building. Imposing. I wanted to stop and take it in for a moment, but Mara didn't pause. She cut across the street through a small break in the traffic and walked straight in. I dodged through the door as it closed behind her.

Three steps into the lobby, Mara stopped and looked around. She made an impression, with all of Jordan's intimidating size. Heads turned and stole quick glances. I stopped beside her, still invisible.

"Man in the suit," she said, just loud enough for me to hear. "Left end of the tellers' counter. He's security. I've got him. Rent-a-guard over there by the door to the offices. Blue uniform. He's yours. Cameras all around, so I'll be seen. On my mark, let's make an impression."

Oh yeah. I was all about making an impression. Particularly at banks, with people who had guns. Compared to what went down at Mara's apartment, though, could this really be that hard?

I shook my head. That was a dumb thought. The plan had been simple, but I realized simple didn't mean easy. Things like *rob bank* left a lot of room for interpretation. A lot of details that could go sideways.

"On my way," I whispered to Mara.

Time to find out what magnificent disaster awaited.

Chapter 24

LIT UP

THERE WERE FIVE tellers behind the long counter. Three of them were serving customers. Opposite the tellers, some desks spread out, two of which had bank people talking to customers seated across the desks from them.

I crossed the lobby with careful, quick steps. It would have been easy to sneak up on Mr. Rent-a-cop even if I hadn't been invisible— he was totally focused on Mara. For her part, Mara just stood there looking like Jordan.

I got to the guard and checked out his gun. It was in a dark holster on his right hip, with a strap buckled over the back of the grip to secure it in place. That was a problem. I leaned in and took a close look. It seemed straightforward. Just a snap on a strap.

The guard took a half step toward Mara, and she exploded into motion. The gun was out and aimed at the other security guy before I fully registered she had moved. The bag hit the floor where she dropped it and her other hand extended toward the rent-a-cop, palm out.

"Hold!" Her voice boomed in Jordan's low range. "No one move, and no one gets hurt."

The security guy froze, his hand just outside of his suit jacket. He'd been going for a gun for sure. Rent-a-cop took a shaky step backwards and came to a stop, his hands hovering near his gun. A couple of the bank customers screamed, but were quickly calmed by the tellers.

"Your gun," Mara commanded, and stretched out her hand toward the rent-a-cop.

That was my cue. I flipped the holster strap open with

one hand while grabbing the gun with the other. I pulled it free fast enough to get it clear before his hand instinctively clamped down on his empty holster. Without pausing, I sent the gun spinning across the stone floor toward Mara. She brought her hand down, keeping it pointed at the gun as it slid toward her, and lifted one foot to trap it. To everyone in that bank, it must have looked like she had called the gun to her.

Well, that made an impression. A couple tellers dropped out of sight behind their glassed-in counter in a dead faint, along with one of the bank customers. Mara bent down and retrieved the gun in her left hand, keeping her other gun trained on the security guy. Several customers started edging toward the front doors. Mara dropped the safety with a thumb, aimed the rent-a-cop's gun at the ceiling, and fired off a couple rounds.

"Everybody on the ground! Now!" As she spoke, Mara strode to the security guy, who dropped to the ground along with everyone else. She stuck the gun she'd just fired into an interior coat pocket as she walked. "Hands up."

He stretched out on the floor with his hands above his head and a look of terror on his face. Mara bent down beside him and her hand flashed into his jacket. It came back out with another gun. "Go get that bag. You have one minute to fill it with cash, or it gets ugly."

The man nodded, and ran to retrieve the bag. Holding it, he crossed back to a door near where he'd been standing and badged through it, appearing behind the counter a moment later. Mara walked to the middle of the lobby and slowly turned in a circle, a gun in each hand. I knew she was doing it to make sure any security cameras got a good look at her Jordan-face, but it was still imposing.

I looked around, too. I didn't like what I saw. Everyone was on the floor, except the security guy who was now behind the tellers' counter emptying cash from drawers into Mara's bag. They were scared out of their minds, and several of them, both men and women, were weeping. Rent-a-cop lay on the ground at my feet, his eyes closed.

It struck me that this whole setup was a bad idea. Sure, it would force Jordan on the run, hunted by everyone and their mother. Hopefully, he'd wind up in jail for just about forever, and I knew he deserved it. Mara and Isabella would escape, and not have to fear him coming after them. Same for me. He'd either be in jail or too busy trying to stay out of jail to come for us.

"Thirty more seconds," Mara said, and the security guy gave her a quick nod while frantically shoveling bills into the bag.

The thing was, these bank people didn't deserve to be terrorized. They didn't know we weren't going to harm them, no matter what happened. In an important way, we were harming them by the very act of putting on this show.

"Fifteen seconds!" Mara said as she set one of the guns on the floor.

That was my next cue. I'd have to think it through later. I ghosted through the counter and hopped over several tellers laying on the ground to stand near the guard. As I reached him, Mara extended her free hand toward the guard. I snatched the bag out of his hand and ran for the door off to the side of the counter and glass that went back to the lobby. It struck me that the security guy had used a badge to get through it. Hopefully it would open automatically from the inside.

It did. I slipped through the door and and tossed the bag along the floor to Mara. As I ran over to her, I wondered if we'd been right. Thomas and I had thought it best to make it obvious to anyone in the Guild who might take notice of the bank robbery that a Seven had been involved. That way, the Guild would hopefully figure out Jordan was a Mocker using Sevens and go after him along with the FBI and cops.

The bag skidded to a stop near Mara, and she dropped all three guns into it. With that, she picked up the bag and turned toward the main doors. I glanced around as I followed. Everyone was still on the ground, except the security guard who stood staring at her from behind the counter, his mouth hanging open.

Movement caught my eye off to the side. Rent-a-cop rose to his feet and ran toward Mara. His left hand flashed down to his belt opposite his empty holster and came back up with a blocky device.

"Taser!" I hissed to Mara and bruised as I stepped between the rent-a-cop and Mara. He gave a primal shout and tased me.

As Mara had so eloquently put it earlier in the day, I was lit up like a Christmas tree. It was like being shocked and punched dozens of times a second. I lost track of time. I lost track of myself. It was hell on earth.

I returned to coherent thought as Mara threw me over her shoulder in a fireman carry and fled the bank. She burst through the doors and paused for a moment, then turned to the right and starting running. She had my legs in a vice grip against her chest, but my upper body was free to bounce around as she ran, so I got a good look down the street behind us.

I realized the loud sounds I was hearing weren't in my head. There were flashing lights and sirens. It looked like the street was full of cop cars descending on the bank. Mara turned to the right again, and my view of the street disappeared. A moment later, she turned left and stopped.

"Can you walk?" Mara asked, still looking like Jordan.

She set me down, but held on to me as I tried to regain control of my body. I lifted one leg, and then the other. My muscles felt on the verge of cramping. The sirens got louder. "I'm shaky, but I can do it."

"Reggie. Hurry." As she spoke, she stepped away from me and disappeared. The clothes collapsed in on themselves in a mound, with the bag beside them. A moment later, a cat fought its way out of the jacket. There was a twisting blur, and Mara stood as herself where the cat had been, wearing the same clothes she'd worn all day.

I tried to ignore that weirdness and concentrated. It didn't seem to help much, but my nerves stopped jangling around, and I felt like I could control my body again. "I'm okay."

"Good. Meet back at the car. Blend and go!" Mara took the guns out of the bag and tossed them up on the roof beside us and then threw the bag of money up with them. With that, there was another twisting blur, and a hawk took off down the alley. In a moment, she flashed out of sight.

I blended and cut back out into the street we'd just left and headed back toward the bank. There were cops everywhere, including two large, black SWAT vans. It took me ten minutes to make my way through the mess and back to the alley across the street from the bank. I hurried through it and out the other end, where our rental car was parked, the engine running. Isabella was sitting low in the front passenger seat.

I looked up and saw a hawk circling high above. I ghosted into the rear of the car and lay down behind the front seats. When I released the ghost and blend, Isabella made a squeaking sound and snapped around to look at me. It was gratifying to see real warmth in her smile.

I yanked off my mask. "Open the driver window. Quickly."

"Mara?"

I pointed skyward. "A hawk."

Isabella reached over and rolled down the window. A moment later a hawk streaked into the car and landed on the driver seat. I closed my eyes for a few seconds, and when I opened them Mara was sitting there.

Isabella started to say something, but Mara flicked a hand up to silence her. She dropped the car into drive and rolled her window up as she pulled out of the parking lot. Mara drove for a couple minutes in silence, taking random turns. The sounds of sirens tapered off until they could no longer be heard.

"Okay, we should be good," Mara said. "Joss, you doing alright?"

"Been better." I scrambled off the floor of the car and sat on the seat behind Mara. "Is it possible to burn out as a Seven? I almost couldn't hold my blend getting back to the car."

"No. You can wear yourself out, but it's not permanent."

"So you robbed the bank?" Isabella interjected.

"Yeah, we robbed the bank," Mara said. "Went well until Joss took a taser meant for me."

Isabella looked at me with concern written all over her face. "You are okay?"

"I'm fine. Just a bit, uh, jittery. Not something I ever want to experience again."

She nodded. "But you protected Mara, yes?"

I shrugged.

"Yeah, he did," Mara said. "All hell broke loose, though, when Joss popped into sight. I mean, all in black, thrashing around on the floor with a taser attached to him? Utter pandemonium. Would have been worse, but the guard freaked out when Joss appeared and dropped the taser."

"So how long was he juicing me?" I asked. "Like, a minute or something?"

"Maybe two seconds," Mara said.

Two seconds? That was crazy. It must have been at least a minute. A very long minute.

"I grabbed him and ran," Mara continued. "Something for everyone. The cops will find the guns eventually with the money on the roof, the FBI will be all over the video footage and go after Jordan, and now the Guild will have definitive proof that a Seven was involved. Hopefully they'll connect the dots and realize Jordan is a Mocker."

"So you'll drop me at home, right?" I asked. "Then disappear into the sunset? Never to be seen again? Just a gun and stacks of cash to see you home?"

"Something like that," Mara said. "I've got your phone and email. I'll let you know when we land somewhere safe."

"Thank you, Joss," Isabella said. "You have meant a world to me."

I wasn't totally sure what that meant, but it sounded good. I gave her a smile when she looked back at me. I realized I didn't even know exactly what time it was. Had Battlehoop ended yet? I pulled my phone out and checked the time. Just after noon.

Wait a second. Twelve missed calls. What? From home. All in the last thirty minutes. My phone was set to *do not disturb,* so I knew I'd miss inbound calls, but I hadn't been expecting twelve of them. All twelve were from my parents.

"Hey, my parents have been calling. Gonna give them a quick call back."

"You think that's wise?" Mara asked. "We can have you home in fifteen minutes. Maybe ten. I don't want them to interfere just yet."

"I'll be careful," I said. I hit the call-back button.

Someone picked up on the first ring. "Hello?" It was Dad's voice, but different. Weaker. Scared.

"Dad? Hey, it's Joss. Saw I missed some calls. What's up?"

"Joss, are you okay?" His voice kept that edge. He sounded scared. My stomach developed a case of the icebergs.

"Yeah, sure, sorry I missed your calls. What's going on?"

"Where are you?"

"On the way home. Why?"

"Are you safe?" Dad asked. "Can you speak freely? Say 'thanks, Dad' if you can't."

My throat tightened. Heat flooded my scalp. My heart tried to break out of my chest. "Dad? I'm scared now... what's going on?"

"Get somewhere safe and stay there. We'll come get you. A restaurant. Store. Anywhere public. Where are you now?"

"Dad?" If it wasn't a whimper, it was awfully close to one. "What's going on?"

"Janey's been taken, Joss. My little girl is gone."

I heard Dad sob as my arm went numb and the phone fell away from my ear.

Chapter 25

THE BEST LAID PLANS

I COULDN'T PROCESS what I'd heard. It was too much. I closed my eyes and shut out the world. So far today, I'd been beaten with a stick, shot, tased, and drunk one too many energy drinks. My body felt hollowed out by pain. The searing heat in my heart, though, overshadowed everything else. My sister had been kidnapped.

"Joss? Joss!" My dad's frantic voice sounded faint. I felt a moment of confusion, then remembered the phone in my lap. I fumbled around for a moment to find it without opening my eyes. I didn't want to see Isabella staring at me, or Mara glancing back as she drove.

I pulled the phone up to my ear. "Hold on, Dad. I'm here. I'm okay. What happened?"

"Where are you, Joss?"

"I'm with Mara. We're on the way—"

"What?" Dad's voice cut in. "Mara? The woman from Battlehoop? Joss, you've got to get away! She's working with Jordan. He…" A sob cut through his words. "He's the one who's got Janey."

"Dad, listen!" I said. "Jordan was holding Mara's sister hostage. They aren't working together, okay? I'm safe. Please." A tear broke free and rolled down my cheek. "Tell me about Janey. Jordan has her?"

"What's going on, Joss? Why are you with her? What have you done?"

I felt a hand on my knee and opened my eyes. Isabella was looking at me, silently crying. Seeing her sadness directed at me had the strange effect of making me feel stronger. *Being a man is being able to stand up under it.*

"I've done a lot, Dad. A whole lot."

I gave him the short version as Mara drove us toward my house. It included most of the main points. Jordan 'recruiting' Mara. Searching for a Thief. Finding me. Making contact with me at the beginning of the summer. Being the Seventy-Seven. Training me at Battlehoop. Sending me on missions. Janey and I encountering the two guys from the Guild. I skipped over Bobby Ferris, and brought it forward to the past twenty-four hours. Suspecting Mara, then finding out the truth. Rescuing Isabella. Robbing a bank.

"You robbed a bank!" Dad yelled it so loudly I couldn't tell if it was a question or a statement. "You knew Jordan was some lunatic killer, and you provoked him? While your sister was with him? How could you? How... how dare you!"

"We were wrong," I said, "but Mara knows him, Dad. Thomas and I didn't think he'd take the risk to expose himself. Mara agreed with us. I guess we were wrong."

Mara pulled into our neighborhood. We were about one minute from my house.

"Joss, if Janey comes to harm..."

"We're here, Dad. Coming in the front door in less than a minute."

A moment later, we pulled up in front of the house. Mara put the car in park and turned to face me. "We're coming in, okay? I'm going to see this through."

"Where did we go wrong?" I asked. "We were so sure he'd keep out of it. Not blow his cover."

"I have no idea, but it doesn't matter. We're going to get her, understand? Let's go."

As we got out of the car, Dad stepped out of the front door. He was carrying my old little league bat like a club in one hand.

"Your *papá*?" Isabella asked.

I nodded and walked toward him. His face somehow looked tight and saggy at the same time. His mouth drawn in a hard line. I hesitated as we closed the distance, but he rushed forward and crushed me in a one-armed hug. With the other he pointed the bat at Mara, who had stopped with Isabella several feet back.

"You're the one?" he asked, though it sounded more like a demand. "Who got my kids tangled up with that madman?"

"I am," Mara said. "And this is my sister, Isabella. She got 'tangled up' with Jordan when he killed our parents and kidnapped her."

I hadn't expected Mara to go head to head with my dad's anger, but it seemed to work. The bat dropped to his side and his shoulders slumped as he let me go.

"Dad," I said, "can you tell us what happened?"

Dad took one last look at all of us and turned back to the house. He waved us with him. "I want you to hear it from Thomas. I may have missed something."

"Wait. Thomas is here?" We stepped through the doorway and I shut the door.

Dad didn't answer, but led us to the family room. Thomas sat on the edge of the couch on one end. Mom was a blur as she swept over and hugged me.

"Oh, sweetie. What are we going to do?" Her voice was low, tilted into my ear as she held me. "I'm so scared."

I hugged her back for a time, and then broke away. "This is Mara and Isabella. They've been held by—"

"I know, sweetie," Mom cut in. "I listened in when you told Dad." She gave Mara a hard look, and Isabella a softer one. "I'm not happy about what you've done, but I'm also not happy about what's been done to you."

Thomas had left his seat at some point and was hovering near me. I reached out to shake his hand, and he grabbed it and pulled me into a serious bro hug. His eyes were red like he'd been crying.

"Thomas, can you tell us?" Mara said. "What happened?"

"Yeah," Thomas said. "You want to sit down?"

"I need food and coffee while we talk," I said. "Can we go to the kitchen?"

"What's this about, Joss?" Dad asked.

"I need to kick my body back into gear. It's been a long day."

We took seats around the breakfast table and Thomas started talking while Mom quietly wept and drummed up some food and coffee for us. "It started early on at Battlehoop. Jordan was acting weird. Real distracted when Mara didn't show up. He kept his phone near him. There was a phone call at one point, then some texts. He had us practice on our own for a long stretch. I knew stuff was going down, and could only hope you'd pull it off."

"So that was while we were at Mara's place, right?" I asked.

"I'd guess so. Anyway, it dragged on. More texts came, and he got more worked up. He stopped training with us at all. Just gave us exercises to do."

"His second crew," Mara said. "They had gotten to the apartment and passed information to him."

Mom put a sandwich and cup of coffee at my place. I thanked her and dug in as she took a seat with us. When I reached for my coffee, Mara put her hand over it. "Wait. Don't drink it yet. Trust me."

I shrugged, but let go of the mug.

"Anyway, I was nervous," Thomas said, "but I wanted to get any info possible. I stayed close to him. Well, as close as possible. Toward the end, he was sort of wandering around in a daze, staring at his phone. The rest of us were up on the platform. I worked my way over to the edge, and he drifted by. I got a glimpse of his phone. It was some news site, and a big picture of him with two guns."

"Right," I said. "That's the bank, so—"

Thomas cut me off with a raised hand. "And I swear I heard him mumble something like, 'They're gonna kill me.' Then things went downhill. He disappeared into his office for a few minutes, then came out on a phone call. When he hung up, he walked over, handed me a note, then just grabbed Janey by the arm and walked out with her."

"What?" I yelled. "No one fought?"

Thomas looked down at the table. "She fought. And yelled. Not at first, but she started up when he dragged her out of the building. It… it was just so casual. Happened all at once. We were in shock."

"Nobody tried to stop him?" I couldn't believe it.

Thomas looked up at me and shrugged. "We did, but it was too late. Frankie got to him first, right as he threw Janey in the back of his car. Jordan beat him. Hard. He'll be okay, I think, but it was bad. It, it scared us. We kinda froze up. Then Jordan drove off with Janey." His chin dropped to his chest. "I'm sorry."

"The note," Mara said. "Let me see it."

Dad stood and pulled a piece of paper out of his pocket. He unfolded it and set it on the table near Mara and me.

Joss and Mara are to meet me at the closed down warehouse at the corner of Wilcox and Auburn to discuss arrangements. Enter through the door in back. Be there by 5pm or she dies. If the police get involved, she dies.

Mara looked up from the note at Thomas. "You're sure he said that? 'They're going to kill me?'"

Thomas nodded. "I'm sure."

"Why?" Mom asked. "Who's *they?*"

Mara pursed her lips and frowned in concentration. Isabella reached out and took one of her hands.

"The Mockers," Mara said. "It must be. When Joss got tased and—"

"What!" Mom said.

"For real?" Thomas asked.

Well, that was inconvenient. I'd left out that part of the story when summarizing things over the phone. Mara should have known better.

"Yes, yes," Mara said. "He was tased. And shot. Now focus!"

"Dear Lord," Dad said. He was staring at my shirt. The part of the shirt with a small bullet hole and a large stain of blood, barely visible in the black material.

"I'm fine. Mom, Dad, really, it's okay. I healed myself. It's one of my talents."

"It makes sense," Mara cut in. "How do the Mockers work? They must have oaths. Ways to enforce secrecy when using Sevens. We exposed Jordan at the bank. We knew the cops and FBI would go after him. Sure, there'd be complexities. He'd have an alibi, being at Battlehoop when it happened. So we made sure there was evidence of a Seven involved to add pressure from the Guild. We wanted to make sure he was either in jail or on the run, too busy to go after us."

"Okay," Dad said. "But the Mockers?"

"Joss had been invisible. He popped into view when the taser hit him. It, I don't know, must have crossed some line with the Mockers. Their internal code. Something like that. Why else would he say 'I'm a dead man'? I don't think the FBI and cops, or even the Guild, would make him fear for his life. The Mockers are going to take him out."

"So he has nothing to lose," Mom said. "You pushed him too far. He's, he's capable—" She broke down into sobs, and Dad reached over and took her hand.

"He's capable of anything," Dad finished.

Chapter 26

THE EAGLES ARE COMING

"WE'LL GET HER back," Mara said. "On my life, I swear it."

Dad stared at her with a hard look for a moment before slapping the table and standing up to pace. Mom slumped into his empty seat.

"Promise me something," Mara said. "If something bad happens and I'm, uh, well… take care of Isabella."

Apparently, Isabella wasn't too happy about that, because she launched into a tirade in Spanish. Mara weathered it, then put her finger across Isabella's lips to silence her, and gave her a big hug.

My dad threw his hands in the air. "Yeah, we'll do what we can. But how do we rescue Janey? He could kill her!"

Mara nodded, then glanced at her phone. "It's 1:00. We have some time, and we'll need it. How far away is that?" She pointed to the note as she spoke.

"It's about fifteen minutes," Mom said, wiping her nose with the back of her hand. "It's an isolated warehouse district. I've got the map up on my laptop. Want me to get it?"

Mara shook her head. "Not yet. First things first. Jordan said no cops, right? And you're sticking to that?"

Mom and Dad both nodded.

"I covered things with Frankie," Thomas said. "To make sure his parents didn't get the cops involved. Showed him the note. He doesn't really know what's going on, but he's covering for us. He'll blame his bruised up face on an accident when sparring."

Mara nodded. "Good for him. Joss, you need to go upstairs and lie down. Put everything you've got into healing. We can do this, okay, but we've got to do it right."

"I'm fine," I said, "but I need to save what energy I have."

"Trust me, Joss. One reggie to another. I'm pretty sure everything's going to hinge on you. We need you at your best."

I looked around the table. Thomas shrugged. Mom looked frail, broken down, and was staring at the note. Dad pursed his lips, then gave me a quick nod. I turned to Isabella and was greeted with a warm smile. Maybe being a hero wasn't as bad as I'd thought it was.

"All right," I said. "I'll lie down and put everything into a reggie, but then I'm coming back down and we're going to get Janey. Understand?"

"Sure, Joss," Mara said. "Just make sure you really concentrate."

I pushed back from the table and headed for the stairs. I didn't know what all this was about, but after the past twenty-four hours, I trusted Mara. I went upstairs and lay down on my bed. After a few deep, calming breaths, I turned inward. *Heal.* I put everything into it.

Mom shook me, and my eyes popped open. "Joss. It's time to wake up. We've got to go. Here's that coffee I made for you. I reheated it. Drink it down."

What was going on? Wake up? How had Mom gotten here so quickly? I'd just laid down. I glanced at my clock. 2:34. What the heck? I sat up and stretched. I felt great. A little tired still, but the hollow ache was gone.

"You've been asleep for an hour and a half," Mom said as she handed me my coffee.

"Mara…"

Mom shrugged. "I don't know about this Seven stuff, but I guess she knew what you needed."

"What about her?" I asked. "Mom, she got shot so many times. She's been through a lot today."

Mom put her hand on my face for a moment. "Joss, I'm so scared for Janey, and then I find out I could have lost you today." She fingered the hole in my shirt and shuddered. "Mara told us what she needed, then went to sleep on the couch for about an hour while we got it all together. She's up now and ready to go."

I took a sip. The coffee was somewhere between warm and hot. Perfect for drinking quickly. I gulped it down. Mom stood, and I hopped out of bed and did some stretches. I was amazed at how solid I felt. I'd have to remember that trick. Big time reggie plus nap equaled feeling great.

"Let's do this," I said, and followed Mom downstairs. As we entered the family room, my dad and Thomas stood face to face in a quiet but heated argument. Thomas seemed to have grown another inch this summer, and he was only a couple inches shorter than my dad. Mara and Isabella sat on the couch.

"There's no arguing," Dad said. "No debate. You are not coming."

"So I just go home and wait?" Thomas said.

"That's exactly what you are going to do."

"And that's safer than being with two Sevens? When some lunatic mobster is out there, who knows where I live? He's got men who work for him. Who says one of them isn't waiting at my house to off me now that I've delivered the note? You can't call the cops. You have to keep me with you."

Dad glared at him for a moment, and then snarled and turned away. "I forget your mother is a lawyer. This is madness. You and Isabella are staying with Jennifer, understand?" He looked at Mom. "Whatever we end up doing, keep them out of it, okay?"

Mom crossed the room and took his hand. "Count on it."

"Someone want to tell me what's going on?" I asked.

Mara stood, and Isabella followed her lead. "*Vamanos*. We'll meet you there. Joss, they can tell you on the drive over."

"I'll lock up behind them," Dad said. "Joss, we're taking

my car."

I shook my head and followed Mom and Thomas to the garage. We piled into Dad's SUV. He showed up a moment later, carrying the baseball bat. As we pulled out of the garage, I decided I'd waited long enough.

"So," I said, "we're just going to drive up and ask for Janey back?"

"There's no plan, Joss," Mom said. "We're meeting Mara about a half mile from the warehouse where Jordan has Janey. Mara's going to scout it out. Then we figure something out."

"I've got all kinds of stuff in the back," Dad said. "Hammers, saws, a crowbar, some rope, duct tape, that sort of thing. Anything we might need spur of the moment. It's going to come down to what Mara scouts out for us."

"Oh, that should totally do the trick." I said, feeling frustration and anger boil up. "They're trained killers! They have guns! What good is some duct tape and rope going to do us?"

"I have no idea, Joss, but it'll have to do," Dad said. "Now, tell me what happened today. Don't skip anything this time, okay? No more secrets. No more surprises."

Thomas wisely kept quiet while we Morgans hashed it out. The drive took almost fifteen minutes, which gave me time to really freak Mom and Dad out. I had glossed over more of the details than I'd meant to the first time, so there were lots of surprises. Somehow, I'd completely skipped the whole bomb-vest with a dead man's switch. Mom had to turn the AC way down and fan herself.

"This, uh, is a bit more than putting your hand in a table," Dad said. "I just don't understand why you didn't talk to us."

"I'm sorry," I said. "I desperately wanted to train. And then one thing led to another. You've got to remember I was being manipulated by a master criminal."

"I'm keeping it in mind, Joss. But I'm disappointed in you."

I was disappointed in me, too. I had nothing to say. Mom

reached back and patted my knee. "I'm proud of you for rescuing Isabella. I got to talk to her a little bit while you slept. It was the right thing to do."

I gave her a grateful smile, but it didn't last. "We're going to rescue Janey, too, Mom. They won't know what hit 'em."

Dad turned the car onto a street with large, windowless buildings. Most were about two stories tall and looked like giant boxes with loading docks. He turned again and we cut between two of the buildings before pulling over next to a railroad crossing. Mara's rental car was the only car in sight.

Mara and Isabella were already out of their car. When they saw us, Mara waved and then shifted into hawk and flew off down the tracks. Mom made a choking sound, her hand to her mouth.

"Never going to get used to this Seven stuff," Dad muttered as he pulled in behind the other car and killed the engine.

We got out of the car and waited. Isabella walked over to us and leaned against the SUV next to me. Thomas gave me a sideways look and raised an eyebrow. I glared at him.

"Joss?" Isabella said.

"Hmmm?"

"You will be careful?"

I thought about it for a moment. "No. Can't say that's my goal."

Her shoulders slumped, but then she nodded. "I understand."

"You'll like Janey. Heck, I bet she could hang with you sparring, even if you've trained with Mara for a couple years."

"I will meet her soon, yes?" Isabella said, and offered me a smile.

A motion caught my eye, far down the railroad tracks. A large bird flying toward us. "Yes, you will."

The hawk landed nearby and immediately twisted and blurred into Mara. We all converged on her.

"Well?" Dad said.

"Did you see her?" Mom asked.

"Janey's in there," Mara said. "No injuries that I saw."

Mom and Dad had a serious moment together that involved hugging and crying. I felt like a weight had lifted off my chest.

"Here's the thing," Mara said, after giving everyone a chance to quiet down. "There's only a couple lines of sight into the building, but I saw her. They'd set it up so I could see her. Understand? It was a message, of sorts. She's okay as long as we do what we're told."

"Should we?" Mom asked. "Give him what he wants?"

My stomach clenched. "Do you want me to turn myself in to him?" I asked. "I'll do it if you want me to."

Mom's eyes opened wide in shock. "No! No, I didn't mean that. I don't know what I meant. I just want Janey safe."

"We go get her, right?" Dad said, looking at Mara.

Mara nodded, but she bit her lip. "I only saw two guys with Jordan. The others may have gotten busted if they'd showed up at the apartment this morning at the same time the cops arrived. But we don't know for sure. And there's a complication. They must have started working on this facility months ago. That would fit Jordan's M.O. He's careful. Covers all his risks."

"So what is it?" I asked. "What'd you see?"

"He's got a wire mesh covering everything on the inside that I could see. Even the windows. It's got to be silver."

"I don't get it."

"Yeah, it never came up," Mara said. "You know all those stories about silver bullets killing mythical creatures? It's loosely based in reality. Silver grounded in the earth is like a talent killer. It leaches the power out of you."

"So I can't, what? I can't ghost through it?"

"You might, but probably not. And if you tried to push through it and failed..."

"Weren't you training him?" Dad said. "How can he just be learning about this?"

Mom put a hand on Dad's shoulder. He glanced at her

and scowled, but settled down.

"What about the floor?" I asked. It terrified me down to my toes, just thinking about ghosting into the ground, but if I had to do it, I would.

"I couldn't see much of the floor," Mara said, "but I saw areas covered with the mesh. The ceiling, though, looked clear."

"So we get me on the roof and I ghost through it?"

"Yeah," Mara said, "I figure that's what he wants you to do. He's leaving you one clear way in. It's a trap, for sure."

"So what do we do?" Mom said. Her voice was edged with despair.

"We spring the trap," Mara said. "We send Joss through the roof."

"You can't be serious," Dad said. Those were the words, at least. His facial expression said something closer to, "Over my dead body."

"Deadly serious," Mara said, "but I'm not saying we have Joss ghost through the ceiling. I've got something else in mind."

She laid it out. It started with Mara and I shifting into giant eagles and her towing me with the rope to get airborne. The plan went downhill from there. I'd been acting out plans that had almost gotten me killed all day. To hear a plan practically designed to get me killed, though, was a new experience. I didn't like it, but it did sound like it could work. Worse, it sounded like our only good option.

"Mara, can we talk for a moment?" I nodded my head off to the side, away from the group. "Seven to Seven?"

"Joss…" Dad said, but Mom laid a hand on his arm to cut him off.

We moved a few steps away and leaned in close.

"I don't like it, but it's a good plan," I said. "Bold, simple, shocking. Just one problem. The part about me shifting into an eagle. Remember? We never practiced that? You guys were too busy turning me into a Thief?"

"You think I haven't considered that?" Mara's eyebrows came together as she spoke. "Joss, all I've been doing is thinking of ways this could fail. But you can do it. Trust me."

"No, I can't."

"You can. You must. Look, being the Seventy-Seven isn't just about having all the talents. It's about your strength. Your ability to learn. You think a normal Seven could ghost like you can after a couple months? It'd take years."

Again with the new information. "Why am I just hearing about this?"

"Jordan wanted you on a tight leash. He didn't want you knowing too much until he had firm control of you."

It made sense. And it made me angry. I shook my head in frustration. "So I'm going to be able to shift? Just like that? Like you do?"

"I doubt it. No way you'll be able to change your weight. At least, not much. We're going to have to go big. It'll make it harder, but I'll be there to help."

I looked back toward my parents and gave them a thumbs up, and then turned back to Mara. "Okay, so I manage to shift somehow. Then what? How do you help me?"

"We use the rope. Once you shift, you'll intuitively know what to do, but the size will be unnatural. It will throw things off. I'm going to tow you to give you some needed speed. It'll work."

"Okay, tell me what to do, I'll do it."

Mara gave my arm a squeeze, and turned back toward the others. I followed her over and gave my mom a big hug. She clung to me like she didn't want to let go, but I finally managed to break free. I gave my dad a more respectable bro hug.

"I don't think waiting's gonna make it any easier," I said. "Dad, can you get the rope?"

"Once we lift off," Mara said, "be in position in ten minutes."

"I'll keep the kids with me," Mom said. "But if I don't hear from you in twenty minutes, I'm calling 911."

"Jennifer, you can't do that." Mara stepped over to Isabella and put an arm around her. "I don't want my sister deported without me."

Isabella gave Mara a hug and stepped away. "It will be okay. We will call the police if we need to, and we will figure out what to do with me."

Mara looked from Isabella to Mom, and gave a quick nod and stepped toward the train track. Dad brought the rope back, tied off a large loop on either end, and laid it out along the track. It was probably fifty feet in length. I pulled my mask out and put it on. I'd gotten used to wearing it.

"You ready?" Mara asked me.

I nodded, and she shifted into a freakishly large bald eagle, almost as tall as me. My parents both took a step back. I didn't blame them. Her beak looked wicked.

Thomas stepped over to me let out a low whistle. "Merica." He held out his fist. I bumped it.

"Can you do this?" he asked.

"Here's hoping," I said.

Mara's eagle-head cocked to the side. One huge bird-eye stared at me. It was my turn. I started my breathing exercise. A count of four in, hold for four, and breath out for four. Repeat. It all came down to this. We'd rescued Isabella and set up Jordan so he'd be hunted down, but none of that mattered if I couldn't make this shift.

While breathing, I tried to let my vision, my entire world, dwindle down to the giant eagle standing in front of me. It should have been easy. It was a giant eagle, after all, but I kept thinking of Janey, scared and alone. Well, not alone, and that was the problem. Jordan had played me from the moment I found the note in my locker, and now he thought he'd just lead me into a trap. It was time to turn the tables on him.

Giant eagle. I concentrated on overlapping that one image with my sense of self. My identity. I breathed out my fears. Actually, I didn't, but I tried to pretend that's what I was doing. I wasn't sure it was possible to breathe out fear. The whole concept seemed weird. And I was getting sidetracked. I had to concentrate! Out with the fears, and in with the monstrous eagle. I closed my eyes, but kept the image of the eagle firmly in mind. Breathe in, breathe out.

I shifted. Just like that. My big bird-eyes opened in surprise. The world was a different place. My field of view was enormous, with rich details popping out into the distance. I saw it all. Mara's eagle head nodding. Dad catching Mom as she passed out. Thomas giving Isabella a high five.

Mara shifted back to herself and picked up the loop of rope near us. She held it out to me. I opened my mouth, now a giant beak, and grabbed hold of it. The strangest part of being an eagle was how natural it felt. The beak felt right. I spread my wings. My *wings*! It felt as though they belonged. Nothing unusual here, just a giant set of eagle wings.

Mara walked to the other end of the rope. "Joss, just hold that rope and do what feels natural." She turned to Dad. "Is she okay?"

Mom was sitting on the ground fanning herself, my dad beside her. Dad gave a thumbs up. "I'll be in place in ten minutes," he said.

Mara nodded, and shifted back to a giant eagle. She grabbed the other end of the rope in her talons and launched herself into the air. I followed her lead, leaping as I spread my wings and flapped down hard. The rope pulled taut and tugged me into the air as I frantically flapped. Being an eagle had felt a lot more natural when I was on the ground.

Mara flew straight down the railroad track as I flapped along on the other end of the rope like a drunken kite, fending off the ground every few flaps with an outstretched claw. The only part of the whole arrangement that worked well was my beak. It was really good at holding on to the rope. Slowly, beat by beat, I found the rhythm, and suddenly we were gaining altitude. My stomach lurched as we rose above the nearby buildings, but the newfound eagle in me rejoiced.

One hundred feet. Two hundred. After that, I had no good way to estimate how high we were. Mara swung out in a broad arc as we climbed, so that we spiraled higher. We followed a broad circle and returned to the track, now far below, and then repeated. Each spiral took us further along the tracks toward the building that held Janey. I had no clue which building it was. That was Mara's job.

Mara was a much stronger flier. If not for the rope pulling me along, I didn't think I could have gotten into the air, let alone soared up toward the clouds. We climbed, and I distracted myself from what I had to do next by focusing on the raw delight of flight. The view was incredible, and my eyes were like binoculars. As we swept around in a curve, I spotted my parents getting into Dad's SUV with Isabella and Thomas. On the next pass, I saw the SUV driving along the road parallel to the railroad tracks.

We climbed higher, now thousands of feet in the air. I finally found a rhythm that worked and was able to gain a few feet on Mara so that the rope went slack. The wind was cold but held at bay by my feathers. My wings cut through the air, holding me aloft. This was what being a Seven was all about. I was flying!

Mara banked hard into a much tighter spiral and leveled off. We had arrived. I didn't feel ready for step two of the plan. How could I? It was suicide.

We circled high in the sky. It was coming. I knew it, and thought I might throw up, which made me wonder what giant eagle throw up looked like. Mara's eagle claws opened, and her end of the rope dropped and whipped back below me. I opened my mouth and let my end go as well. The rope tumbled toward the earth far below.

I closed my eyes and pictured Janey. Now or never. I shifted back to little ol' me, and tumbled from the sky.

Chapter 27

ICARUS

WHEN I WAS little, Dad had read me the story of Icarus. There was a super important point to the story, but I didn't remember what it was. I had latched onto that scene of Icarus, flying high, then falling from the sky. I'd secretly wondered if that fall had made it all worth it. I'd always loved the big drops on roller coasters. Icarus had taken the ultimate big drop.

My first impression of dropping from the sky was buried under a horrific scream. It took me a moment to realize I was the one screaming. Then the cold hit me. Thankfully, my work clothes and mask protected me. Eventually, I ran out of breath and quieted down.

I wondered if I could survive without a stomach, because I was pretty sure I'd left mine behind when I started falling. After a few seconds of windmilling my arms, I managed to orient my body head-down and stretched to my full length, like a rocket falling back to earth. I caught fragments of the earth far below, but the wind and cold made my eyes sting and water, so I had trouble keeping them open.

An eagle's cry cut through the sound of rushing wind. I twisted around and saw Mara the eagle directly behind me, wings folded, keeping pace with my fall. I straightened back out and held my arms rigid along my body. Her claws grasped my upper arms and adjusted my course as we fell. I glanced down and got a good look at ground, still far below, rushing up toward us.

Little rectangular and square roofs sat between a road

and the railroad track. Mara adjusted our angle a bit more, and we lined up with a large, blackish roof sitting at the intersection of the road with another road that cut across the tracks. I blinked away tears and stared down at the building. It was getting larger. Approaching fast. Mara had thought we'd have between thirty and forty seconds of falling, and I guessed I had about ten seconds left. I thought I saw someone running toward the back of the building.

The talons released me. That was my cue. Mara had done what she could to aim me, now I just had to bruise like my life depended on it. Because it did. I tucked my knees up under my chin and wrapped my arms around my legs, pulling them tightly against my chest.

I glanced one last time toward the ground. I was definitely going to hit right in the middle of that roof in a few seconds. Mara had been certain she could keep me away from the area of the building where Janey was held. I tucked my head against my knees, closed my eyes, and willed my body to harden. To become steel. No, to become diamond. Diamond was supposed to be really hard. Wait, diamond could shatter, couldn't it? I went for it all. Diamond steel.

Jordan wanted me to come through the roof? To walk into a trap? Wish granted. I hit the building like a diamond-steel asteroid.

Pain. For a time, that was all I knew. Then confusion. I opened my eyes, but I saw only a warm, beige light. The pain tried to conquer me. A single thought rallied me to fight back—Janey! I had to move. To act. To rescue her.

I reggied. It turned out that the sound of bones popping back into place was loud, and the feeling was worse. I vomited. With that out of the way, I tried opening my eyes again. This time, my brain kicked into gear and helped me figure out what I was seeing. A heavy mist of dust swirled around in the air, but was clearing. I sat at the bottom of a shallow pit made of shattered concrete, twisted rebar, and scattered pieces of a silvery mesh. I stood so my head cleared the top of the pit, careful to avoid the mesh.

A man limped toward me, a gun clutched in his hand, dangling from a bloodied arm. Our eyes locked. The gun came up, aided by his other hand, and pointed at my chest. Seriously? I'd survived skydiving without a parachute just so some dude could shoot me?

A little league bat took him on the side of the head and he dropped. Dad stood behind him, looking near panic and very angry. He looked up and ran toward me. "Joss!"

I heard a menacing popping sound, and Dad twisted and fell toward me as blood sprayed from his shoulder. I'd seen the flash off to my right of the silenced gunfire. Dad collapsed a few feet from me, and his head hit the floor hard. He lay there, unmoving. I screamed and kinneyed. Time slowed. Dust motes hung frozen in the air.

I surged out of the hole and ran toward the source of the gunfire. Two steps out of the hole, silver mesh covered the floor. Ahead, I saw the murky shape of the man who had shot my dad. I leapt.

The speed from my kinneying shot me forward like a crossbow bolt. The man came into sharp view as I sailed through the air. He was a big guy, and had a big gun. I floated through the air, and he gradually raised his gun toward me. It was going to be close, but I thought I'd get there before he could get off a shot.

I hardened my fist and arm, dropped the kinney, and took a swing at him. I was moving with incredible speed. My fist connected with him as I flashed by, and the force of the impact sent me into a tight spin as I tumbled to the floor. It had happened so fast, I wasn't sure which part of him I'd hit.

I spun across the floor on my belly, my guts screaming in pain from having the wind knocked out of me when I landed. I hit a doorframe and ricocheted a few feet into a room before coming to a stop. My head was facing back the way I'd come, and a smear of blood marked my route. My right thigh was on fire, and I was doing a solid impression of a fish out of water as my lungs struggled to draw in air.

I tried to reggie, but nothing happened. I rolled over and

glanced around the room. A window provided a little light on the wall opposite the door. Janey sat on a wooden chair in the middle of the room. I scrambled to my feet, but my leg gave out and I settled for crawling over to her.

"Janey!" I gasped. She didn't respond. I looked more closely, and saw the rope securing her to the chair, and the duct tape across her mouth. Her eyes were locked on me. I hauled myself up using her chair and slowly pulled the tape off.

"Joss!" That's all she got out before she started crying.

I gave her a fierce hug, then looked around the room for something to cut the rope. There was silver mesh covering the floor and walls, but nothing else in the room. Wait. Silver mesh. No wonder I hadn't been able to reggie.

"Janey, I've got to get off this silver to heal, okay? I've got to, uh, sit in your lap."

She nodded and tried to stop her sobs. I dragged myself up onto her lap, and used a hand to lift my bad leg clear of the floor. My pants had a four inch cut in them, and blood leaked out of my leg. He must have shot me just as I hit him.

I reggied. Relief and weariness flooded my body. I looked back at my leg. The blood was still there, soaking the area just below my knife pocket, but it didn't seem to be getting worse.

My knife! I pulled the knife out and made short work of the rope binding Janey. Once free, she jumped up and grabbed me in a hug. "What happened out there? It sounded like a bomb?"

"Yeah, that was me. Mara dropped me on the building from over a mile up."

She pulled away and looked at me, her eyebrows pulled together. "I don't understand."

"Later. We've got to get out of here. Dad needs help."

We stepped toward the door and stopped. Jordan stood in the doorway. It looked like someone had attacked him with scissors. He must have been hit by flying debris when I had made my entrance through the roof.

He stepped forward and raised a gun. "Time to cut my

losses."

I stepped in front of Janey and bruised. Nothing happened. I looked down at the silver mesh on the floor. We'd come so close. It was the end of the line.

A blur of motion caught my eye and Jordan grunted as he twisted down and away. Something hit Jordan's head and the big man stumbled toward me out of the doorway. Thomas stood behind him holding my Dad's bat and took another swing, this time at Jordan's knee.

Jordan fell to the side and yelled as his knee gave out, but he still managed to swing his gun around toward Thomas. Isabella leapt past Thomas and kicked Jordan's hand, sending the gun skittering off to the side.

Jordan roared in anger and swung at Isabella, but she dropped to the floor and rolled away. He tried to kick her, but the knee Thomas had hit buckled, and he barely kept his feet. Thomas took another swing with the bat, but Jordan leapt off his good leg and kicked out with that same leg to knock the bat out of Thomas's hands. He landed awkwardly facing away from me.

Janey sprinted forward and kicked him on the side of his good knee. I said a word I'm not allowed to say and ran to join the action. Jordan spun toward Janey, but she twisted out of the way of his fist. I didn't. It felt like I'd had a close encounter with a bulldozer.

Janey and Isabella danced around Jordan as I stood back up and tried to get my eyes to work together. Two Jordans were having trouble standing, but their fists were still in full effect, fending off two Isabellas and Janeys. Where'd Thomas go? I looked around and saw twin Thomases as they took their shirts off and used them to pick up Jordan's gun.

I couldn't seem to get my eyes to uncross. I needed to get back into the action. I was the Seven, after all, but my feet didn't want to walk in a straight line. Then, for a moment, my vision aligned and I saw Jordan clearly. He was facing away from me. I took two steps and leapt onto his back

I hadn't really thought about what came next, but once

on his back, I got an arm around his neck and held on. I reggied, clearing my head and vision in a rush, and then bruised to harden my body just before Jordan delivered a vicious punch to my face. I have no idea how he pulled off punching me that hard while I was on his back, but it must have hurt him, because my face was rock hard when he connected.

"Joss!" Thomas called. "Get clear."

I looked to my right. Thomas knelt about ten feet away, the gun aimed low down at Jordan. Isabella and Janey were on either side, out of the line of fire.

"Just shoot!" I said as Jordan reached back with both hands. "Now! Shoot now!"

Jordan grabbed me just as Thomas started firing. If Jordan managed to put me in contact with the floor, I was done for. All my powers would leach away. I tried to kinney, but I just didn't have it in me. I threw everything I had into bruising and clung to Jordan's neck with both arms while he pulled at me.

Thomas pulled of shots at a steady pace. The fourth one hit Jordan near the knee. He collapsed like one of those buildings that are taken down with explosives. I shoved off him as hard as I could, fell to the floor, and rolled away from him.

Profanity and threats streamed out of Jordan's mouth as he rolled on the floor and clutched his knee. Thomas wasn't done. He scooted over a few feet and lined up another shot while Isabella and Janey both came over to me. Thomas still held the gun with his shirt. Isabella grabbed one of my arms, and Janey the other. Three shots later, he hit Jordan's foot on his other leg.

Thomas stood and nodded at us. He pointed the gun at the far corner and squeezed off six more shots before the gun's clip was emptied. He tossed the gun toward the same corner and pulled his shirt back on.

"Dang, Thomas," I said, pulling my hands away from my ears. "That was legit."

He shrugged and looked toward the doorway. "Dad

loves to take me to the shooting range when he has me for the weekend. Joss, your dad looked hurt. And I didn't see Mara. Let's get out there."

Isabella made a squeaking sound and dropped my arm. She and Janey raced after Thomas as he went through the doorway, going wide around Jordan. I stumbled after them.

"I will hunt you down," Jordan said through clenched teeth. "Every one of you."

I ignored him and headed after the others. The dust had settled, and I got my first good look at the space. It was just a giant room. A gaping hole in the roof was directly above a crater in the concrete floor. Near the hole, my dad was sitting with his head between his knees, holding the back of his head with one hand, and clutching his shoulder with the other.

A quick glance showed four of Jordan's men. One lay near my dad, still unconscious. Another was face down on the floor near the doorway where I stood. A third was on the other side of the pit, covered in a layer of dust and debris. I'd been facing the other way when I'd gotten out of the hole and never seen him. He must have been knocked out or worse when I came through the roof. The fourth was on the far side of the room, laying in a twisted heap next to Mara, who was stretched out on the floor, unmoving.

Janey went to Dad, while Isabella and Thomas ran to Mara. Mom came through a door at the back of the building and stopped. Her eyes went wide as she surveyed the room, and then she rushed over to Dad and enveloped Janey in a hug.

Isabella wailed as she collapsed beside Mara. I hurried over to her. A pool of blood blossomed beneath Mara, and a smaller, matching pattern soaked the lower part of her shirt. "Is she…"

Thomas looked up at me from where he knelt beside Isabella. "She's still breathing. Barely, though."

Mara lay there on the floor, bleeding out. She was going to die. Why didn't she reggie? Of course. She was lying on the floor covered in silver mesh. "Quick! Help me pick her up."

Thomas looked confused, but he helped me hoist her up off the floor. Isabella stood with us and cradled her sister's head in her hands. Within seconds, Mara's breathing deepened and her color started to improve.

"Carry her toward the hole," I said. "No silver there."

Thomas and I lurched our way over to the hole. We set her down at the edge where the silver mesh had been torn away by my impact, and I went to check on my parents. Mom was holding Dad's shoulder with both hands, compressing his wound, while he winced and tried to smile at me.

Janey looked up from beside Mom. "Is Mara going to be okay?"

"Oh yeah," I said. "She can reggie when unconscious. Just had to get her off the silver. How bad is it?" I nodded at Dad's shoulder.

"Not very," Mom said. "Muscle tissue only. Needs maybe five stitches. I'll take care of it at home."

Dad reached out with his good arm and pulled me into a hug. A moment later Mom and Janey piled in. A Morgan group hug. It felt great.

Chapter 28

LOCAL NEWS

WE PULLED APART after a few seconds, and I was surprised to see Mara already up, an arm draped over Isabella, the other over Thomas.

"We need to go," Mara said. "Now. These guys could wake up. Or cops show up."

Mom continued to apply pressure to Dad's shoulder while I helped him to his feet. An ugly lump stood out just below his hairline, and he wobbled a bit. I pulled his good arm over my shoulders and walked him toward the back door.

"What happened in here?" Janey asked as we cut across the room. Her eyes were wide as she looked around.

"Later. Okay, sweetie?" Dad said. "We need to get out of here now."

We all walked out the back door and down a few steps to the parking lot. I stopped and looked around. No car. But there was a small stash of rope, duct tape, and miscellaneous tools piled nearby.

"Thomas," Mom said. "The duct tape, please."

Mara pulled her arm off Thomas. "I'm fine now. Go."

Thomas hustled over and brought the tape to Mom. She placed a few strategic pieces on Dad's shoulder and around his arm to hold the wound shut and keep pressure on it.

"Thanks, Jenny," Dad said. "Much better." He pulled his arm away from me. "I'm fine now. Seem to have found my feet."

Mom looked doubtful, but kept quiet. "The car's one building over." She pointed vaguely toward a nearby building.

"I'll bring it," Mara said. She was standing on her own now. "Keys?"

Mom dipped into her purse and tossed Mara a massive bundle of keys. Mara caught it and started flipping through the keys. She held one up for my Mom to see and raised an eyebrow.

"That's the one," Mom said.

A short time later, we were all piled into Dad's SUV with Mom driving. Thomas and I were stuffed into the third row, with Mara, Isabella, and Janey across the middle. Mom drove us back to where Mara's rental car waited, and Mara and Isabella got out. The moment Isabella closed the car door, Mom started to pull away.

"Wait!" I said. "We need to say goodbye."

Dad looked back and frowned. "More like good riddance."

"Dad!" Janey said. "She's a friend."

"They don't even have a home," I added. "Or clothes. Or anything. Well, other than a bunch of cash."

Mom sighed. "They're right. We need to invite them over. Give them a meal and a place to sleep tonight."

Dad's eyebrows got even closer together, but then his face softened. "You're right."

I folded the seat forward in front of me and climbed out, with Thomas right behind me. "Mara!"

She stopped, the car door about to be pulled closed. "Right. Sorry, Joss. We should say goodbye, but I want to clear the area first, okay? Can we meet somewhere for a few minutes?"

"How 'bout my house? For dinner? You and Isabella can crash there tonight, then disappear tomorrow."

Mara looked dubious. She was going to say no. Then I heard a burst of Spanish from Isabella, and Mara turned toward her in the car for a moment before turning back to me. "Thank you, Joss. We'd be delighted. We'll see you there in a couple hours, okay?"

"Yeah, that's great. Couple of hours."

Thomas and I clambered back into the SUV, sitting in the middle row this time with Janey.

"So?" Janey said as Mom pulled the car around and headed for home. "Pretty obvious something big went down today. You know, beside me being kidnapped. What happened?"

"I'll tell you what happened," Thomas said. "Joss is a flippin' superhero!"

"What I want to know," I said, "is how you and Isabella showed up just when you did. I thought you were going to stay with Mom."

At that, Dad twisted around and gave Thomas a hard look, and Mom stole a quick glance over her shoulder.

"Whoa," I said. "No hard feelings, right? Dad, you'd be down two kids if he hadn't shown up right when he did. Isabella and Thomas more or less stopped Jordan from killing us. I just want to know how it went down."

""Not yet!" Mom said. I realized she was quietly weeping. "I need some distance. I don't want to know just yet how close everyone came to dying. I want to know we're safe. I want to feel safe. Are we safe? Is that Jordan character coming after us?"

"Doubtful," Thomas said.

"Because?" Dad said.

"Thomas drilled him in the knee and foot," Janey said. "It was awesome. Looked painful."

"Wait," Mom said. "Drilled him?"

"It was like a gangster movie," I said. "Thomas used his shirt to pick up Jordan's own gun so there'd be no prints, then shot him in the knee on one leg and foot in the other. Just..." I held my hand out like a gun. "Blam! Blam! Blam!"

The car started to gently swerve back and forth, and my mom's sobs got a bit louder. Dad reached over and put a hand on her shoulder. "Steady. We're almost home. We're safe." Dad turned back to us. "Let's hold off on retelling everyone's adventures until we're home, okay?"

"You bet, Mr. Morgan," Thomas said.

I leaned in close to Thomas and cupped my hand by my

mouth to contain the sound. "How'd you and Isabella get there? Weren't you supposed to be with my Mom?"

Thomas followed my lead. "She stood there staring down the tracks after you flew off and your dad headed toward the building. We cut back to the main road and jogged down the street. Saw you coming down like a comet. It was insane. Guess we got there just in time."

"But our car was only a building over," I said.

"Yeah," Thomas said, "I'm guessing your mom raced over there as soon as she noticed we were gone to come get us out of trouble."

"So you just talked to Isabella and decided, hey, let's throw ourselves into a war zone?"

Thomas shook his head. "We just looked at each other and knew. Then we went."

"When you showed up, I thought we were..." I couldn't finish. It was all too fresh.

"I get it," Thomas said.

We rode the rest of the way in silence. Thomas texted his mom and found out she wouldn't be home until late, so once we got home, Mom invited Thomas to stay for dinner. There was a fragile silence as Mom got out her medical kit and stitched up Dad. After that Mom and Dad went to work in the kitchen pulling together a meal. Dad didn't help much with his one good arm, but his presence seemed to help Mom. Janey hovered in the kitchen with them, and Mom gave her a big hug about every five minutes. For our part, Thomas and I played video games with the sound off. It was very therapeutic.

By the time Mara and Isabella showed up an hour and a half later carrying bags full of clothes and other stuff, dinner was ready, and Mom and Dad were acting more normal.

"I'd like to declare an amnesty," Dad said as we all sat around the dining room table to homemade spaghetti, garlic bread, salad, and veggies. "Mom and... Mrs. Morgan and I are so overwhelmed, so horrified, by what has happened, we don't know what to think." His eyes locked on mine. "We aren't happy how things were handled. But, we also witnessed everyone work together, to the point of risking their own lives."

He paused to wipe his eyes, and continued. "I do not expect to ever, *ever* find out again that one of my children has been secretly working for a criminal organization. But for tonight, I want to give thanks to God that we're all here. Sure, we're still unsure what happens next, but tonight, we are alive, and more or less well."

He raised his glass, and we all gave a quiet cheer.

"And to new friends," Mom said, looking at Mara and Isabella, "and the new life in front of them. May God grant them a peace they have not known in a long, long time."

After that, a couple of the women cried, and a couple of the men had wet eyes, but it was okay. We had good food, and soon we were all eating and talking. Janey peppered everyone with questions until she had a good sense of what had happened while she sat tied up in the building most of the day. Mom hounded Mara into promising to stay for a couple days, and after dinner the two of them went off to set up the guest bedroom.

"When do I need to take you home?" Dad asked Thomas once we were seated in the living room. Janey had Isabella off on a tour of the house, so it was just us men.

"Mom'll be home around midnight," Thomas said. "I'm not sure I want to get there much before her."

"Understood," Dad said. "I'll drive you over and make sure everything's okay after the news. I wonder..." Dad trailed off as he picked up the remote and turned on the TV.

A picture of Jordan dominated half the screen, while scenes from outside the bank took the other side. It was footage from just after we'd robbed it, with police cars swarming, and uniformed men running around.

"Jennifer!" Dad called. "You'll want to see this!"

Dad fiddled with the remote, and the volume came up as first Mom and Mara came into the room, and then Janey and Isabella.

"... the manhunt ended definitively early this evening at this abandoned warehouse," the reporter was saying. The screen cut to an aerial shot of the warehouse, now surrounded by police cars, the hole in the roof in full view. "Here, the body of Mr. Jordan Johnson and four presumed accomplices were found. All had been shot and killed at close range. But mysteries remain, not the least of which is this: what caused the hole in the roof, and the matching impact crater inside the structure."

Thomas silently reached over and gave me a fist bump.

"I guess you heard him right," Dad said, looking over at Thomas. "Jordan had reason to fear for his life. Mara, you're sure the Guild doesn't do this sort of thing?"

"As far as I know," Mara said.

The reporter was still talking, but I didn't pay attention. Jordan was gone. Permanently. He wasn't going to make good on his promise to hunt me down. I was safe, at least from him. The tight coil in my chest relaxed.

I started crying. Tears leaked out of my eyes, and I couldn't stop. I wanted to—why cry now, when it was finally over?—but I couldn't seem to get control of it. I tried to reggie, but it didn't help. Then Mom was there, and Dad, too, so I rolled with it. Janey hovered nearby, but let me have a little space.

When I was done, I realized it was just us Morgans in the family room. The TV was off and the others had made themselves scarce. It was a relief. I'd just cried in front of Isabella and Thomas. The last thing I needed was to have to meet their eyes right then.

"How long's that been building?" Dad asked, giving me a firm pat on the back.

I shrugged. "Weeks?"

Dad nodded. "I understand. Look, I need to get Thomas home. I hate to leave you guys alone, but I don't feel right just dropping him off. I'm going to wait out front in my car until I hear from him that his mom's home."

"We'll be fine," Mom said, reaching over and giving Dad's hand a squeeze.

And we were. Mom finished getting Mara and Isabella set up in the guest bedroom, Dad took Thomas home, Janey moved a pallet into my folks' room to sleep on, and I went to bed.

I slept for fourteen hours.

Chapter 29

THE END OF THE BEGINNING

THE COPS SHOWED up the next day. We had Mara and Isabella hidden upstairs in my room when my dad invited the detectives into the house. Dad had anticipated they'd be coming by, and drilled Janey and me on how to discuss Battlehoop, and called Thomas and went over it with him.

Detective Young and Detective Malick sat on the couch, a man and a woman, each holding a pen and small pad of paper, while Janey and I sat on a couple chairs we'd pulled in from the kitchen. My parents sat on their recliners. It felt like there was enough nervous energy in the room to start a lightning storm.

"So, Joss," Young said, "Where were you yesterday?"

Dad had told me to be polite, but answer every question with as few words as possible. "Here at home," I said.

"I'd thought you were in this, uh, class at Battlehoop," He said.

"I was."

"But not yesterday. Why not?"

"I felt bad," I said.

Young glanced sideways at Malick, and she sat even further forward on the couch. "That squares with what we heard from some of the other members of the class," she said. "Janey, I heard Jordan kidnapped you. Can you describe what happened?"

"It was terrible," Janey say. "He was so calm about it, I didn't know what was happening, but he grabbed me and dragged me over to his car. Just threw me in the back seat. The door handles wouldn't open. I really did try to get out."

"How did you escape?" Young asked, and Malick frowned, her mouth open, ready with another question.

"I didn't," Janey said. "He just got angrier and angrier, and then he dumped me out of the car near our neighborhood." A big tear tipped out of her eye and traced a line down her cheek. "I was so scared. I ran all the way home."

"Are you okay, honey?" Dad asked. That was her cue. Janey started crying in earnest.

"I think that's enough for now," Mom said, rising to her feet.

"We have some more questions," Malick said. "About the class. How they got involved."

Janey cried louder. It was an incredible performance. Mom waved the detectives toward the front door. "Of course," Mom said. "I can answer any of those questions for you. Let's just step outside to talk and give my daughter some space."

Both detectives frowned, but Malick gave a small shrug and Young nodded in response. They both stood.

"Shouldn't take long," Young said.

"However long you need," Mom said. "We're here to help." With that, Mom led them outside. Janey's tears stopped like a switch had been flipped.

"How do girls do that?" I asked.

"No idea," Dad said, "but your mother has used it to great effect a few times to get out of speeding tickets."

"It's a girl thing, Joss," Janey said. "You wouldn't understand."

We both ran upstairs to let Mara and Isabella know we were in the clear. They were sitting side by side in the guest bedroom bed, looking intently at Mom's laptop.

"Whatcha looking at?" Janey asked.

"Planning a route to drive home," Mara said.

"So how much money did you end up with, anyway?" I asked.

"Enough," Mara said.

"Lots," Isabella said at the same time.

"Enough," Mara repeated, giving Isabella a small frown. "And we'll be going out to spend some of it as soon as the coast is clear. We need to go back and get my car as well."

"More shopping," I said, my voice flat.

Isabella's eyes sparkled. "Yes! Do you like the shopping also, Joss."

"I don't think that's what he meant to imply," Janey said. "But I do. Can I go with you?"

Mara shrugged. "If your parents are okay with it. I'm not sure your dad wants me responsible for either of his children any time soon."

Mom came back in after about fifteen minutes and gave us the all clear. Janey asked about the shopping, and it turned out Mara was right, but Mom had a private discussion with Dad for a while, and then he agreed. An hour later, the house was quiet. I messaged Thomas to see if he wanted to come over.

In brief sentences on my phone, he told me about his encounter with the police investigators, his mom's intervention, and how his mom had left for an important meeting and he was home alone. I texted him back.

So is that a yes? You're coming over?

An hour later, Thomas knocked on the door. I opened it and waved him toward the stairs. We headed up to my room.

"What took you so long?" I asked. "Thought you'd be here half an hour ago."

"Had a couple things to take care of," he said. "Where is everyone?"

"Mom and Dad are downstairs, probably in their room. Neither of them went to work today. Janey went with Mara and Isabella to shop. Mara's trying to get them set up so they can leave in a couple days and have what they need for the trip and basic living once they get home."

"And Janey went on purpose? Shopping?"

"I know!" I said. "Women. Hey. You heard from any of the others?"

"Yeah, I talked to Frankie after the cops went by his

house," Thomas said. "They went straight from my house to his. He told them what he knew. We talked for a while. He was so relieved to hear Janey was okay. He thought Jordan still had her when he'd been killed. He didn't know Jordan had 'dumped her off in our neighborhood' and whatnot."

I smiled. "Good enough. How'd he look?"

"Like a raccoon. Two black eyes."

I winced. "I need to get to know him better, don't I? He's a good guy."

"He is," Thomas said. "I knew you'd see it one day. Hey. I've got something."

He reached into his pocket and pulled out a ziplock bag. It held a ratty looking folded up piece of paper. Something tickled my memory, but I couldn't place it. Thomas waved it in front of me and raised his eyebrows. Apparently, he thought I should know what it was, too.

"It's making me think I should know what it is," I said, "but I give. What is it?"

"I swung by Beckler Park on the way here. Checked that hollow in the tree."

It clicked. "Bobby Ferris! I told him to leave me a note in the tree if he needed help. Wait. How'd you know about that?"

"You told me, doofus. Here." He held the bag out to me.

I stared at it. Why had I expected everything I'd done this summer to just pack up and go away? Bobby Ferris. I wondered how the past few days had gone for him. Hopefully better than the ones before.

I reached out, hesitated, and took the bag. "This should be interesting."

I opened the bag and pulled the paper out. With careful movements, I unfolded it and held it so Thomas could read along with me. It was written in a messy scrawl that was barely legible.

Bobby here. You told me to write if I needed help, so I'm writing.

My dad's done good the past few days, but it's been hard. He's going to see it through. That's what he said. He's going to do the right thing.

But he's in big trouble. I always wondered where his money came from. He didn't have much, but he never worked. Now I know. He was doing stuff for some sort of criminal organization. Dad needs to get away from them. Get a clean start. You can help with that, right?

"Well, that's a pickle," Thomas said.

"I don't even know what that means," I said. "Where do you get these expressions?"

Thomas frowned and stood up straighter. "My dad. Everyone knows what it means to be in a pickle."

I shook my head and smiled. "Well, if we're in a pickle, it's a pickle for another day. For now, Joss the Seven is signing off. I'm just Joss until further notice."

Thomas nodded. "Good idea. Hey, after everything that went down, there's just one thing we forgot to do."

"What's that?"

He held his arm out, forearm angled on the diagonal. I smiled and banged my forearm into his.

"Battlehoop!" we both yelled.

About the Author

J. Philip Horne probably shouldn't be alive. Born in Florida, he grew up overseas for the most part, spending much of his childhood in Liberia and Micronesia. During those years, he experienced numerous attempts on his life. The wannabe killers included malaria, spinal meningitis, blood poisoning, a staph infection in his heel bone, a close encounter with a green mamba, and other cold-hearted foes.

From his earliest years, his parents read to him fantastical stories from wonderful worlds. Narnia and Middle Earth featured prominently, and had his youth been a generation later, he would have certainly encountered Hogwarts at a young age. Through his teen years he read stories by many other authors and experienced a host of new worlds.

After dabbling in writing for many years, he finally got serious and wrote his first novel in 2011. He has continued to write ever since. He currently lives in Dallas, Texas with his wife, four children, two dogs, two rabbits, and several literary aspirations. For news of upcoming works, please join Mr. Horne's email list at jphiliphorne.com or visit him at facebook.com/jphiliphorne.

Made in the USA
San Bernardino, CA
28 March 2017